The Last Lamp

Also by Sue Robishaw

HOMESTEADING ADVENTURES
WITH JJ AND CHICKB

The Last Lamp

by

Sue Robishaw

ManyTracks

~~~~~~~ NEANA'S PROLOGUE ~~~~~~~~~~~~~

The lamps. That's what comes first to my mind when I think back on those days. A previously pleasant but minor item in the background of my life. The lamps that gently lit the nighttime activities in the town Square. Music, poetry, dances, discussions. Fun and interesting activities for a gentle and diverse community. But occasionally, as I found out, the setting for something not so peaceful. For someone with a hidden agenda, a deliberately destructive one. Someone named Caljn. Who preached the worst of the old religions mixed with the worst of the old scientific beliefs. Caljn and the Power Movement, who wanted to recreate in our lively but peaceful community his distorted and destructive version of the late twentieth century.

Not that we really know what life was like back then, so much has been lost, so much has changed. The land masses are different, of course, and the weather. And apparently so is our awareness and psychic knowledge and spiritual consciousness. At least, that appears to be the case. We certainly have our troubles and challenges to deal with today, but I guess it was much worse back then. Though certainly it wasn't as bad as Caljn depicted it. With repression and narrow-mindedness and intolerance as the blueprints for living. Why would anyone want to live that way? Especially today.

But Caljn wanted to, and Valjar, and the others.

And it was my community, my friends, my life they wanted to destroy. When I fell into their world, when I discovered what they were up to, I had no choice but to get involved. It was too important to just walk away.

Trouble was, I wasn't prepared for people like that. Even if I'd had more than my twenty-seven years of living behind me, I don't think I would have known how to deal with them. How to deal with their effect on me. Jahon still says I was wrong in the way I went about it. Some days I agree with him. But some days I think I would do it the same way again. Maybe Shahvid, my older brother and the whole of my family, is right, maybe I am just plain stubborn. I prefer to think of it as living life artistically and independently. But I did learn. We all learned. Some lessons were easier than others. And some I'd rather not think about at all.

I came into the middle of it all several months ago when I first heard Caljn speak to a small crowd in the Square. But my part and this story really began the night I took my information, and plan, to Starpeace. When, by putting into words those well hashed out thoughts, I put into motion the events that added a few new experiences to my life, and the lives of my close friends. Stress, chaos, anxiety, confrontation, violence. Previously abstract words, soon to become familiar companions.

Starpeace. The underground fighters for freedom and peace. Real freedom and real peace. The kind that comes with responsibility. The kind, and the people, that Caljn and his Power Movement were working so determinedly to destroy. Regular people, yet not so regular when you looked close. People like Chanthan and Sinat and Sushati. Even Rafnon. It's hard to believe that I didn't know who they were then, who Starpeace was. Knowing now that they had never been so very far from me at all. But I didn't know, and that night I headed into a new part of my life. Thankfully more positive than my association with Caljn had been. But at the time it was simply another of the growing number of challenges I had to deal with.

The fight of people like Starpeace against the Power Movement types is not new of course, above or below ground. It has been going on for centuries. But this battle was mine, was ours. It was too real and too close.

Thinking back to that night, my first meeting with Starpeace, I can almost feel the soft, warm breeze against my face as I had walked along the paths. The anxiety churning inside me that didn't match the calm and peaceful surroundings. A different path and it would have been a different story, a different ending. But these are the decisions I made, and these are the paths I took, independent of, yet closely entwined with those around me.

~~~~~~~ *SUNDAY ~night*~~~~~~~~~~~~~~~*one*~~~

The decision had been made and there I was. Walking along a path in near darkness, from lamplight to lamplight, heading toward Starpeace, whoever they were. The soft light from the lamps didn't seem to help much as their daylight energy was fading naturally into the night. I wished for some moonlight. But it wasn't really light I needed, it was courage.

Caljn and the Power Movement had to be stopped. I knew I couldn't do it myself. But it wasn't the kind of thing I wanted to share with my friends. The Power Movement were not pleasant people. And any association with them could have been dangerous. Certainly trying to stop them would. Starpeace was my hope. But I didn't even know for sure who they were. Just a sort of underground reputation. And an overheard comment or two. A little deliberate digging. And not a little luck. It would all bring me, I hoped, to them, to their meeting that night. I was sure it was the right thing to do.

So why was I shivering in spite of the warm breeze? I turned onto a lesser used path. The packed earth felt firm and comfortable beneath my sandals. There was no reason to be afraid. This was a safe and peaceful community. I'd walked all over it, day and night, for most of my life. Of course, I hadn't known about Caljn and his friends all those years. But they weren't into individual attacks, their goals went much higher. Or lower as the case may be.

But my anxiety was real and I knew the cause wasn't just the Power Movement. I hoped I was blending into the night as Kasho says I do, with my brown robe, dark hair and brown skin. I didn't mind occasionally being the center of attention, but not that night, not on my way there. If Caljn or the Power Movement had found out what I was about to do . . .

It was no use dwelling on that, I told myself, or them, or their plans. They were a reality but they would be stopped. They had to be. I wouldn't think of any other possibility. I slowed my steps and turned onto a path beside a wide alley. The houses and yards sat comfortably back on my left, close enough together, but not too close. They looked shadowy in the dim light, with all their trees keeping a sentinel watch. I shivered again.

I was being ridiculous. It was time to get something less negative in my mind. Jahon floated through, my brother's best friend and, usually, a comfortable friend of mine. But his harsh comments the previous week about my association with Caljn jumped out at me, again, and I shoved him and them away. He, and my brother Shahvid, could be so irritating and overbearing at times. I was glad they didn't know what I was involved in. That was one confrontation I certainly wouldn't have wanted. But there was no reason to think they would find out.

That line of thought wasn't helping. I put my hands in my pockets and concentrated on where I was. I knew I must be getting close. I looked carefully at the houses in the area. But which one was it? And how was I going to get them to let me in? This wasn't exactly a public invited meeting. I shrugged. It would work out when I got there. I certainly hadn't come this far to turn back just because I was nervous. Or because Jahon or Shahvid might have disapproved. Not that they would disapprove of Starpeace. But of what I had planned I wasn't so sure.

The wind picked up for a moment, busily rustling the bushes beside me. I stopped and scanned the nearest house. That had to be it. Turning, I retraced a few steps and started down the stone path toward the place. It was a low, quiet building, set into a small rise. I didn't see any lights on inside, but I was sure this was the one.

Suddenly I felt . . . something. I hesitated and looked carefully around. There were no lamps glowing here, just pale starlight. The bushes and plants, close on either side of the walk, were quietly alive with night life. I smelled lavender, and maybe basil.

Two men jumped from the shadows. Startled, I almost screamed then caught it back. I whirled around but before I could think one of the men had his hand over my mouth and my arms pinned to my side. His partner tied a cloth across my eyes and another across my mouth. They didn't give me a chance to say anything. I struggled. One of them tied my wrists together. They weren't small men, and certainly weren't gentle. Without saying a word they hurried me between them down the uneven stone path. My feet automatically kept pace.

I was so shocked at the unexpected attack that my mind stopped for a moment - then made up for it with thoughts and images chasing each other in and out. Nightmare thoughts. Meantime, my body continued to react hard, struggling with all it had against the bonds. One of the men gave me a shake and hissed a quiet "Shsh!". They were apparently concerned about keeping the encounter quiet. I just wanted to pull this suddenly chaotic experience together, and get free. This wasn't what I had planned, to say the least. And I hadn't a clue as to what to do.

Struggling, pulling, twisting, our strangely silent battle moved quickly on toward the house. My captors pushed and pulled me along, not responding to my restricted fight.

We reached the door and the men pulled me into the house. We started down some wooden stairs. My mind settled on what was happening. My stomach cramped with fear, and my energies whirled. This just didn't fit with what I knew about this group. Could I have been so wrong? Or had I chosen the wrong house? Was I headed for the wrong meeting? The thought turned my whole body cold.

The men stopped at the bottom and I checked my awkward descent. One of them opened a door and stepped through, bringing me with him. His partner was close behind. Brightness came through around the edges of the cloth across my eyes. As I fought to get my bearings I was hit with a storm of emotions and impressions which collided roughly with my own. The world whirled uneasily. I felt voices rather than heard them.

One of the men said something and gave me a small push forward. I stumbled as I tried to bring everything together and step ahead. My eyes strained uselessly to see. The world was tipping. I pulled desperately to free my hands and catch myself. As I fell toward the floor I heard a strong voice near me ringing, "What the hell . . . ?!" I thought I felt a hand, but I was on the floor before it connected, leaving my body resting at the man's feet. My mind and self felt like they were somewhere else.

"Well?" The man's voice was quiet, strong, tinged with anger. He knelt down beside me and started working on the knots of the gag. I very carefully kept still, my eyes closed. I could feel my hair and robe were spread brown across the floor and I wanted to pull myself back in. But my wrists were still tightly bound, and I felt it safer to keep quiet. I was disoriented. I couldn't see the people in the room but I could feel the emotions, and it felt crowded. The silence was tight as no one said anything. I thought I should recognize the voice of the man who spoke but I couldn't focus. Yet I felt I was watching the whole scene in a strange clear way, as if from a corner of the ceiling. Hearing not only the words but the thoughts as well . . .

~~~ ~~ ~ ~~ ~~~

Chanthan gently removed the cloth then looked up again at the two men. They glanced at each other uneasily.

"I'm sure she's part of the Power Movement, the inner group!" one of them hurriedly explained. "I've seen her often with Caljn. We saw her spying around here just as we were coming in. She could be dangerous!" He looked at the others for support as Chanthan's stare didn't waver. The woman looked much smaller lying on the floor than she had outside. Suddenly it appeared that maybe their actions had been over-reactive, and it wasn't a comfortable feeling.

Chanthan turned to Sinat as he started forward, having gotten past the first startled moments. Their eyes met and Sinat's dark eyes mirrored Chanthan's blue, anger knowing no color difference. Sinat said to him, in a quiet, controlled voice, "I know who she is. You can take the blindfold off also."

As quickly as his anger had gone out Chanthan pulled it back in. Not to be rid of it, but to use it. He knew that not everyone felt as he did about this battle with the Power Movement. Some were into it because they enjoyed the conflict, or thought they did. He didn't try to pretend that he understood that part of the group. But they were a reality and one he accepted. Starpeace was made up of a diverse people. He knew they were all going in the same direction. Sometimes, however . . . He carefully worked the blindfold loose.

Sinat had subdued his own sudden anger. Why did there seem to be only a small group of them who felt the real cause, who really hated the violence? Even if he hadn't known who the woman was he felt there was no excuse for this kind of treatment. But he *did* know her. What could have brought her to them, alone? Why hadn't she come with Shahvid? Or Jahon? Whatever the reason, he knew he had better take care of Shahvid's sister if he didn't want to lose himself a good friend. But he didn't say anything to the others. He would let her speak for herself.

As Chanthan worked on the ropes he turned to the men across the room, one of whom had left the doorway to sit astride a wooden chair, and nonchalantly rub the bruises on his legs. "I don't care *who* she is, there is no reason for this type of treatment." His voice was firm and measured. "We can be safe without being brutal."

Sinat headed across the room. No one else moved. The only sound was Chanthan's indistinguishable words as he swore under his breath. The cord was thin and coarse, and had in that short time rubbed the skin raw.

Chanthan spoke again, his voice sounding loud in the quiet room, "Sinat, there is some liniment in the cupboard behind Rafnon . . ." He stopped as he realized Sinat was already there. Sinat crossed the room and handed the jar to Chanthan.

A man, neatly but unimaginatively dressed, not a large man, casually leaned back against the wall across the room from Chanthan, trying to hide his first startled gasp beneath his usual cool demeanor. At least that was his view. He, Rafnon, finally spoke, "I doubt that she is all that dangerous, or a part of the inner group." He almost obtained the casual tone he sought as he added, "I wouldn't trust her though."

He started to say something more but Chanthan interrupted, "We have a job to do here, all of us, and we must not let our emotions get tangled up in the wrong direction. We need to keep in mind what it is we are striving for and why. We need to keep our fears out in the open where we can recognize them for what they are. We need to act for the cause, not react to our fears."

Chanthan was deliberately calm as he talked, removing the last of the ropes as Sinat wiped Neana's face with a cool, wet cloth. He accepted Sinat's apparent trust of her in spite of Rafnon's words. They were close enough not to require explanations. The details could come later.

~~~ ~~ ~ ~~ ~~~

The suddenly clear words, burning salve and wet cloth on my face jerked me abruptly back to myself. My body's awareness jumped from one sore spot to another, reminding painfully how alive I was. My mind whirled and focused, trying to take in all at once the room, the people, and that voice.

It hit me. Of course! I knew the voice, though I had seldom been very near the man. Why hadn't I thought of him before? He would be the one, the head of Starpeace. Even without my strong admiration for his work, it made sense. He was a well known, and admired, leader of the community. Chanthan. A feeling of relief swept through me. My instincts hadn't been wrong. I was in the right place.

Thoughts of pain fled as what I had come to say came flooding back. Chanthan sat back and then stood as I moved to scramble up, almost falling right back down as the room tilted and swirled for a moment.

"Easy there," Chanthan said, offering a hand.

Sinat moved to place a chair behind me. As I started to speak, he stopped me, "Here, take a breather for a moment, there's time," and he handed me a mug of water. He had a calming smile.

I was feeling somewhat disoriented and shaky, my normal strength apparently deserted. I took the mug and worked to keep everything together. The anxiety that had been building in me for weeks was taking its toll now. It wasn't a good feeling. A long drink helped. I smiled at him in gratitude. My green eyes felt as dark as his. This wasn't exactly how I'd planned to get in, but I had apparently successfully arrived at the Starpeace meeting.

Remembering that there were others in the room I looked around. From the men who had brought me in (neither met my eye) to a woman sitting across the room (she gave me a rather sad smile), another man and . . .

"Rafnon!" My eyes widened as the exclamation burst out. I steadied the mug against my thigh and stared at him in surprise. Rafnon?

Chanthan watched carefully as Rafnon responded. "Hello Neana, rather surprised to see you here." He hadn't moved from his stance against the wall but he didn't seem all that easy.

"Hello," I replied rather lamely. Well! Rafnon. Here. Our friendly relationship had cooled awhile ago. At my request. He insisted it was because of Caljn. But we both knew it had been because of his relationship with my sister-in-law, Careen. I didn't want to deal with him right then. I drew in my surprise and turned my attention back to Chanthan. He had moved over near Sinat, and in spite of all that was going on the artist in me had to take a moment to admire the picture they made. Chanthan's more gray than blond unruly hair matched his large build, loose clothing and fair skin, as Sinat's smooth dark hair blended with his dark skin, tight build and neat tunic and pants. The inner strength that emanated from the two of them did much to calm me.

I took a deep breath and addressed them both, not deliberately excluding the others but intuitively knowing that these two were the core, the heart of Starpeace. I had already pushed aside the earlier attack. The only thing that mattered at that moment was what I had to say. My strength had returned. I was myself. The bruises would wait until later. I dove in.

"My name is Neana and I have something important to tell you. I have some information. I think you can do something with it. I had to bring it to you." Words almost tumbled over themselves as I hurried to get them out. Now that I was here, I wanted to get it over with.

But my mind hesitated, and I glanced around. Why *was* Rafnon here? I trusted Chanthan of course, and the dark man standing near him, but the others? My fears and doubts surged forward. I had to work to stay calm. I started to speak.

"We don't have time to listen to her," Rafnon interrupted as his repressed emotions boiled up. "We have more important things to attend to, and I told you she's not to be trusted anyway." He was angry and was having trouble with his cool, detached act. He knew he walked a fine line sometimes between Starpeace and the others and he didn't want anyone disrupting his plans.

Rafnon's outburst surprised me. Maybe he was still angry with me, but the cooling of our relationship had been his own fault. And that didn't have anything to do with these people. I didn't say anything.

Chanthan glanced at Rafnon then turned to me,

"Take your time, we will hear you out. ALL of us." The last words were spoken in a quiet, firm manner that they all understood. They had seen his anger let loose but few times and none of them wished that upon themselves now. The room quieted.

With a mental shrug I continued, calmly this time. I knew what I had to do. Whatever Rafnon's problem was it would have to wait.

"I've known of your group in an abstract way for some time. There are many like me I think, not members of your organization but a part just the same by our thoughts and feelings and beliefs. I hadn't planned on it being any more than that. But I fell into some information that you might want to know. I am here on my own, no one else is with me in this." I glanced at Chanthan, then away.

"My involvement in the community is mainly as . . . a painter . . .," I hesitated over the word. To call myself an artist didn't seem right in front of the great Chanthan. His paintings had inspired me since I was young. "I'm aware of the views of the Church of the Final God but had never paid them much mind. Until I came to know of a small faction within the organization. A much more fanatical group than the whole. Of course you would know of them but I just recently found out how dangerous they are. And how intent they are on undermining and destroying our . . .," I groped for the right word, "culture I guess. Not just mine but most everyone's."

I paused but no one interrupted. So I went on, holding the mug firmly on my lap. It seemed to help. "On the surface they are just a small group under the design of a church with rather odd, old ideas. But the faction, the Power Movement, is using the church as a cover. Not that the Church of the Final God isn't repressive enough in itself but most of the people there are just unhappy maybe, not, well, not evil."

A slight sigh escaped and I could feel myself frowning. I didn't know what all they already knew, or wanted to hear. They were all so quiet, and intent on what

I was saying. It was rather unnerving. "Well, I came to know the one who is the internal leader, more dictator I think, of this inner group. Caljn, the 'poet'. He knows a lot, and it is his interpretations and teachings of the old documents that they go by. And many of his close associates are scientists who embrace with a vengeance some of the old ways. The ways before science was dispersed and let free. Caljn is the one pushing them all. But of course it is their own choice to be involved." I stopped. "You know this?" I asked Chanthan.

He replied with an encouraging smile, "Some of it, but please, do continue."

I nodded, answering his smile briefly. Talking about it didn't make me want to smile. But they seemed to be taking me seriously so I continued. "The more I learned the more I felt I had to find out more. So I deliberately got close to Caljn, and so his group. Listening, trying to be as much a part as I could, without actually being one of them. At first it was just an exercise in trying to understand people who were so different. But I ended up learning more than I had planned." I shivered involuntarily as the feelings of that came back to me, all those weeks.

"Caljn's direction is not just a philosophical one. He and his group have very concrete plans, some they've already carried out, or tried to. You're probably aware of some of these. But there is more coming." I paused a moment and took a drink. My throat felt like a cat's tongue.

Chanthan and Sinat's frowns were deep, and the others were listening intently. Even Rafnon came out of his private world of troubled thoughts as it sank in, what I was saying, where I had been. This had nothing to do with him and Careen. He knew that I had been with Caljn a lot these last months but he hadn't realized how close I'd gotten, or why. No one had to describe to any of them the danger and destructiveness of Caljn and his friends. They knew too well. But none of them had ever managed to get into that inner group.

"Caljn has been using the others to set the stage for his coming 'great act'. Only a few of them know what he is really doing. The rest just seem to think that they are 'righteously right' and everyone else is wrong so what they do is OK and all that. They follow him pretty much without thought. He has plans to use them all eventually, even those least connected. But this event involves only Caljn and his closest associates.

"They have been working on and perfecting a weapon system, one that will not only destroy the main target but will spread to those around him and on from there. A pyramiding pattern of destruction. They've tested parts of the system in the past, sometimes successfully, sometimes not. But they feel the whole thing is ready now for a 'trial run'." I stopped a moment, putting my thoughts in order. The room was quiet. I realized my hands were tight on the mug so I made them relax.

"My knowledge of how it all works is unfortunately sketchy but I'll draw out for you what I know. My familiarity is more with what they expect it to do. The main weapon is a small, hand held piece programmed to zero in on a particular person. When hit, that person would be incapacitated both physically and mentally, but not killed outright. The weapon's combination of rays and viruses will radiate from there and attack those around that person. And continue to spread until the power fades, connecting wherever it can to do whatever damage it can.

"Caljn plans to make this first attack this coming Friday evening, in the Square, just at sun-fade. As you know, the Square will be filled with people on their way to the Gallery Reception." My voice quieted, feeling, thinking, of what was planned.

"I wasn't sure before who their main target was. Thought viruses have already been sent out in several stages these past weeks. Not that they normally would be a threat to anyone not choosing them. But they are one part of the system and can possibly draw the main weapon rays and viruses further out.

"But it is the attack Friday that will be the catalyst, the disaster that people won't see right away, so they won't be able to fight it off. The source, and cause, of the debilitation isn't going to be obvious. They hope it is never discovered, of course. So they can attack again, and again. Until they have the community under their control.

"The main targets, and the timing, have been chosen in order to hurt the community the most. The people Caljn will hit, the individuals programmed into the weapon, will be the most active and creative leaders. I don't know how many other people will be hurt or destroyed. *They* don't know. This is to be the first test of the whole thing."

It was even worse now, to know who that first target was, and to see that I should have known before. Not that it made any real difference all in all, still . . . I turned to Chanthan, silent.

He smiled, "So it is to be me. I wasn't sure. We were working on it. And of course I knew at some level that something was coming." He chuckled, "I'm happy to hear that my recent indigestion has a source other than my own cooking." No one else shared his humor. He sat down in a chair half facing me. Sinat still stood listening intently, as did Rafnon at the other end of the room. There was movement amongst the others as positions were adjusted. They didn't like the implications of what I had said any more than I did. Chanthan leaned back and continued, seriously, but calmly.

"Don't look so stricken. In a way it is not news to me or the others. Though certain important aspects and details *are* new, and are very important." He thought a moment, then asked, "Is there anything else of importance to the matter? The time is getting late and it seems we have many decisions and plans to make now. And you want to get home before light I think."

"Oh!" With a start I looked at the clock. I would have to be leaving soon. I didn't want another argument with Shahvid as to where I'd been. Not this night. I didn't think my inner resources would be up to that. But there was one more thing to say.

"I know Caljn must be destroyed, and the weapon

too. I think they only have one, and without it the rest of the system falls apart. Not knowing your capabilities, I don't know exactly how it can be done. But I do know the details of his plan for Friday, and I can be close to him without suspicion. I've been thinking a lot about it and I know that his destruction must happen at just the right time, just as he aims. It has to be then. It is important that it appears he destroys himself. It all has to be stopped right then.

"Caljn will be where the lamps form a circle around the small raised area. It is his favorite spot. I often light the lamps in the Square in the evening so possibly you could use that in some manner. As a signal, or a direction.

"Since I can be beside him without drawing attention or questions, I can help carry out whatever action that you plan. No one else need be there so it will be safer. Except for you of course," I nodded soberly to Chanthan, "but you will be at a distance and they already expect you."

I was afraid they wouldn't understand, wouldn't trust me. It was so very important but I didn't know what else to say. I had gone over it in my mind so often it was almost boring. But there was much I didn't understand. And so little time to prepare.

I was all of a sudden very tired. It wasn't easy to decide to murder someone, especially someone you knew. A new dimension in my life. I knew what kind of man Caljn was. But I also knew him as a real person. I looked down at the mug in my hands, then up at Sinat, then Chanthan.

They trusted me. But there was also some doubt. Not of me, but of my plan, my participation. I could handle that. I had gotten this far. I would get through to the end.

Chanthan slowly nodded his head. He saw, he understood. Maybe he saw too much, more than he could cope with. But he knew he'd never be handed more than he could handle. Nor would any one of us.

Everyone was silent as they thought about what had been said. Sinat looked from me to Chanthan. "It is a good idea. We have the equipment and organization to do it, but . . ." He stopped, then said to me, "It is just that this is not a matter to be taken lightly. Not that I think you are. But we must be sure of what is right to do."

Chanthan nodded agreement, then asked, "Are you sure of this plan? We trust you. But are you sure you want to be involved? I will admit that it would make it easier but I will not minimize the danger. You have done much in bringing this to us and we would well understand if that would be all the farther you wished to go. It would be enough." He looked briefly at Rafnon who was frowning intently at the floor. His gaze came back to me.

I looked at him steadily, "I am sure. I have already decided that I will be involved to the end. I have an advantage that no one else here has. I can easily get close to Caljn. I think you need that. And," I added quietly, "I am already very much involved."

Chanthan took a deep breath. He looked at Sinat, then at the others. Friday. Five days. That didn't leave much time. And it had to be carried out with precision, the whole operation. There was no room for error. A wrong move and the destruction could be worse than even the Power Movement hoped for. More time would have helped, but they didn't have it. They all had to pull together, every one.

He missed Sushati. They could have used her calm awareness and insight. She picked a fine time to be gone. But it wasn't her fault, he knew that. There was a baby to deliver and her job was there. No, not her job. It was her main interest in this life, along with Sinat. She and Sinat had a special relationship which he respected, as he did their skills, and of course their friendship.

Chanthan spoke out loud through his thoughts, "Friday. It doesn't leave us much time, but I think we can do it." It came out somewhat as a question as he looked around.

They were all there with him as he should have known they'd be, as each person agreed in their own way and with their own commitment and talents. Other emotions and thoughts were set aside. Apologies were offered, accepted. Belated introductions made. Earlier mistrusts vanished. The room became alive as they settled in to the discussion of just what to do, what each person's responsibilities would be. How each skill would be utilized.

Sinat took part in the discussions but his mind was also on other concerns. He was quite uneasy about my vulnerability in the plan. But no one could come up with a better program, and Chanthan was right, they hadn't much time.

He wondered what to do about Jahon and Shahvid. Apparently I didn't know of their association with Starpeace. Nor did they know of my involvement. I had insisted that I was, and intended to remain, on my own in this. He had to respect that but he wasn't happy about it, and he knew neither Shahvid nor Jahon would be either. He would talk it over with Sushati and Chanthan later, but he knew that unless I changed my mind, neither Jahon nor Shahvid would be included in this event. He felt an added responsibility to see that I came through it all safely.

The scout rays of the sun were just lighting the tops of the trees as I let myself quietly into my brother's house, and my home. I hardly remembered getting there. I felt thoroughly drained. I was glad my entrance was separate from the one Shahvid and Careen used. Still, Shahvid was up and around at all hours and his study was near my rooms so I took special care to not make any noise. I was tired and my meeting with Starpeace was too alive in my mind. I didn't want to try a side-stepping conversation with my brother right then.

It wasn't long before I sank thankfully into bed. My mind wondered if I would be able to sleep but my body took charge. As I closed my eyes I drifted off into a much needed world of dreams.

~~~ ~~ ~ ~~ ~~~

At the sound of the door and quiet footfalls Shahvid looked up from his drawing board. His world of walls and windows and rooms changed abruptly back to the present. He half rose, frowning, then settled back down. No, it seemed his and Neana's talks the last weeks had all been at cross purposes, and he didn't feel up to it that night. He was worried and he knew that got in the way of his conversations with her, or *at* her as she told him.

He sighed, ran his fingers through his unruly brownish hair, his thoughts jumping around here and there, always coming back to Neana. His mind had been there a lot lately, and not often with ease. Her independence, which he respected, was more often now a source of worry. Or rather, he admitted, her actions, and lack of communication with him, was the worry. The independence had been with her even as a young child, before their parents had died when, at nineteen, he had become responsible for her. She had been ten. There had been no question of her living with anyone else. It hadn't occurred to either of them and had been accepted by the others. They were their family. They had been friends before and that feeling deepened over the years. It was something his wife Careen never could understand. But that was an area he didn't want to think about, not right then.

As he had done so often lately he tried to put Careen, and his sister's activities, from his mind. He turned back to his drawings. It seemed a long time since he'd created a building on paper with real life, the kind that came from deep inside. He thought of those times at night, alone, when he would lose himself in it all and it would come.

Maybe once he and Careen straightened their lives out he could set about getting his own on a more stable line. It looked like their marriage was going to be over soon. Or had it ended some time ago? He wasn't sure. He knew he'd ignored the growing schism for too long. When she had started in on her all too common harping the other morning, he had just exploded. He hadn't meant to do that. The words had needed to be said, but not in that manner.

Careen had seen him as a slick successful architect, builder of houses for the rich and famous, or at least those *she* saw as rich and famous. She had never been able to see how he felt about his drawings, his creations. How he needed to have a certain rapport with the owners. Something he just wasn't interested in doing with those people she thought important. But then again, maybe he hadn't tried very hard to explain. He was probably just as guilty of reading her wrong, seeing what wasn't there.

She especially wanted him to be The Architect for

her church, The Church of the Final God. But he couldn't find much common ground with those folks. He didn't want to. He tried to respect her right to her choices but that was one association he really didn't care for.

And then there was her dislike of Neana. That was something he never could figure out. It had too often caused discord in their household. A home needed to be full of laughter and joy and good conversations. That's what he had told her. But he wasn't sure she knew what he was talking about. She had been too angry to listen.

She had moved out, temporarily, to stay with a friend. He probably should have told Neana about the situation. But he wasn't sure he knew exactly how he felt about it himself. And things were not settled yet between him and Careen. Besides, Neana and Careen lived quite separate lives. Even though they lived under the same roof, Neana may not have noticed Careen's absence. Funny thing was, he hardly did himself.

He thought about how he and Neana used to have great, long conversations. He'd like to be able to talk with her like that again. About his dreams, his drawings. Maybe even about Starpeace. He thought she would understand. That would be a pretty serious step though. Before he considered bringing Neana into Starpeace he would talk it over with Jahon, and maybe Sinat and Sushati. But he could talk to her about Careen. But then, they never had talked much about Careen. And he and Neana had been drifting apart. Besides, there were those rumors of her friendship with Caljn.

He *had* tried to talk with her about that. But every time she had firmly changed the path of the conversation. And Jahon had been little help, bristling whenever Neana and Caljn were mentioned in the same sentence. Shahvid did have some thoughts about that, but he kept them to himself.

Sighing, he put his pencil down again and went along to Neana's room. A light knock brought nothing and he quietly went in to find his sister, fully dressed, fast asleep on her bed. She looked worried. Or was it his own worry he was projecting onto her?

He gently drew a cover over her and quietly pulled the curtains tight so the sun wouldn't waken her in the morning. He knew she'd be angry, but he felt she hadn't been sleeping much lately, and certainly hadn't been tonight. He told himself firmly that he simply had to find a way to reach her, find out what was going on. He'd talk it over with Jahon soon. Even if he was prickly about it, Shahvid trusted him.

~~~ ~~ ~ ~~ ~~~

When I awakened something didn't feel quite right. I opened my eyes, lying quietly, trying to figure out what was wrong. Then I noticed the drawn curtains. I hardly ever closed them in the warm months. I lived with the sun's movements and tried to always be within its reach.

Getting up I pulled them open, letting the light pour in. It was mid afternoon! How could I have slept so long? I had planned to be at the Jansoon's home first thing that morning. The memories of the night's events waited while I grappled with the immediate problems. Shahvid! Shahvid must have pulled the curtains, darn him anyway. Did he think I was still a child to be taken care of? I had things to do, a painting to work on, and . . .

As I hurried around and started to dress for the day I realized I was still dressed from the night. I stopped then, sinking to the bed as the previous hours', and days', happenings flooded in. And I knew Shahvid was right, even if I wasn't going to admit it to him. I wouldn't have been worth anything that morning. And he would no doubt have questions about my whereabouts the previous night. With some exasperation I pulled my tunic off over my head, and immediately my sore wrists caught my attention.

They hurt, and probably should have been bandaged when I got home. Though the wounds were probably the least of my problems right then. When I thought about what could have happened . . . But at that I shook my head and stood up. It wasn't going to do any good to worry about the night before, or the next Friday. Events would happen as they happened. Better to just concentrate on the day at hand. There was time to get in some good work before sun-fade, the Jansoon home wasn't far, just across the Square. A quick shower and breakfast and I would be on my way, my thoughts only on present actions.

But I knew I would need to think seriously, and soon, about what was to come. To study the Square. And the lamps. How long it would take to activate them. And in what order they should be lit. Would Caljn be where I thought he would be? And what would actually happen when I lit that last lamp? The thoughts went round and round till I determinedly set them aside and went to take my shower.

As I walked briskly along the paths between the houses the sun felt warm, and welcome. I thought about the paintings I was working on. They weren't very difficult which certainly was a blessing right then. And the Jansoons were nice people. Their commission of two medium sized paintings, one of each of their children at play, was one of those satisfying jobs. The children were chubby, cute and usually laughing. Young enough to give freely of what was inside them at any given moment, and often changing minute to minute, yet old enough to communicate with whatever world was around them. Their liveliness had prompted so many sketches that it had been hard to choose just two to turn into the paintings.

I had brought along my 'traveling studio' the previous week and had begun painting. I like working in my client's home when possible. That way I can keep in touch with my subject, though I prefer not to have anyone in the room with me while I'm actually working.

A lively striped chipmunk skittered across my path, almost under my feet. Startled, I had to skip a lively step to avoid him. I had to laugh as I stopped to look after it, long enough to hear its chittering back at me. "Same to you," I replied out loud, "and I wish you also a good day." I continued on, my mind going back to the Jansoon children. They had a lot in common with that energetic chipmunk!

As I entered the Square I was drawn to the lamps. But I didn't want to think of that right then. I wondered if I would ever feel the same way about the lamps. I'd always had a special fondness for them. I slowed my steps as I crossed over the eastern end of the tiles, and looked back through the people at the Square. The chipmunk and children faded from my mind. I stood, staring, shading my eyes with my hand, thinking.

The lamps in the central area are of the older type. You have to use the long activating wands to light them, and the energy only lasts about three hours. The wands have to be recharged periodically, as do the hand lamps and portable energy carriers. You just take them to one of the spots of concentrated electrical activity to charge them up. There are a number of different areas, and it doesn't take long. There is usually a lot of conversation and community available there too, which can be fun. Then there are the times when you want a quieter spot. I have two favorite areas that I can usually count on being free of other people. It isn't just the tools that are energized there.

But, I thought, what about Caljn, and his close friend, Valjar? Where did they go? I had never seen them at any of the charging areas. And how would they feel if they went to one of the quieter spots, how would it affect them? Not enough public for Caljn, and too much for Valjar I'd guess. I couldn't picture either of them there.

I turned my thoughts back to the lamps. I could light the lamps that evening if I returned from the Jansoons at the right time. Anyone could do it who wanted to, whenever they wished. There was hardly a time when they weren't lit for the early evening, even during storms sometimes.

And at night, especially during those lazy, balmy times, a group or more would meet in the Square, light a few lamps and enjoy a more private public get together. A quiet one of course. Although the homes begin a good distance from the Square (places of commerce surround the immediate area) it was known and agreed that more riotous gatherings would be held in one of the outlying parks, far enough from homes not to disturb them.

It was at one of those late, quiet gatherings in the Square that I first ran into Caljn. And began to learn more of that small part of the community that I wished wasn't there.

I put my hands in my pockets and leaned back against a post, remembering . . .

I had been working on a painting in one of the large houses north and west of the Square. An area where people live mostly on the outside, seldom admitting to an interior self. I occasionally do a painting for one of those people. I feel sorry for them somewhat, and maybe I feel I can share something of my philosophy of life with them that way. It is draining but I fill in between with a lot of jobs that add to my being instead, like the Jansoon children.

But it wasn't an uplifting job I came from that night. It had been late because the woman felt she had to be too busy during the sunup hours to "sit" for the painting. And she did insist on "sitting", though I didn't want or need it. It was one of the woman's many beliefs that she clung to so hard, at the expense of reality and her happiness I'm afraid. It wasn't worth fighting her for but it hadn't made the job any easier. I usually left feeling frustrated and irritated, and that night was no different.

I'd taken a path that went around and through the Great Hall, a large, covered area connecting the main roads and paths with the Square. Outside the Hall are most of the town's stables, pastures, runways and parking areas. An amazingly calm conglomeration of beasts, bicycles, sail planes, and electric vehicles, none of which are allowed in the Hall or onto the Square. Except for those run by people who couldn't get around on their own of course. There were enough lights lit that night to make the path easy to walk.

The Hall's lights had been glowing softly. And as I came through onto the Square I noticed a small group gathered around a man, off to the side, where the lamps circled a small raised area. It appeared to be a reading. I felt that might be just the thing to lift my spirits and calm my irritation. I usually enjoyed such things even when they weren't along my own beliefs. It didn't hurt to see other perspectives and it helped me to organize my own views.

No one had paid me any attention as I came up and sat down on a bench in the shadows, near the edge of the people. A rather thin, pale man was standing under a lighted lamp speaking to the group, or maybe preaching *at* the group was a more apt description. His name was Caljn. I thought I had seen him in the Square before, but I didn't know him. He had a sheaf of papers in his hand which he waved around now and then for emphasis. His voice wasn't very strong, and not musical at all. Actually, it was rather hard and whining.

I was disappointed. I could have used a nice pleasant, rhythmic voice that night. The man was dressed in a colorful tunic but it didn't fit him very well. Most of the people listening were late middle aged, a few older, a few younger. Many of them were overdressed in rather stiff clothing. There are some groups that adopt that kind of dress, sort of as a statement I guess. Certainly not to be comfortable. Tamoi says it's not unlike clothing of some of the cultures in the old civilization so it could have a historical basis I suppose.

Only a few lamps were lit and it seemed a rather melancholy crowd. It wasn't what I needed. But something held me. Sort of a morbid fascination with those thoughts that were so alien to my own.

I finally decided to stay awhile and just let it all flow in and out without criticism. But I couldn't stay detached. I became more uneasy with his words as the minutes passed.

Caljn was lecturing on some teachings of The Church, but they sounded a bit off to me, something in his words didn't quite fit. More of a feeling than an actual physical difference. I felt him notice me and his words changed a bit, coming from a direction just slightly to the side of where they had been. No one else seemed to notice. They all appeared mesmerized by him. I could see how he might have that effect, and I knew that he knew that too.

But what he was saying! The teachings of some of the old religions were rather stilted and narrow I knew, but most of them had their good points. They hadn't discovered all that much from the old church-based religions, but of what there was the 'Church of the Final God' had picked out what they wanted and founded their religion on that. They hadn't chosen the parts I would have but then they weren't me, and I wasn't much for organized religion anyway. At least most of the other religious groups had a base that made sense to me.

But this was obviously a group from the Church of the Final God. I was familiar with it through talking with clients who belonged. Like the woman I had just left. For that matter my sister-in-law Careen was a member.

Caljn seemed to have taken the church's teachings and mixed them with some old scientific views, and was spewing them out. Intent, it appeared, on soaking everyone around with them.

Where the ideas came from didn't matter of course, it was the ideas he was currently handing out that were of importance. I sat listening, and shivered in spite of the warmth of the tiles. The ideas were awful. But even worse was that these people were hanging onto the man's words as if they were great truths.

How could anyone want to believe in such repression, such anger against other living things? Especially in view of the world we were living in now, such a freedom that wasn't known in the old civilizations apparently. Or at least was ignored. No one really knew. There are some who just don't want the responsibility that comes with the freedom I guess. I decided to go on home.

I got up quickly to slip away. Caljn abruptly ended his talk and sent his followers away, saying he'd see them there night after next. He slowly hurried along beside me and spoke, inviting me back. He gave me the chills but I smiled politely and said maybe, and that I really did have to be going. I left and tried to put aside what I'd heard. I certainly hadn't planned to be with *that* group again.

But I went back. Even after the painting was done and I had no reason to be out so late (for some reason these meetings were almost always held late at night). Part of me was appalled and insisted I stay away. But another part said it was important. I didn't pretend to fully understand but I had learned to listen to that second part of me. My paintings often came from there, and the ones which did were my best.

After his lectures Caljn would talk with me. I listened, and kept my distance as he seemed to grow more and more impressed with his words, seeming sometimes to talk just to hear himself talk. He insistently pushed, apparently not able to stand that I wasn't falling in line like the others. He seemed to think that was a natural thing for those around him to do. He lived in a very narrow world.

I grew more and more distressed by what I was learning, almost against my will. But it wasn't against my will, I knew that. I made the decision to let myself go and learn all I could. To feel what was going on with this man. Not just his words but what was behind them. To try to understand where it was going. I felt it was important to know.

Caljn and his group became more and more a part of my life. The bits and pieces piled up. It was a small group actually, and ignored by most. But as I became more immersed in their world the size of the group grew proportionally in my mind. I had to remind myself again and again that they were a minority.

I sat down on a nearby bench and watched the people, working to put Caljn and his group in perspective.

During the sunup hours if I ran into Caljn we seldom spoke but a few words. He seemed to operate best in the dark. He was known around as an eccentric, or just plain untalented poet and was often found in the Square, throwing words out to no one in particular. Again, there, he just seemed to enjoy hearing himself talk.

The time spent with Caljn and his group had not been pleasant. I was glad I had my work to bury myself in for relief. It helped. Though it was hard to avoid Shahvid and his questions. He knew I had been out late a lot since he was often up and working himself at that time. That schedule seemed to suit him and Careen.

So often I had almost talked to him about the whole thing. But it just wouldn't have fit into his world, or my friends' either. Caljn and the Power Movement were so negative. At first I just wanted to figure those people out. And it wasn't something to share with friends. Then I realized if I confided in them I could also be involving them in something far more dangerous.

Besides, I didn't know what they would think of my involvement. It was best just to avoid the questions by avoiding my friends. It wasn't easy. Especially with Kasho, with whom I was quite close. But, I told myself, after it was all over I could get back to my old life, reestablish my friendships. Meantime, I simply had to do a better job of reassuring Shahvid, of not letting him know of my problems and anxieties. Careen was enough of a problem for him without worrying about me.

And then there was Jahon. Shahvid's closest friend Jahon. Damn. I wished I could put our "talk" out of my head. Or *his* talk rather. It hadn't been my idea. When Jahon had angrily confronted me about my meetings with Caljn I had just blown up. It certainly hadn't been a pleasant fight. I guess no fight is But I couldn't make much sense of our confrontation.

I shook my head. I didn't want to think about Jahon, or why our previously easy relationship had changed. Or how, and why, he knew about Caljn and me. The public relationship that was. I was sure no one knew of my attendance at Caljn's more private meetings. I stood up, the frustrating thoughts and feelings swirling.

I knew this was doing me no good. And certainly wasn't my intent when I left home. Deliberately, I put my mind on the paintings and what I had planned to do that afternoon, then continued on my way.

I took leave of the Jansoons and headed out. It was almost dark. A brief interruption earlier for tea and cheese had managed to stay my hunger for a while but it was time for something more substantial. As I walked along, I thought about the paintings. The afternoon session had gone well. I figured I should be able to finish them by Friday.

When I reached the Square there were quite a number of people around, going here and there, some hurrying, some not. The air above was fairly quiet with few gliders or electric planes in sight. The lamps had already been lit. They were such a pleasing sight in the darkening evening. The soft light from the lamps and the soft light of the sky blended to make a beautiful backdrop for the people. I picked a bench from which to watch. Sunday night's Starpeace meeting seemed long ago.

I enjoyed the scene. The people and their clothing were so varied. You could paint your whole life and never capture it all. How boring it must have been back when communities were mostly of the same color, and dressed in the same costumes. There are a few groups that organize that way even now of course, but they're a minority. Most folks seem to enjoy the differences as much as I do.

I had to smile as I watched the ebb and flow in the Square. There were mainly adults and older youngsters, the youngest people being home that time of night, or with their families in one of the many green areas scattered among the houses. There were a lot of loose robes, tunics and shifts moving across the tiles, in every shape, size and color imaginable it seemed. Tighter, more confining clothing was interspersed along with striking one-of-a-kind costumes.

For myself I prefer my soft hooded robes, the lengths of which vary with the seasons as do the layers under or over. In the warm months I usually wear one of loose neck and moderate length with sleeves that easily roll up. Although I enjoy others' clothing adventures, I'm not much interested for myself. My wardrobe is simple. And easy. I like it that way.

I tend to the earth colors. Maybe my painting takes care of any need for brighter hues. But when I'm at the easel I wear a loose, light colored smock with tight cuffs which is usually a riot of colors. It happens to be a handy place to test a new shade or tint of paint.

A cool breeze meandered by and I fastened my robe closer around my neck. I drew off my sandals and sat with my feet drawn up on the warm bench, my robe wrapped around my legs. The heat felt good. My body still ached from the rough treatment the previous night. But I quickly thrust the thoughts of that away.

The paving tiles and the benches are made to absorb the heat of the sun during the day and gently give it back in the evening. When it is cloudy there is some other arrangement to heat them from solar energy stored in a building south of the Square. I closed my eyes and relaxed against the bench, enjoying the gentle heat and the movements around me. I deliberately set aside the thoughts of Caljn. I felt the flow of people moving and talking. It was comforting, and I let my mind wander.

I remembered the planning some years ago, when it was decided to renovate around the Square. To give the breezes more room but calm the storms Shahvid said. He and Jahon had sure been involved in the project. How ignored I'd felt during that time! I had finally joined in by helping Pia and Brant with the layout and planting of the vegetation. They had been in their glory, and fun to work with.

It was a great success too. Each business around the area has its own ecosystem now with lots of plants and bushes and small wildlife. Yet each seems to complement the others. It's amazing how it all came together in the end. Some of the people had gotten together to plan their spots, but most came up with their own creations to suit their business and themselves. There were no set rules as everyone understood the spirit of the plan, and had a good time with it.

It's fun to wander around to see what changes are being made. I especially like the 'Signs of Commerce'. The different groups who serve and trade with the public came up with symbols to identify their particular activity. Then each owner added their own design or symbol to individualize it. It's so much nicer than the lettered advertisements. Harmonizes well with the varied environments too. There are so many talented folks around this community. And then there are people like Caljn, and his friends.

My daydreaming ended hard with the thought, and I landed back in the current world. My stomach growled its irritation at so much neglect, a loud reminder of how hungry I was. I sat up and stretched. As I relaced my sandals I noticed my wrists. The marks from the ropes wouldn't be gone soon but at least they didn't hurt any more. I pulled my sleeves down carefully to cover the bandages. I could just see trying to explain those wounds to Shahvid, or any of my friends.

On an impulse and with little thought I decided to go to the Harmony Tea Establishment. I'd left a note at home saying not to expect me till late, having no idea when I left what my plans were to be. I'd been avoiding the Harmony Tea the past months. It just hadn't fit well with my life at that time. But right then I felt a sudden need of food and comfort, the kind of comfort you get from friendly souls of your own persuasion. I quickly headed toward the southeast area beyond the Square. I wondered what kind of soup they'd be having. And I hoped there would be some bluesy music.

The Harmony Tea doesn't have an extensive menu. You can get whatever kind of soup was made that morning, and maybe yesterday's if there is any left. Also cheese and breads, the kinds depending on what Chan felt like buying and what Salti felt like baking. And teas of course. The choices are almost overwhelming. I think Chan and Salti spend most of their creative energy looking for different and varied herbs, leaves, berries and flowers to put together in an infinite variety of combinations. I suppose as I use my paints, they use the plants.

And then there is the music. A small stage is in the corner of the room where various musicians add music of their own making, quietly, so as to not override the conversation flowing around the room. There is a sign-up sheet posted so sometimes you know ahead of time who is going to be playing or singing, but usually it's more informal, more spontaneous. The variety is almost as vast as the teas with instruments of many kinds, some from the old civilization and some newer creations. Mostly stringed but also reeds and flutes. The singing covers the range of the singer's emotions and talents, always a little different from anything else you've heard.

It is a great creative atmosphere and the need to soak some of that up washed over me. And the desire to just relax. To set aside the events of late, and the events soon to come. I needed to shake off the hopelessness I absorbed whenever I was around Caljn.

The room shared its warmth and happiness with the evening outside as I pushed the door open and went in. A feeling of missed familiarity hit me. There were people at quite a few of the small wood tables and I waved greetings and smilingly declined invitations as I made my way across the room. A quiet table along the wall caught my eye and I settled into the chair. It was that type of place. Invitations to join were usually there, but no hard feelings if they weren't or you declined. I wasn't ready that night for intimate conversation.

An older man was on stage singing a soft, meandering tune to a rather large stringed instrument that had a low, deep tone. I just sat there letting the music and the conversations and the noises of the place soak in. Not thinking of anything in particular, just being. Then my stomach rumbled, reminding me of why else I was there. So I nodded a yes to Salti's questioning look and raised soup ladle, then rose to make my way to the bread and cheese bar.

Salti registered the order without missing a word in her conversation with several people. And she dished soup, made tea and sliced chunks of cheese off a large wheel, seemingly all at the same time and with no hint of hurry. Salti was setting the soup on the table as I returned laden with my bounty.

"Hard day, eh?" Salti perused my heaping plate with amusement. It was a joke among them all how I could eat so much and weigh so little. Salti's weight went the other direction. "We've missed you, glad to see you tonight." No questions, neither Salti nor Chan would think of it. But if you wanted to tell them, they would listen.

"I got involved in my painting and forgot about dinner," I explained as I arranged my soup, cheese and bread. "Is this some of Phielon's goat cheese?"

Salti sat down for a minute, "No, his new cheeses won't be ready yet for another month. This is some from across the valley, I can't think of the name but Chan says it's pretty good. Maybe a little stronger than Phielon's."

We chatted on a bit about the cheese and bread and soup. It was that kind of conversation and Salti understood. She stood up as someone across the room headed up to the soup counter.

"Something different to drink tonight? Or you want to stick to your Blackberry & Rose Nights?" Salti headed to get the tea and dish the soup almost before I could answer. She would know that it was not the night for a new tea.

You couldn't hide much from her if she knew you. And I guess I didn't care to.

As I ate, my body felt both drained and renewed. I took the empty bowl up to the kitchen window and poured hot water into the small ceramic pitcher containing the herbs for my tea. Weaving amongst the groups of people I made my way back to the table, nodding here and there at a word or smile. Someone else was on the stage now, a young woman sending out a golden, rather melancholy melody on a reeded instrument. She seemed too young to have feelings so sad, and all of a sudden I felt close to tears. All my own conflicts washed over me. My life seemed for a moment almost overwhelming.

I drank my tea and let the music and conversations blend in, firmly pulling up my inner reserve of security and wrapping it tightly around me. I wasn't used to this type of emotional seesawing. So intent was I on getting myself back in control that I didn't notice Jahon till he pulled up a chair to the table. Startled, I just stared, missing his greeting. For some reason I couldn't think of a thing to say.

Jahon moved the honey jar and helped himself to a piece of cheese from my plate. "What's wrong? Do I look that rough? I was out at my parents place and tried to beat the dark back here. Forgot to charge up the bike's headlight battery and almost ran over a cat down by Neisar's place." He stopped talking, looking both disconcerted and irritated when I didn't speak up. He reached for a slice of roll.

I fought to find my voice, and my composure. It was ridiculous, you would have thought I was sixteen and he my current hero. It occurred to me that it maybe hadn't been such a good idea to eat at the Harmony Tea. I took a breath and managed to say "Hi, how are your folks doing? I haven't seen them in quite awhile." For some reason my words just wouldn't flow. Frustrated with myself I felt on the edge of tears again. Damned emotions. I got up, "I'll get you some more bread and cheese."

Jahon moved to stop me, then pulled back. He didn't say anything out loud but his look said enough. I knew he was concerned and maybe frustrated but I just couldn't find an easy path to tread with him right then. The shadow of Caljn seemed to be there between us. It was as if we had suddenly become casual acquaintances. But we weren't. That was the trouble.

Jahon had been around for most of my years. He and Shahvid were close friends. Naturally, with no pretenses. Their relationship just was. Jahon is a bit younger than Shahvid though they look the same age, Jahon's black hair being partly gray already. He's about the same height, though leaner, more muscle than flesh. Shahvid tends to be heavier, and is a lighter complexion compared to Jahon's bronze. They have a good relationship. Shahvid designs the buildings, and Jahon gets them built, doing much of the finishing work himself.

It was because of that friendship that I had seen so much of him over the years. I had also spent much time with his family after my parents had died. His mother and father were a somewhat calm oasis and they had a happy family. His sisters are older than I but they had easily and naturally shared their home with me. No one pushed, no one tried to take the place of my parents as so many adults had tried to do.

Shahvid used to consult with Jahon about me when I was growing up, and Jahon's parents had shared helpful advice whenever needed. To my advantage I'm sure. It had been a pretty good atmosphere. I knew of their love, friendship and help but I also knew I was pretty much responsible for myself. And it all helped to make me the independent person I am. Trouble is, neither Jahon nor Shahvid seems all that comfortable with my independence. They say I am stubborn. Well, maybe they're right, but I'm certainly old enough to be my own person. If they could have both just seen and accepted that I think things would have been easier.

Maybe if Jahon hadn't been so demanding and direct when he had confronted me about my relationship with Caljn, I might have been able to come up with an explanation that would have satisfied him. But it wasn't the first time he had questioned my friendship with a person of the opposite sex, though never so violently. I didn't feel it was any of his business, or Shahvid's either. I was certainly the one to choose my friends, not them. Though I would hardly have called Caljn a friend, no matter what Jahon thought. Oh well, I don't think our clash had been any easier on him than on me.

"I tried to bring you a little of everything. This cheese here is new and very good, especially with the pickles." I was in control once more. I sipped my tea while Jahon ate. We talked of his parents, my recent painting, the work he was involved in now. But he was being intensely gentle and I couldn't relax. I kept waiting for him to mention Caljn.

When he was done eating I excused myself, "I want to get going early tomorrow. The room where I'm painting has the best light in the morning."

"How about if I walk you home then, it's pretty dark out tonight," Jahon offered.

I laughed, shaking my head no. That's all I needed right then, a nice friendly evening walk. And talk. There was no doubt who would have come up in the conversation. One fight with Jahon was more than enough for me. "Thanks, but you know I'm almost as comfortable in the night as the day walking around here. Besides, you have to accompany your bicycle home. You can't expect it to find its way alone. Go ahead and finish your tea. I'll see you later." And with a wave to Salti and several others I dropped some coins in the box and made my escape out the door.

Jahon sat frowning into his tea mug for quite awhile, hardly aware of the surroundings. Salti headed his way once, but changed her mind. There wasn't anything more she could offer that would help, just what was already there. After a bit Jahon abruptly got up and walked out into the night, almost forgetting to greet her as he left.

My mind was an uneasy jumble of emotions, feelings and thoughts as I headed down the path toward home. I felt that I needed a good night's sleep. But I couldn't kid myself. That wasn't the problem, and it wasn't the answer. Though it couldn't hurt.

I thought uneasily of Caljn. The last time I'd seen him he'd been even more insistent on seeing me again soon. And that had been Friday night, three nights previous. Saturday night had been drizzly and I'd used that for an excuse to stay home. I'd taken a long sauna alone, relaxed, hoping for a good night's sleep.

But then I'd spent most of the night sitting at my desk, staring out the window at the barest sliver of a moon, thinking of what I planned to do the next night. Arguing, discussing, pro and con, back and forth. Trying to get straight all I knew, from outside and inside, about Caljn and his group, his plans. Actually, the decision had already been made, but I had to go through it all again.

Sunday had been a long day. I'd slept some and worked a bit in the garden. When I had caught a glimpse of Jahon riding toward the house with Kasho, Tamoi and Binjer, I'd taken refuge in my studio. I didn't feel I could handle a fun, friendly bike picnic. Not with what all was on my mind.

When the group had left with Shahvid, I had felt a strong mixture of relief and disappointment. I felt left out, knowing of course that it was my own choice and there was no reason to feel that way. Conscious reasoning seldom changes the feelings inside however.

I ended up spending the afternoon reading and dozing. Waiting for nightfall. Trying not to think any more of my decision. Going not to Caljn Sunday night, but to Starpeace.

Caljn had wanted me to join him Saturday and Sunday nights, but had been quite insistent about Monday night. I thought uneasily of how he might react when I didn't show up. The get-together was to be at Valjar's house. Caljn had said only a small number of followers had been invited.

I wished I hadn't been one of them.

I suppose I should have gone. It was important that everything run smoothly, that there be no suspicion of anything wrong. But I just didn't feel like facing that crowd, not right then. Not right after the Harmony Tea, and Jahon.

Besides, I thought, maybe it would be good that I wasn't there. It was also important to keep them from suspecting how much I knew. Although I was sure Caljn didn't, and the others thought whatever he told them. He was so terribly 'man-minded'. I was sure he thought most of his rambles had gone far over my womanly head. But that prejudice had served me well thus far. That, and my inner feelings. Not to mention that conversation I had overheard, between Caljn and his closest associates. When I learned of their weapon system, and Caljn's *real* plans.

The thought of that night makes me cold deep down, even now. The unaccustomed feelings of hate and destructiveness. The fears as I realized exactly what I had heard and, as it all came together, a terrible crash deep inside me. It had been hard to continue after that.

I shivered, shook my head pushed the memories aside as best I could. It wouldn't help anything to go over it, nor to worry about it. I deliberately took a detour to Pasic's Fruit and Juice Market. Pasic usually left some of the day's offerings out for her night owl customers. Sure enough, when I arrived there were several small crates of fruit in their special 'cage'.

Pasic also provided for her smaller, more furry, friends and she preferred they ate from their own plate. Since they didn't see any difference between theirs and the human's she built a strong, so far effective, cage for her people fare.

I undid the latch, lifted the heavy lid and chose my breakfast, filling my pockets till I felt more like a lumpy potato than a woman. I dropped my coins in the mini-crate provided for that purpose and walked on home. I put my mind on hold and concentrated on the world around me.

By the time I reached the house I felt better, ready

for a night's restful sleep. I quietly let myself in. The faint
notes of Shahvid's guitar drifted down the hall from his study.
I thought briefly of going in to talk with him but decided
not. The time wasn't right yet. After Friday I would turn my
energies into renewing my relationship with my brother.. It
was past time to do so.

The first of the morning sun woke me, or rather the morning light. The sun had decided on a day off and the patter of drops introduced the day before I opened my eyes. I laid there a moment thinking of my dreams but they had fled as I woke, mixing with the rain into the day. That was OK. It had been a while since I had spent much thought on my dream world, and hadn't written any down for months. Later, I told myself, along with so many other things. I hadn't been around anyone to share and discuss them with anyway.

I tossed off my quilt and donned a long robe. It was chilly. I guessed that the fans on the heat storage unit had stopped again. I knew Shahvid had been working on them. Like most houses built at that time ours had a large area of rock that collected heat from the sun then released it when needed, when the sun wasn't shining. It was an old, simple system but it worked well. Usually. Even the new renovations often had something similar. I simply washed and dressed quickly. It wasn't that cold.

The kitchen was quiet but warmer than my rooms. I chose some fruit from the cooler to wash for breakfast and wondered where Shahvid and Careen were. Careen wasn't often in the eating area at that time. But she could usually be heard in her rooms getting ready for the day. It was amazing how long that took her. I had never been able to figure out what she could be doing all that time. Didn't matter

I guess. I turned my attention to my tea.

I thought about the day ahead as I ate. It was hard to believe it was only Tuesday. It seemed like I had lived two weeks since my late night meeting with Starpeace, instead of only two days. In a way, I wished it were already Friday, just to get it done with. But a part of me also wished that Friday would never come.

But the day was not Friday, and I had a day to plan. I would start at the Jansoon's. The window in the room where I was working was large enough to let in adequate light. Of course, I could work by lamp light but it just wasn't the same. After lunch I would go from there, depending on what the weather did.

My life is woven, for the most part, around the weather and the seasons. As is true with most folks. We don't hesitate to venture out in rain or storm, if we want or need to. But neither do we hesitate to choose inside jobs on stormy days, or take the day "off" on an unusually nice one. I've had some really nice afternoon swims on those nice days, sometimes alone but usually with friends.

There are a number of good swimming spots and the town seems to naturally organize into groups of like swim habits, each having its own favorite areas. Our group can usually be found in the more secluded locations, deep and wide enough for some serious swimming and diving, yet with a clearing large enough for some non-serious fun, games and picnicking. The children are mostly old enough to swim well, so shallows aren't important. The planned swims are always fun, but we've had some great spontaneous gatherings too.

It must have been odd in the old days when everyone wore 'swim clothing'. Most folks now don't go in for that archaic habit. How could you have a spur of the moment swim if you had to first go find a 'bathing suit'? There sure were some strange habits back them. On a really nice, warm day most of the town closes down, businesses are left unattended, and the waters and favorite shady areas become full of people! Tamoi says that back then people just didn't do that. They had to plan their 'days off' in advance. How could they possibly know ahead of time when it would feel good to go swimming? Or do anything else for that matter? It doesn't make sense to me. I sure wouldn't want to only go swimming on planned days.

Well, the day wasn't a day to spend swimming anyway. It was raining. And it didn't sound that warm a rain even if I was interested, which I was not. I was not going to take a chance of being with friends, not until after Friday. After that I was not sure of anything. But the struggle the previous night against the warmth of Jahon's friendship had been too much of a strain. I was not going to try that again.

As I finished my tea, a thought stirred in my mind. If something was such a strain then maybe it was because I shouldn't be doing it. I put the thought down. I felt it best right then to keep my close friends at a distance, and I didn't feel like questioning that decision. My involvement with Caljn and his crowd wasn't to be shared and that was that.

Speaking of Caljn. I knew I would have to see him again, keep up the relationship. I considered that if it really stormed then that would be a good excuse to stay home. But that was pretty cowardly. Besides, it wouldn't have solved anything. I needed to keep in touch with how things were going with the group. I got up and cleared the table. It was decided. I would go that night. They would be at Valjar's again.

With that decision the day turned gray and dreary, inside and out. The rain sounded harder and colder than earlier. It would have been nice to be able to just tesser myself to the Jansoon's.

I decided the heating fans could wait till later. I pulled on boots and shrugged into a long coat, pulling the hood tight around my face. Even in that kind of weather I preferred to walk. I loaded my pack with sandals, dry socks and a towel.

Before I went out the door I added a couple of the small bright yellow fruits I'd brought home the night before.

The children would enjoy them. To them anything that had traveled in my pack was special. Once I was outside the rain didn't feel as bad as it had sounded.

At the Jansoon's I donned my smock, tied my hair back, and settled in to my painting. The gray receded, the day and my work satisfied me. A very pleasant break for a long lunch with the family didn't hurt. Both adult Jansoons worked out in activities that were slow during rainy weather, so they often chose to stay home on stormy days. It was a nice time spent together. And my painting went well afterwards.

The portraits were almost done but I couldn't do any more on them till the current layer of work dried. I cleaned my brushes, set my painting area in order and went to find the family. I told the Jansoons I would be back Thursday morning, and that I should be finished Friday afternoon. Though the paintings wouldn't be dry, varnished and framed for a while yet.

With a final hug for the children I left them looking forward to Friday, and discussing how they should celebrate the occasion. The children didn't really understand about the paintings, or rather they weren't important to them. But they knew about celebrations, and they were excited.

The rain had lessened to a cold drizzle and the people in the Square were hurrying through, not spending much time in socializing. Their interests were more in the area of a dry home or other place of congregation, especially one that included food. My feelings matched, but I thought of my plans for later that night and decided against going home. It was easier to just stay out and come in late, thereby avoiding Shahvid and his questions. I hoped. So that left food.

Well, the Harmony Tea was out, too many friends to run into. I especially didn't want to run into Jahon again. A good possibility since he frequently ate out. He is a good cook, but says he doesn't like to waste his talents on just one person. And Shahvid was often with him since Careen had so many dinner meetings to attend. And neither his nor my schedules were set enough to plan on many meals together. I didn't want to meet him for dinner either.

I stood in the Square trying to decide where to go. The drizzle had turned back to rain, light but gusty, and not very pleasant. In exasperation I chose the Flying Fish and Such. They usually had a good choice of vegetable dishes. Besides, it was in an area where I wasn't likely to run into many friends. It wasn't that it was an ugly area or anything, but it seemed to be maybe louder, and not so relaxing as the southeast section. I turned to go to the restaurant, then stopped as I heard my name called. My instinctive first reaction was a joy at the sound of a friend. Then almost on top of it, the thought to ignore it and pretend I hadn't heard.

But Jahon was beside me before any decision could be made, "Hey, why are you standing around in this rain? Come on, I've just finished for the day and was thinking of the Grape & Stew for dinner." Intent on his own thoughts and direction he didn't wait for an answer but turned to go, asking, "How are your paintings coming? The frames are ready whenever you want them."

I didn't know whether to laugh, cry or scream. His easy inclusion of me in his plans without even asking would more than bug me at the best of times, and that night my mood was in line with the weather's. But the wind was picking up as the rain came down harder, and he looked so funny with his long raincoat alive with protrusions. He apparently had underneath it his backpack full of tools. I certainly didn't want to stand out there and argue with him. And besides, the Grape & Stew had good food.

So, full of apprehension because of my later plans, but looking forward to being out of the rain, I fell in beside him and we hurried across the Square.

"I'd just about forgotten the frames," I spoke above the rain, "I should be done with the paintings Friday, so I'll plan on picking them up sometime next week if that's OK."

I used to make all the frames for my paintings myself using Jahon's shop. It had been important to me at one time. Then Jahon started doing some for me now and then, and it evolved to him making almost all of them. I still enjoyed working in his shop, all full of wood smells. But I had to admit that Jahon did a better job with the frames. He has a good feel for my paintings and for the wood.

As we entered the Grape & Stew we were greeted by a homey mixture of people, warm food, and wet clothing. It was crowded, but we found space to hang our wet coats and packs. We made our way toward the back to a small table.

Like most of the eating establishments in town the

Grape & Stew's menu is small. The owners have a small vineyard so a dish of fresh grapes accompanies any order whenever they are in season. At other times other fruit is substituted, and in the winter you get raisins. And always available is a small selection of their own wines, which was possibly the reason for the inn to begin with, a place to share their wines with people. The meal is 'The Stew', the contents of which varies with the seasons, but which is always thick with vegetables, and served with dense dark bread.

We both ordered a meal and hot tea, declining wine but asking after the early grapes (an inquiry rather expected). We laughingly agreed that the yellow fruits on the table were rather gaudy compared to a fine dish of grapes, but they would do until harvest time.

The atmosphere was friendly but not as intimate as the Harmony Tea. Thank goodness. I nibbled a fruit while we waited for our dinners. It would be a bit of a wait since the room was full and no one hurried. Rushing would have been out of place. But I wished the food would arrive to offer a distraction. I uneasily thought of the meeting later that night, and knew I couldn't relax to enjoy the evening.

Actually, it had been awhile since I'd had an open, relaxing evening with Jahon. As I talked with him, a little uneasily, I felt a sense of loss. My involvement with Caljn and the Power Movement was between us. And being with him for dinner just made it worse. He was being quite friendly but I was on needles waiting for him to mention Caljn or the meetings. Our last argument had not been pretty and I didn't want to repeat it. It had ended with bad words and bad feelings on both sides. Jahon hadn't mentioned it since. It wasn't as if he had forgotten, or let it go, just that he had chosen not to mention it. Yet.

Our conversation finally settled in to an acceptable groove, and it was easier than the previous night. He told me about the project he was just finishing, and his plans next. He had some of his tools along with him since he had stopped by to do some small repair work for a friend before coming to dinner.

Jahon's circle of friends includes most of the town it seems and he has no lack of projects to choose from to satisfy his interests. He seldom has need to use coin for any goods or services as he barters his talent and creations for nearly everything he wants. Most people of the town work it that way, trading their wares or services, using coins only when necessary or convenient.

The soup arrived and we busied ourselves with our dinners, both of us absorbed by our own thoughts but at the same time strongly aware of each other. Each of us wondering what the other had in mind. And both worried about the meeting later that evening, but from far different directions.

I figured I had about a half hour before I had to leave. I wanted to get to Valjar's just as the meeting started. I was not anxious to spend any time alone with Caljn, but didn't want to miss anything either. My stomach worked on tying itself in knots as I finished my meal and sipped my tea. I had a feeling I might not be able to get rid of Jahon so easily this night. I knew him well enough to know he had something on his mind, and I didn't pretend to think it had nothing to do with me. I also knew how difficult he could be once he'd decided on a course.

I had never stopped to think how he knew of my meetings with the Power Movement, and that if he knew chances were that Shahvid would know also. My anger at his demand that I stop seeing Caljn and to stay away from that group had clouded all else. He hadn't been very tactful. Jahon was by nature a direct person, though he wasn't one to feel he had to always state his views. But he seemed rather emotional about the whole thing and it had come out as a rather direct attack.

My mind was busy with my thoughts as we talked and ate. Jahon seemed preoccupied also. I think we both had too many thoughts left unsaid. They probably would all come out someday. I just didn't want it to be right then. I tried to concentrate more on our somewhat shallow

conversation, and less on my choppy thoughts. I realized
he had stopped talking and was staring rather intently at
me. Neither my nerves nor my temper were up to that kind
of scrutiny.

"Do I have soup on my nose or something?" I asked
him rather irritably.

"Huh? Oh, sorry, I was just thinking," Jahon finished
one of the yellow fruits. "Since it's Tuesday Andon and Lex
will have their sauna going tonight, and that's just the thing
to go with this weather. How about going with me?"

~~~ ~~ ~ ~~ ~~~.

He tried to be offhand about it, as if he hadn't been
planning it since the day before, when Kasho had told him
of the meeting that night. She also knew and was concerned
about this situation with the Power Movement, though from
a different perspective than his.

Kasho had been keeping him informed about what
was going on, whenever she knew anything. He hadn't
questioned why, or how she knew what she did. There were
many of his friends in the outer circle of Starpeace, quietly
supportive and there if needed.

He knew his last confrontation with Neana hadn't
been a good idea. He had a hard time keeping his temper
in line whenever he thought of Caljn. He was sure she didn't
really know what the man was about. But *he* did. Enough
to make his blood run icy hot whenever he thought of him.
Why in the world did she want to be around him and his
crowd of blind followers anyway? Something different he
supposed. Well, Caljn and crew were certainly different
enough.

He had to find a way to get, and keep, Neana away
from them. If she just wasn't so darned stubborn. He'd
thought about discussing it with Sinat but didn't feel it was
necessary. It wasn't as if there was a real danger. He couldn't
put his finger on exactly what the problem was, he just knew
that it was there. He couldn't even discuss it with Shahvid
for some reason. ·

He had hoped that by some miracle things would

have righted themselves, and she would be back to her old self. That everything would be as it was. But he knew it could not be. Time may be relative but it didn't run backwards, not in this life. He waited, somewhat tensely, for her answer. Afraid that he already knew what it would be. But hopeful nonetheless.

~~~ ~~ ~ ~~ ~~~

    I toyed with my tea, feeling suddenly very depressed, a feeling that *used* to be alien. Oh, damn, damn, damn! The thought was so strong I almost said it out loud.

    But to Jahon I replied quietly, "I guess not, thanks anyway. I already have other plans for tonight." No use pretending otherwise.

    Jahon sat staring at me for a moment, his brown eyes alive with carefully reigned in emotions. "Fine." He dropped some coins on the table and stood up. Turning, he walked away without another word, and without looking back.

    I sat there staring into my tea mug, fighting back tears, again. I had never felt so alone. The feeling that I had made a big mistake, taken a wrong turn, enveloped me. Part of me wanted to hurry after Jahon, talk to him, tell him . . . Tell him what? Everything? Get him involved? No. This was something I had to take care of by myself.

    Dainon quietly came by and filled my mug. They may be busy but Dainon was always aware of what was going on around his room. I barely acknowledged him but he didn't expect anything more. I drank the tea and finished off the fruit.

    Somehow I made my way out of the inn, and found myself outside with raincoat and pack, walking toward Valjar's place. The rain had lessened once again to a drizzle. I made my way diagonally across the Square, not even noticing the lamps. In fact, I didn't notice much of anything. I was numb, inside and out. I knew where I was headed and was simply going there, with no thoughts in my mind at all, about anything.

I stopped when I came to the tall square white house. Valjar's house. I stood a moment outside the sturdy fence, thinking. Many folks fence in areas of their yards, usually to keep animals out of the gardens, but they seldom fenced the entire place like Valjar had. But then people like Valjar and Caljn weren't like most folks. Thank goodness. Tamoi says there were once many more like them though. I could hardly imagine it. But then again, those ideas of Caljn's, and his 'old science' friends came from somewhere. I had to keep in mind that they *were* a minority, no matter how pervasive they seemed sometimes.

I pushed open the gate and it closed behind me. I knew my entrance was being watched as I made my way to the side door. The few trees around his yard made the house seem oppressive. But what a terrible thing to think about a tree. It just was. It was the people inside who were oppressive of course. Interesting how you could feel that even out there.

Someone I didn't recognize opened the door for me and I followed him down the hall to the meeting room, slipping out of my wet pack and coat as I went. I had to consciously not show the uneasiness I was feeling, as I always did when I was around this group.

About twenty people sat around the room, mainly men, as usual. It would be interesting someday to figure out why. Caljn was already talking, standing beside the table as if he were some great important wise orator. Guess he thought he was.

He stopped when I entered, but I just briefly nodded to the room as a whole and slid into a seat farthest away from him. The room was crowded with furniture, extra chairs and people. And harshness. I mentally pushed the harshness away from me, preparing myself to listen to the words without letting their feelings get to me. I glanced around, thinking about the group.

This was the middle layer of the organization. Caljn and a few of his old-school scientist friends and followers were the inner. He had told me once that they met most every night that was not taken up by middle and outer group meetings. The outer circle included many of the church's members, and those who stopped by the lectures in the Square but weren't really involved, either because of their lack of interest or because of the inner group's distrust.

Caljn had pushed at me to be a part of the inner circle but I had refused to even talk to him about it, which I think was his main reason for wanting it. I sincerely hoped he hadn't mentioned it to anyone else. Being as involved as I was made me nervous enough, though necessary for what I had to do. I didn't think the members of this group were much aware of the inner circle, and knew nothing of their activities.

And good old Caljn kept preaching, that night as wordy as ever. And they keep listening. It was mainly along the same old lines, how important it was for them all to get out among the population and spread his word. Interesting that he called it 'his word' instead of 'the sacred teachings of the old church', or some such thing that he used to say.

The civilization was too loose, it was a wreck, the people had to be brought in line. I was used to it by then but still, hearing it again . . . It was all such a big bad joke. Unfortunately, one that had gone way out of hand.

Oh, there were other groups here and there that thought they had the final answer to everything, the only answer, and that it was their duty to push it off on those other poor souls who didn't happen to believe exactly as they did. Problem was, those 'other poor souls' were as a whole quite happy and contented people who continued to live their own lives. It was rather hard to 'rule' other people when they weren't the least bit interested in being ruled, and simply ignored you. So why did these people here want so much to be ruled that they would follow someone like Caljn?

You would think hearing Caljn droning on and on about 'duty' and 'responsibility' and how terrible it would be for them if they didn't do what he said (I never had understood that part) would make them all just want to get up and leave. Or throw up. That's how it affected me.

What was that? Caljn was saying something about Friday. I tightened. He wasn't going to tell them what he planned to . . . No, it was something else. I wondered what he was up to.

Then I saw it. He wanted to get them all there to see him do his great act. After all, it wouldn't be worth as much without his loyal audience watching. How could he just ignore the lives and people he was so coldly planning to destroy, just to have one great 'show off'? I wanted to grab him and shake him till every thought in his demented head spilled out on the floor. Then throw him in and let him drown in that stinking polluted pile.

I took a quiet, deep breath. A few more minutes along that line and I would have done it. I carefully put my mind elsewhere. Jahon came through, and his workshop. No, not Jahon, I couldn't deal with him right then. But his workshop, that would do. He was never angry there and neither was I. I concentrated on it, and calmed down.

It appeared there would be little discussion that night (not that you could call their ignorant parroting of Caljn's ideas discussion). No, this was all Caljn's. Nothing new either. At least he had verified by what he had said that the Friday plan was still on. Three more days. I wished I had some hope that something would change before then. But

I didn't see any.

I cautiously looked around at the others. There didn't seem to be any indication that the people here thought of me as anything other than a fringe of their group. That was good. They would all expect me to be in the Square Friday, just like them, because Caljn had said to. But nothing else. If they thought of me at all, which wasn't likely. That was just fine with me.

Caljn ended his talk by saying he would see them all next Saturday night in the Square for an open meeting. To go over their successes of Friday evening, when they would All, of course, work together to Share The Views' with the Ignorant Populous. So, he wasn't going to tell them *he* would be there Friday. Maybe it was just a childish desire to 'surprise' them with his presence. That would fit.

But they would be in as much danger as the rest of the people in the Square. The destructive rays and viruses that Caljn planned to shoot at Chanthan would radiate off him to *all* those around. What could Caljn be thinking? Unless . . . I wondered if they had an antidote? He would then be a hero and "heal" his followers after the event, leaving the rest to suffer. Could that be?

I felt my face flush with sudden rage. I closed my eyes and roughly brought my emotions back down. Not here, and not now. All of a sudden I knew I would no longer question my own role in Friday evening's event. It was the right thing to do. And it *would* turn out OK. It had to.

I opened my eyes and looked at the paintings around the room. Pretty awful, but they fit both Valjar and Caljn well. I wanted to walk out. Right then. But that would have just angered Caljn needlessly. He expected me to wait till he talked to me. And he, of course, had to talk to most of the others first. Low person on his totem pole. Good place to be.

So, no meeting till Saturday he had said. That would mean the inner group would get together Wednesday and Thursday nights. It made sense considering what was coming Friday. I felt a sense of relief that I wouldn't ever have to be in the same room with these people again. And never again, after Friday, have to see Caljn in his ill fitting and off colored tunic.

I stood and mingled with the others, keeping to myself but not obviously so. Just a part of the backdrop. I felt hot and sticky. I concentrated on blending in.

I watched Caljn as he made his way to me, and I realized what those people were to him. It didn't have anything to do with that other, terrible plan of his. They were just a playground for his ego. An ego that was terribly bent out of shape. An ego that was trying the best way it knew how to project the man's distorted inner world. A world so lopsided with his beliefs of evil and demons and devils that it was not worth working for. He was leaving this life, no doubt, and going to take all he could with him. And he believed they would all end up in some frigid black void when they went.

As I patiently continued my inconspicuous waiting, my mind continued its frustrating circle of questions. How could anyone even begin to help a person like Caljn? I couldn't come up with a hint of an answer. Besides, I knew that the bottom line was that Caljn, like everyone else, was wholly and totally responsible for the world that he had made for himself. And that world seemed to be creeping in through the cracks and crannies of my own mind, dragging me down.

Caljn finally made his way to me, breaking off my thoughts. He steered me into a quiet corner. I saw Valjar watching us intently, his normally dark features stormier than usual. I hoped I wasn't the cause. Caljn seemed oblivious to his stare, but I certainly wasn't. I knew Valjar didn't like me, and only put up with me because Caljn insisted.

Caljn didn't waste any time, "I'll see you tomorrow night, here, same time." The inner circle meeting. He turned to go. I was too amazed to feel anger. Besides, he wasn't worth wasting my anger on.

I said quietly, "I guess not, thanks anyway. I already

have plans for tomorrow night." That had a strangely familiar ring to it.

Caljn turned back in angry surprise. He was engulfed in his world and wasn't used to having anyone question his demands when he was there. He didn't like it.

"I'll probably see you Saturday night though," I continued, strangely in control. It's amazing what kind of reserves you find in yourself when needed. And I needed it then. Caljn's look was not frier.dly. I seemed to have the touch that night for making people angry. I ignored his manner and smiled gently, refusing to think of the danger.

"Guess I'll be heading out now. See you later." I followed another woman out of the room, trying not to hurry, trying not to feel the angry stare that followed me. The anger that I knew could quickly and easily turn violent.

Out of the corner of my eye I saw Valjar walk over to Caljn. Though he was a much larger man than Caljn, one usually didn't notice him. He was always in Caljn's shadow. It came to me, for the first time, that Caljn wasn't the only one of that inner crowd who could be dangerous.

When I got outside it was raining again, which seemed appropriate. I took the path toward the Square, adjusting my pack over my rain coat. It seemed a long walk home. It was hard to believe that it was the same day as the one that morning when I had dropped the fruit into my pack to give to the Jansoon children. The same day as the one I had spent so many hours blissfully lost in my painting. The same one that had held my dinner with Jahon. How could anyone seriously believe that every day was the same length as another, that time was a constant, a concrete fact, never changing?

I woke late Wednesday morning to sunshine and warm breezes streaming in my window. I stretched, rolled over, threw my quilt off and enjoyed the simultaneous feel of warmth and gentle coolness on my skin. I couldn't remember any of my dreams but I felt rested and content. All the dark emotions of the previous night had apparently been dispersed while I slept. I enjoyed the cocoon of contentment, even if it was probably short-lived. It sure had been rare the past weeks. I let my thoughts drift nowhere in particular.

I felt like I had been given an extra day, and I didn't want to waste it. After all, one wouldn't want to ignore a gift from the gods. I sat up and arranged the pillows, leaning against the wall so I could watch and hear the birds flitting among the bushes outside my window.

It was a nice area out there. A large part of the yard was left pretty much to its own. I looked out on a variety of fruit trees, bushes and plants. A stone walk meandered through from the north entrance of the house (the one I used) to the garden shed then on to a small storage barn. It continued on through the garden, finally connecting with the lane that led to the house. The whole area was alive with creatures both furred and feathered.

I'd often thought about building myself a place on the outskirts of town, near where the forests begin. Where there was lots of room for the birds and animals. Or rather rebuilding a place. No one builds on fresh ground. After all, nature's other creatures have to have room to live too. But if you wanted to move, there were always a few places available to live in as is, renovate, or take apart and rebuild. And occasionally there was a spot where a building had been, but had been moved, torn down or destroyed. Nature has been known to completely rearrange an area with her storms. And, though rare, fires do occur.

I had a folder full of drawings and ideas for my place. The sketches had changed over the years but the basic layout ended up being much the same. I'd never shown the sketches to anyone, not even Shahvid or Jahon or Kasho. I didn't know why, it just hadn't come up. Maybe because no one seemed to expect me to leave Shahvid's house, my home since soon after the death of our parents.

When I was young we lived on the other side of the Square, in a larger house. But when it came to be just the two of us, Shahvid traded with a family who wanted more space, and we had moved. The house isn't now much like it was then. Shahvid and Jahon have rebuilt it often over the years to fit the changing needs.

Actually I did move out once, nine years ago, when Shahvid and Careen married. I was eighteen then and, though involved in many directions, was settling in to young adulthood and a narrower focus. As a child I had been given a good measure of freedom to explore whatever interested me, as is common with most children. I had taken full advantage of the encouragement. It is interesting how the more I explored different areas the more clear my real interests became to me.

By the time I was in my teens I knew I wanted to paint, had been painting off and on for some time, and had worked with an array of teachers. Anyone with an interest is a teacher, needing only to have something to share and someone interested enough to share it with. Most teachers simply set aside some time out of their regular lives to accommodate one or a few students.

My painting teachers had been quite a varied group. There was Deita Kim, who traveled all over collecting materials from earth and nature to mix into paints, allowing an occasional student to accompany her now and then. She would also make time when she was back in her cottage to let students assist in and learn how to mix the colors. I had spent an adventurous five months traveling with her when I was fifteen, and had learned a whole lot more than just paints and painting! I wonder if she is still traveling? It has been some time since I've visited with her.

And then there was the elderly Paclerei who had shown me how to feel the harmony and discord among colors. He would have me randomly and freely fill canvas after canvas with different shades and tints and intensities of color after color, on top of each other, beside, over, under, through. All the while he accompanied whatever I did on his piano, another great interest and talent of his. That experience had been greatly refreshing. And had relieved me of the mechanical pattern of painting I had gotten stuck in. A habit I had acquired by spending too much time with a few established painters who had simply taught me their style. The mechanics of it are important of course, but painting isn't much without the feeling. Whenever I think of him I'm newly grateful. He has gone on from this life now but I have no doubt that he is still actively pursuing and creating.

I also remember the many hours spent in and out of Jahon's workshop. I liked working there, carving or making small items. I'd spent some time over the years with various other woodworkers, but I knew it was more a hobby than an inner direction. And of course I had grown up with Shahvid's love of creating buildings on paper and having them become a physical reality. Often with Jahon's help.

I had learned much from them both, working with them on several of their joint building projects. I got involved from the design, to the drawings, to the actual construction and finishing of the building. It was fun, but again, it wasn't like my painting. I could do it or not.

Then there were those numerous 'odd jobs', doing this or that, helping out where a little extra help was needed. And always learning, feeling out the world, seeing where my interests would lead me. Then Shahvid had introduced Careen.

He had met her through a renovation he'd designed for one of the big houses. It was her Aunt's house, and Careen was spending a lot of time with her Aunt then. She had just left an unhappy marriage and Shahvid ended up spending almost as much time counseling Careen as overseeing the renovation.

A month after the project was completed, Shahvid announced his marriage plans to Jahon and me. Jahon hadn't been involved in that project but he knew Careen somewhat from around. She was older than either of them but the town isn't that large. He hadn't been very happy about the marriage.

But I had been excited for Shahvid. I had only met Careen a few times, which seemed odd, but this was Shahvid's life and I was young, full of romantic visions.

And then, with the marriage just two weeks off, Careen and I had a private 'talk' and Careen had left no doubt that I was to move out before she moved in.

Deeply wounded, I had lined up a small apartment in one of the big houses northwest of the Square. It wasn't my favorite area of town but it was available right then. It wasn't that I hadn't planned to move anyway, after all Shahvid was on to a new life. But I had thought I'd wait to find a place that fit me.

I hadn't said anything to Shahvid, or to anyone else. I just borrowed a small van and moved my belongings one day when he was out. What could I have said anyway? I certainly wouldn't repeat what Careen had said to me, after all Careen was to be Shahvid's wife. Besides, I half believed her words.

Only a week previous a friend of Careen's had bluntly told me I should stop tagging after Jahon, that he had a life of his own and shouldn't be saddled with his friend's little sister hanging around his shop. I hadn't had much defense for that type of thing then, and the two talks had hit me hard. I hadn't known how to react. I hardly knew either woman and they were both much older than I. Not that it should have made any difference since I had friends of all ages. But these two were different. And I was eighteen, with emotions every which way more often than not.

A sigh slipped out as I thought of that time and the years that had followed. I wrapped my arms around my legs, chin on knees. I don't know even now why Shahvid married Careen, none of us did, maybe not even Shahvid himself. There were other single women in our circle of friends, all nicer than Careen. I knew it wasn't right to compare, but I'd long ago given up my fight to try to see the best of my sister-in-law. I tried to accept her as she was. Not that she didn't have any good points, but basically it turned out she just wasn't a very nice person.

But back then I had stayed in my tiny apartment, avoiding Jahon and spending little time with Shahvid. He had been livid when he had come home to find my note saying I had moved. Jahon had been with him and they had stormed over to bring me home (I got this by way of several friends who had met them on their way there). But I carefully wasn't around and neither was the family who lived there.

Careen hadn't mentioned her talk with me to Shahvid of course, so all he knew was what he saw on the outside. And he wasn't about to have his sister move out to some strange house. When Jahon told him what he knew of the family who was renting the apartment to me, he about tore the door down to get in. But, there was really nothing he or Jahon could do but go home. And come back the next day, early.

I had finally faced the two of them, calmly telling them I was my own person and would live where I wanted to and do what I wanted to do, and that was that. Well, it wasn't exactly that simple but I had held my ground and they had finally given up and left. I then went inside and cried off and on for three days.

But life went on, as always, and Shahvid and Careen were married. Within a month I knew my hasty retreat had not been a good idea. But it was seven months (after a long talk with Jahon's mother) before I quietly moved back to my brother's home. The suggestion that I move out was never brought up again.

My thoughts were silent for a moment, listening to the birds. Why was I thinking of such down times on a beautiful day? There were more important things to think of, like working in the garden, or taking a jaunt to the forest, or going for a swim, or . . . All sorts of images faded in and out of my mind. I carefully set aside any pertaining to the events of the last months. This was my free day, and I wasn't going to think of anything not pleasing, or do anything that didn't feel good.

I got off the bed and opened the window all the way. It was warming up already, and the mixture of morning cool and midday warmth breezed in to tickle my skin. I laughed at a small furry creature tunneling through the low foliage of the ground cover below the window, poking its nose out now and then to sniff the air. Good idea. I took several long deep breaths, then turned back to get dressed for the day.

My light, tan tunic under the green robe seemed adequate for the day's weather. I pulled on socks and sandals, then brushed my hair, leaving it to fall loose around my shoulders. Other items went into my pack, to take care of whichever direction I decided on. Then I headed out the back door. I didn't want to talk to anyone who might dispel my magic day. I decided to eat breakfast "on the road" so took a path leading to Pasic's Fruit and Juice Market.

I skirted the busier places, eating my breakfast and enjoying the day. I kept to the narrower paths, meandering in and out, not in any hurry to be anywhere. I had enough fruit and rolls, having also stopped at the Dough's On Bakery, for a small party. I just had to fill up my canteen at one of the fountains and I'd be all set. For what I wasn't sure yet but that didn't matter.

My first stop would be the Library. I had some books to drop off and maybe I'd take out another if something struck me as fitting the day. The Library is a great, large building filled to the brim with books and cozy spots to curl up and read. There are nooks with small tables and comfortable chairs if that's what you wanted. Or an area where everything is scaled down to fit you if you are of a younger age, and smaller size. It is a contented place and one I have spent much time in. It is also very popular so is open early to late to accommodate the people.

I made my way to the corner of the Square where, backing up to the Great Hall, the Library sat waiting between the Meeting Room, Council Rooms, and Maintenance Shop.

When I came out of the Library the day was noticeably warmer. I decided a swim would have to be fit into my plans. And a long walk before that would be just the thing for my body and my mind. As I went through the corner of the Square and into the Great Hall, I waved and greeted several friends. But I didn't stop to talk. I needed the day to myself.

I slowed down in the Hall though. It is an interesting place, about 80 feet wide and four times that long. The sides are the back walls of the two-storied connecting buildings; to the south the Meeting Room, Library, Council Rooms, Maintenance Shop; and to the north Public Services, Communications, Help Center, Theater Halls. They are all covered with a sod roof alive with wild flowers all of the warm months.

The Great Hall, in addition to being a connecting tunnel between the Square and the paths and roads leading out of town, is also the main communications area for the population. Its walls are covered with lists and signs and information. The areas above and overhead are alive with works of creativity from the town's artists. I even have a spot to display one of my paintings, which I change every month or so, as do most of the artists. Along the upper edges of the Hall are clerestories which let in whatever light nature provides, supplemented with soft electric lights when needed.

The information areas are as varied as the townspeople. There are lists of teachers, what they have to share and other related data; and lists of potential students, what they want to learn. If you want to hear some music, or see a play, or share in a reading, this is where you look to find your spot. Or if you are interested in something more physical you can look for a game or activity to suit you.

There are notices of Council Meetings and minutes of the meetings held recently. And notices of any meeting that would be of interest to any one of the townspeople. Visitors also have an area which includes a large map of the town with all the shops and markets and public services marked on it, along with other information a person new to the area might want. And much more.

I love to stand at one end of the Hall and view it as a large creative sculpture. One that is ever changing. The committee who oversees the Hall are a talented group.

My admiration was short that day though. My mind was on the day ahead and I wasn't interested in distractions. I decided to take my favorite series of paths that lead to an upper branch of the river, and a small clearing hidden in the brush and trees of the lower forest.

It was a good distance to hike, and by the time I arrived the sun had started down the other side of the sky. I lowered my pack to the carpet of pine needles on the edge of the clearing near the river. My sandals and tunic followed. The North Branch was deep enough here for a welcome shallow dive into the cool water, which didn't take me long to achieve.

I drifted with the current a ways, then slowly swam back upstream. The dragonflies kept me company above, and the minnows below. The water slid by my skin, taking with it some of the buried tension. I climbed out onto the bank and shook off the drops. Stretching, I slowly turned around and around, letting the sun dry me with its soft towel.

The rays glinted off of two small gold pendants I wore around my neck, one on a shorter chain, the other hanging beneath it almost to my breasts. I took a long drink from my canteen, then spread my robe on the grass. I was soon asleep, my body wrapped in the warmth of the sun and the friendly companionship of the woods.

The sun was far to the side of the sky when I awoke. For a few minutes I laid still, watching some birds playing in the branches nearby. Then I got up, stretched fully, and dressed quickly as I became aware of the cooler air.

I settled back down on nature's floor, warm and contented, and laid out my banquet from the selection in my pack. As I ate I blended with the life around me. I and the area knew each other well, and we didn't have the need to explain or question anything. I relaxed. I didn't think of anything in particular.

But the sun soon told me it was time to be going. I drew myself back in and got up. Leaving some offerings for the local inhabitants I slipped on my pack, and made my way back to the world of people.

The lamps were already lit in the Square by the time my walk brought me through the Hall and onto the tiles. There was a small crowd at the far end through which I could hear some music. It sounded like Lex and Kasho with baklia and flute.

I shrugged off my pack and sat down on a near bench. Watching the people, trying to decide what to do, and listening to the music as it floated my way. The mellowness I'd picked up out in the woods was still with me.

There are many groups who get together to play various types of music, sometimes in the Square, sometimes in a home, sometimes just off in one of the parks. The music I was hearing was from one such group, and they were the friends I had pretty much avoided since that night I had met Caljn. I hadn't played any music myself since then either. It was quite possible that Shahvid or Jahon would be coming along to join in. The sounds of guitar and harmonica appeared, then a bass lutimer.

I pulled my feet up on the bench, wrapping my robe around my legs. The evening wasn't cold but it wasn't warm either. As the people and sounds drifted around me I leaned back, and looked at the lamps.

I had to decide on my course of action for Friday, and it seemed a good time, while I felt calm. As detached and methodically as I could I thought the scene through, over and over, this way, then that.

Was I absolutely right about Caljn's intended actions? What if something had changed since my last talks with him, and the overheard conversation? I wrestled with the idea of going to Valjar's, either directly as Caljn had invited me, or as before, silently on my own.

I shivered, and drew my robe tighter around me, pulling the hood onto my head. I was a coward. But I knew what a chance I had taken before, and how close I'd been to being caught. I refused to think of what would have happened then. I'd heard enough to easily imagine the consequences, and it wasn't something I could handle. It had been so hard to continue the relationship with Caljn after that night.

I closed my eyes and hugged my knees. My calm mood was gone. The thoughts and feelings were so at odds with the scene around me, with friends not so far away, yet too far.

I brought myself sternly back in line. I couldn't afford to be uncertain. The community couldn't afford it. I wasn't going to Valjar's that night or the next night either, so no use playing the 'what if' game. Back to my role Friday.

The timing of the lighting of the lamps wasn't too hard to figure out. I'd done it often enough to know about how long it would take. And no one would notice, or care, in which order they were done. Or if I skipped a few. As long as I lit that last lamp of the group, within which Caljn would be standing, at exactly the right time. That was to be Starpeace's signal to aim. Their special low-impact electric plane would be following the lighting of the lamps in order to be at that spot at the right time. The plane was swift, small, and quiet. And would, hopefully, not be noticed.

I had the target device already. The small box that would draw the Starpeace weapon's fire directly to the intended target. I had only to set it behind Caljn without being noticed. Sinat had assured me it was a very accurate weapon.

No one had contacted me since that night. Chanthan had said I could assume it would be as we'd agreed, and if there were any changes then Sinat would let me know. I trusted them. And I had no questions, no reason to make contact. But I was a little uneasy. There were so many variables. And this wasn't in the realm of my normal activities. What the Power Movement might do . . .

Someone sat down next to me and I opened my eyes with a jump. So many possibilities went through my mind at that moment that I couldn't catch any one of them, which was just as well considering the directions they took. But it was Sinat's friendly dark eyes that met my own.

"Sorry, I didn't mean to startle you so. Did I catch you sleeping?" Sinat's dark skin and his dark gray tunic and trousers seemed to blend into the black bench as he smiled at me. I blinked and it took me a moment to come out of my thoughts.

"Or were you expecting someone else maybe?" Sinat asked, hoping my reaction wasn't because of him.

"No, no, I'm fine, I was just thinking. I wasn't expecting anyone but I'm glad it's you." My words stumbled. It was disconcerting to have Sinat suddenly appear. Not that I should have been surprised considering my thoughts. "I mean, it's nice to see you," I managed to add as I smiled back.

"Sushati wanted to go over and listen to the music so I thought I'd stop and see how you were doing," Sinat explained. "And to let you know that everything is all set and as agreed from our end. Is it all going well with you?"

I half smiled at his question. Was it going well with me? That depended on how you looked at it. Since I hadn't been able to bring myself to share my troubles with even my close friends I simply answered, "I'm fine. I'm glad things are together on your end. I haven't learned of anything new so my plans are still as we discussed."

Sinat nodded. "I'll be on my way then. If you feel a need to talk to me before then, please do so. Anytime. You know where to reach me? Good." He had explained that night at the Starpeace meeting exactly where he'd be for the next week, in case I wanted to contact them. "Don't hesitate please, for any reason. And again, any time."

"I promise. But I think I'm all set now. Unless something changes." I smiled, reassuringly I hoped, and he rose and walked off across the Square toward the music.

I stayed where I was on the bench thinking of Sinat, and Sushati. I knew of her but we had never met. They seemed like people I would like to know. After a few minutes I rose and, avoiding the group of music makers, made my way toward home.

I hadn't heard either Jahon or Shahvid with the group and hoped I wouldn't run into either of them on the paths or at home. My desires ruled, and a short time later I slid into bed in a quiet house, without having seen anyone I knew since my conversation with Sinat. Sleep didn't come quickly, and it wasn't an easy night.

~~~ ~~ ~ ~~ ~~~

Sinat stood by Sushati listening to the music, and thinking about the coming event. The more he had thought about it, the more he hadn't liked Neana's involvement in the operation. Although she seemed to have a pretty good idea of what was going on, he didn't think she really understood her position, and how dangerous it was. If those people ever suspected what they, with Neana as the center, planned to do . . . He didn't care to think of the consequences. Not to mention what could happen if anything went wrong Friday.

They seldom used this particular weapon. And did not decide to do so now without a great deal of careful consideration. But it was needed. Caljn had to be stopped. And Sinat did have confidence in both the weapon and the people involved.

Sushati had laughed at his worries, telling him it was some of that old prejudiced chauvinism coming through. But he didn't think it was that. He wouldn't have been so worried if it had been Sushati in Neana's position, and she was half his life to him. No, it was Neana's innocence of such people as Caljn and his friends that bothered him. But it was that innocence that had let her get so close, and learn so much. If only she had not insisted on going it alone.

He was sure Neana had her reasons for not confiding in Shahvid or Jahon. As he knew they did for not having previously brought her into Starpeace. He may not agree, but he had to respect their decisions. And he would not betray their trust. No matter how hard it was to keep quiet. And no matter how much easier it would have been to have Jahon and Shahvid in on the event. But then, he also knew that if they had been, Neana would not be. And Starpeace needed her.

~~~ ~~ ~ ~~ ~~~

I rose soon after the sun did to a beautiful Thursday morning. The sky was full of big fluffy clouds. It looked like it would be a beautiful day. I dressed quickly, then walked out into the cool morning air to pick breakfast.

The berries were ripening in force and they're at their best first thing in the morning. At least that is my opinion. Binjer disagrees. He says fruit is worthy of eating only after being warmed by the sun. It's one of those no win but harmless arguments we engage in.

It was so calm and quiet I could hear the birds getting their own breakfasts. I didn't appear to be disturbing them at all. They were busy with their lives and had no reason to pay any attention to me.

When my basket was full I went in through the side door into the kitchen. I surprised Shahvid making his first cup of tea, or so I thought till I noticed the two bowls and a bottle of milk sitting on the table, waiting.

Shahvid smiled, "Saw you out in the berry patch. Figured no matter what you brought in it would be better than the cold leftover broccoli casserole I was headed for."

I snorted, "The berry bushes don't bite you know. And, your beliefs to the contrary, the early morning sun doesn't hurt you either." I gently tipped the berries into some water to wash them. "Leftover casserole indeed."

"Well, you never know. Apple mint tea? I made

extra." Shahvid filled our mugs as I set the bowl of fruit on the table. We sat down to enjoy our breakfast together. It had come to be a rare occurrence.

"Do we need milk? I can stop by the Dairy Coop on the way home from the Jansoons. I noticed we were out of cheese too." I made a mental note to take the milk bottles with me.

"Sounds fine, this is the last of it. How are your paintings coming?"

We lightly discussed the paintings, the weather, the garden, the various household chores to be done. Anything but the activities that had been occupying so much of our thoughts. I wondered briefly where Careen had taken herself off to so early in the morning. Or maybe she just wasn't up yet. One way or the other I didn't want to bring her into our breakfast by asking, and I suppose I really didn't care.

The conversation lulled into silence as we finished drinking our tea. I thought about my involvement with the Power Movement and Starpeace. But I was no closer to sharing all that with Shahvid than I had been. So I asked him about a friend's house he had been working on. Our conversation drifted to things that didn't matter much, and avoided those that did. An unfamiliar and uncomfortable position. We were close enough to each other to know that something was troubling the other person, but too respectful of privacy to pry.

When the breakfast dishes were done we parted pleasantly, though a bit uneasily, to head out into our separate day's activities. I to the Jansoons and Shahvid to evaluate some homes for Kasho, who was thinking of moving. My concern about what was on Shahvid's mind was dumped into my already tangled and overflowing kettle of worries. It made it difficult to appreciate the day.

I parked my bike outside the Square. My morning's painting had gone well. Now it was time to check on the activating wands, and let Pia know I planned to light the lamps the following evening. I didn't want any last minute problems. And since lighting the lamps in the Square was something I often did there wouldn't be any questions as to my purpose.

I walked across the Square toward the Maintenance Shop, fitting myself in with the flow of people moving about. Pia was coming out of the door just as I opened it to go in. Her hands were full with a bucket of small tools and a flat of plants.

"Oh, hello, Neana, haven't seen you in awhile. How've you and Shahvid been?" Pia set her load down on a table beside the door. Pia and Brant lived in the home nearest the Square and had been in charge of general maintenance of the Square, Hall and surrounding grounds, including the Hall's roof, for as long as I could remember. They knew most everyone around, and made it a point to do so. I smiled back as she closed the door. This wasn't a stop you made if you were in a hurry.

"Hi Pia. We're both fine, thank you. And you and Brant? Can't see where you're going to find room to put more plants, everything looks great." I nodded toward the flat of green.

If you chose not to talk about yourself, all you had to do was mention the greenery around the place. Both Pia and Brant were happy to follow either lead. And actually, it had only been maybe two weeks since I had last seen Pia.

She went off on an explanation of the plants, and where they were to go, and why. After a bit I fit in, "By the way, I want to light the lamps in the Square tomorrow night, if that's OK, and I wanted to make sure there was a wand available. Do you have one charged up that I can use?" I hoped she did. A good charging day only happens a few times a month.

Pia assured me they were all set, and she would set one aside for me. They didn't get as much use now because of the long days, she went on. And people weren't using them as much as they used to anyway. But before she could get started in that direction I thanked her, wished the new plants well, and with a wave and a smile headed back across the Square. It wasn't hard to carry on and get out of a conversation with Pia, it was all in the timing.

I wheeled my bike onto the bike path and headed for the Dairy Coop. It was located east of the Square in a cool, wooded area. Those who had extra milk, cheese, or eggs would bring them to the Coop building where they would be traded or sold to people of the community. I thought back to my conversation with Pia as I rode along and I had to smile. Pia was a nice person, as was Brant. They did a good job with the grounds, and were well suited to the position. But their interest in everyone else's lives could be a trial. Especially when it was directed at me.

I parked the bike and unloaded the bottles. There were a number of other customers inside, so I looked over the cheeses while I waited. There was quite a variety. I picked out a few old favorites and a couple of new ones. When it was my turn I indicated to Sojo those I wanted. He cut off slabs while telling me about the unfamiliar ones, and the people who made them. He wrapped them in cloths for the ride home, then exchanged my empty bottles for ones full of fresh milk.

Sojo tapped my purchases into the computer. "It shows that you have a notice on the system. Do you want to see it?"

"No thanks, I'll just bring it up when I get home." I smiled a friendly farewell and he went on to the next customer.

I carried my bottles and packages to my bicycle and secured them on the back. As I pedaled home I thought about the notice, hoping it was a request for a painting from someone living out in the country. It had been awhile since I'd spent much time very far from the Square. A feeling of nostalgia came over me, almost of loneliness, and I slowed my pace. I thought of past hikes, get-togethers, visits. It was as if I'd moved away and was longing for old friends who were far from me. The feeling was so strong it hurt.

I pulled my bike to the side of the path as I came to

a crossroad. Several people rode by. I mentally shook myself. What was the matter with me? Most of my friends were within easy traveling distance. All I had to do was go and see them. Sure, just go see them. Why not? I shrugged and started my bike rolling again.

I certainly had gotten out of the habit of visiting. Except for Caljn. Well, after Friday. Just one more day. Then I'd worry about visiting friends. I moved my thoughts to another line as deliberately and smoothly as I shifted gears and picked up speed.

I thought instead about the Coop. About their system of trading, how well it worked and all the people who were involved. When someone delivered their goods to the Coop they were credited with the agreed upon value of that product. The value was based on the approximate number of hours of a person's time it took to produce that item. Purchasers could then either pay in coin for their milk, cheese and eggs, or they could enter into the system the services or products that they had to offer in trade.

The Dairy Coop producers could then draw their pay from the money collected, or from the services and products offered by the customers. Between my paintings and Shahvid's architecture work we never had to think about paying in coin. And we usually had extra credits available for those who had need of them. It was a common system. I wondered how it had been to live with the old economic systems. When everyone had to pay in, and work for, money. It was hard to imagine a society where trading and sharing weren't common. That line of thought got me the rest of the way home.

The house was quiet when I carried my purchases into the kitchen. I wondered again where Careen was. I hadn't seen her in quite a few days, though that wasn't all that unusual. I was somewhat aware of Careen's activities but I refused to dwell on it. As I often reminded myself, it was Shahvid's choice to be married to the woman.

As I put the milk away, I remembered the time the previous winter when I had almost given in and talked to

Shahvid about Careen. It was when I had become aware of her relationship with Rafnon. I had been with Rafnon off and on for a few months and he'd been pushing me for more. Then I had found out about him and Careen. That had put an end to my relationship with him. Not that I had ever pretended that it was anything more than a friendship on my part, but even that had soured.

I certainly didn't feel that a married person couldn't have friends other than their partner. A person's life needed to be filled with friends of all levels. But I did feel that there was a point where if your relationship with your partner wasn't the closest and most intimate of all of your friendships then it was time to change partners. And my feelings about Careen and Rafnon were pretty strong since Shahvid was involved.

But I hate gossip and just hadn't known quite how to bring up the subject. If Shahvid already knew then he had made his choice, and it was none of my business. And if he didn't, then should I tell him? It hadn't been second hand information so wasn't really gossip.

But Kasho had taken care of it for me. At a gathering at Binjer and Tamoi's, I inadvertently walked into an argument between Kasho and Shahvid. As soon as I realized the subject of the conversation I had turned away, but not before I'd gotten the gist of the talk. That was pretty easy since Kasho and I had been talking about that subject, Careen and Rafnon, the night before. Apparently Kasho hadn't had the same reservations as I had, and had taken it out of my hands.

I trusted and liked Kasho, and tried not to think too often about what a good couple she and Shahvid could be. I hadn't seen Kasho for a while. It would have been nice to get together with her, discuss my worries, Caljn, Starpeace. But I immediately put the thought down. I had already decided about that.

I sliced off some of the new cheese I'd brought home and opened a jar of pickles. The rolls I had left from my trip yesterday completed the menu. With a tall glass of water and a blanket I was ready. I found a comfortable spot under the trees in the yard and settled down to eat my lunch.

I tried not to share too much with the insects as I ate and relaxed into the world around me. But the thought of Caljn and *his* world came too readily to the surface. I worked at not letting it bring me down. It wasn't easy. Sometimes it seemed almost impossible to stand back and be objective.

I woke from my after-lunch nap a short time later at the hail of a visitor. It was Binjer, coming up the lane toward the house. Pedaling at a furious rate but not going anywhere fast, on a bicycle two sizes too small for him. I rose and waved, laughing at his act.

He pulled up and parked the bike. He greeted me with overdone indignation, "How could you laugh at a friend in dire straits? Do you know what it's like to travel all the way from our school to here in lowest gear? You'd think I'd get a little sympathy, but no, I get laughter."

I grinned back at him, "Just thought you'd come up with a new exercise plan. You know, if you didn't grimace so bad while doing it, it might catch on. The new 'Binjer Style of Bicycling'. You could teach it between your regularly unscheduled classes."

"You may have something there," Binjer joked back. He undid his helmet and wiped the sweat off his forehead with a flourish.

I gestured gallantly toward the house, "Could I interest you in some iced water, tea or fruit juice?"

"Most certainly." Then he added, "After you of course."

I laughingly gave him a shove and followed him into the kitchen. "So did your bike shrink or *was* that a new style of exercise?"

Both Binjer and Tamoi love to cook and the eating that follows. They are always joking about ways to lose weight so they can eat more. Although neither of them is fat, they are both too active ·for that, they do lean toward the thick instead of the thin.

"Thanks, that's just what I needed." Binjer took a long drink and settled into a chair by the table. I set a crock of cookies between us.

"Actually, it's Mastal's bike. Something broke on the way to school and he had planned to ride out to his uncle's place right after classes to help in the orchard. Some special project going on today. So, Jojo lent him her bike, she took mine, and I brought Mastal's here for Shahvid to take a look at. I was hoping Shahvid would show Mastal how to fix it. I could let him know when to come here if he would."

Binjer and Tamoi are both teachers of the younger folks and usually have several children staying with them in addition to their own three. Not many of their circle of friends have chosen to have children, and we often joke that we didn't need to since Binjer and Tamoi make up for most of us. But we are often recruited by them as temporary teachers. It is done so nicely and good naturedly that even those who might be reluctant don't mind. We all take it as part of our friendship. Besides, it is an opportunity to be with the younger people that many of us don't normally have. For Binjer and Tamoi it is just a natural extension of their lives.

"I'm sure Shahvid will be happy to help Mastal with his bike, you know how he loves to tinker with the things. He's out today with Kasho looking at houses. She wanted to get his advice on a couple that are available. You know she's looking to move? I don't know when he'll be back but I'll make a note for him to give you a call when he gets home. And I'm sure there's a bike here for you to get home on. Hopefully with a little more grace!"

Binjer just grinned. He had no trouble laughing at himself. A trait both he and Tamoi shared. "That will be fine. I should be home this evening."

I took his glass as he declined a refill, and asked him, "Are you on your way then?" Binjer was a good friend whom I thought a lot of. But, like many of my friends, I hadn't seen him much the past months, and that seemed to leave a small chasm in our usually easy relationship. I tried to ignore it, but it was there. That and my own despondency which, in spite of Binjer, I was having trouble shaking.

"I wouldn't mind staying a bit, seems like a long time since we've talked, but I told Tamoi I'd have dinner ready by the time she and the youngsters get home. She and some others took a group on a hike in the woods this afternoon. I had some errands to do, other than the bicycle, so had to beg off. My payment for that is to have dinner and a bottle of wine ready when they get home. And to be with the young set while the olders recover in the baths." Their home is built around several naturally warm mineral springs which they have corralled into several 'baths'.

Binjer rose and his smile turned serious. He studied my face for a moment. "You know Neana, you have a lot of friends who have missed you lately. No," he raised his hand as I worriedly started to interrupt, "I'm not going to pry, I hope you know me better than that. But I want you to remember that there is an ear always available if you should want to talk. I know you have closer ears around also but I think you're not using those much either."

I jammed my hands in the pockets of my tunic and my eyes moved to the window. I couldn't meet Binjer's, and couldn't think of what to say.

Binjer continued gently, "I'm not trying to lecture to you, heaven help me if I start that, and I don't mean to make you more unhappy. I just think you're maybe not giving your friends enough credit for the amount of understanding they have to offer. Especially Jahon."

That brought my eyes back to his with a frown. Binjer laughed, "Oh, Neana, don't look so serious, life isn't you know, not really. And if it seems that way then it's past time to share it and get it down to a manageable size again. Here, how about a 'Binjer you don't know what the hell you're talking about' hug and I'll get out of your day."

I didn't say anything but responded with a sincere hug, working to control tears that his words had brought to the front. I didn't follow him out the door. Binjer knew where the bikes were. I sat back down at the table and let my pent-up feelings go. The tears came and I let them. It was a foolish reaction, but I was beyond reasoning myself back in control.

Binjer and Tamoi are both people who feel strongly about letting others live their own lives. But they would be the first to be there when needed. I didn't take Binjer's words, or what was behind them, for granted. Nor did I ignore what he had said.

Some time passed before I rose, feeling drained. I washed my face with cold water and changed into a work tunic. I headed out the back door. I didn't care that the short sleeves exposed my wrists. The garden wouldn't care about those marks any more than it would comment on my swollen eyes and red nose. I didn't care either.

I got my tools out of the shed, and spent the rest of the afternoon and evening with the plants and insects in the garden. I stopped once for a drink, and to add a warm robe as the air cooled. I wondered briefly where Shahvid and Careen were. Then back to my thoughts and the plants.

I had much to think about, and it wasn't just my involvement with Caljn that occupied my thoughts. Binjer had broken loose a lot more than my tears. The very air seemed to echo my uneasy feelings. The garden understood and enveloped me in a blanket of security while I worked. My mind and my muscles were stretched in many directions, both hurting and healing.

~~~ ~~ ~ ~~ ~~~

Shahvid didn't return until late evening. He went right to bed, but was awake far into the night with thoughts of the day and evening. With feelings at the same time both excited and unsure. On the other side of the Square Kasho sat in her room, quietly echoing many of Shahvid's emotions. The day's house hunting had given them both more to think about than they'd planned.

The very air of the town was charged with emotions. It was affecting many people while they were affecting it. It was a feeling shared by many individuals, but few realized where the energy was coming from. Each person utilized or ignored it as fit their being.

Caljn felt it, as he and Valjar sat talking after everyone had gone. But he attributed it to the demons and devils of his world, and he was nervous, anxious. It was this energy that he would use to go forward with his plans for the next evening.

Binjer had used the same energy earlier to talk with his friend, but he called it love. The garden hadn't called it anything, it just was. Each person of the town picked it up in their own way, and used it however they knew how, consciously or not.

Jahon felt it as he sat alone in his living room, in the dark, his hands playing the guitar while his mind played with his thoughts. The furnishings around him were simple, straightforward. They fit him. He sat on a pillow on the floor, leaning against the wall.

He recognized the charged air and wondered where it would lead. Nights like that didn't come often and it always meant something. Either a lot of individual actions or a mass event, maybe both.

The harmonies from the strings rose and fell following his thoughts. Skaduter, his feline companion, prowled around uneasily, finally settling down as close to his side as she could get. He repositioned the guitar to accommodate her, enjoying her small closeness but not stopping to talk. He had already asked her for an opinion but she wouldn't say. She felt humans had to work out their own lives.

He thought of many things, but had trouble carrying any one very far. It would have helped to talk it all out with someone. But Skaduter was the only one there. And she had already made her point by falling asleep.

He concentrated on the music for a while, feeling its rhythm. His thoughts went on, from what he had heard about Careen and Shahvid, to what he had seen when he'd run into Kasho and Shahvid that day.

On to his current work and his future plans. To his friends, his talk with Binjer, what Kasho had told him, what he knew of Caljn and Valjar and the others. And of course, Neana.

He had trouble there, couldn't keep any thought straight and was uneasy with those that came. It was the air of course, he told himself, and his natural worry about a friend. His fingers found a song she liked and he smiled. But he made his thoughts move on.

He tried to think of the woman he'd met last month, a friend of the owner of a building he had been working on. They'd been together a few times since, nice person. But she was fading in his thoughts already. As they all did. Maybe it was just his lot to be single this life. Sighing, he put all thoughts aside and lost himself in his music, long into the night.

~~~ ~~ ~ ~~ ~~~

Friday morning. I was awake but I kept my eyes closed. I tried to follow my dreams as they were fading away, but it didn't work, they were gone. I didn't feel up to the day yet. But the day had started, and my thoughts were intruding. I was uncomfortable. I sat up and opened my eyes.

When the fading sun had finished my work in the garden the previous night I had come in, washed up and gone to work in my studio. I hadn't wanted to think any more, and had lost myself for hours in my painting. Sometime in the early morning hours I had put my brushes down, and fallen asleep on the small couch in my studio.

I yawned and stretched, trying to get some of the kinks out. I didn't feel very rested. But I knew I might as well get up and going. Sitting there worrying was less than useless.

I heard sounds of Shahvid stirring, but by the time I had washed and dressed he was gone. That was fine, the fewer people I had to deal with that morning the better.

I made myself a large mug of tea for breakfast. I considered doing some laundry before heading to the Jansoon's. It was usually fairly quiet at the laundry house at that hour. And hanging clothes out always settled me. Something about the smell and pattern of the chore; first the socks and underwear, then the tunics and shirts, then the towels, then the pants. It was comforting. Crazy maybe. But it would help me get into the day. It was going to happen with or without me. I figured I might as well be an active participant.

Several hours later I was in the back yard hanging up the last piece. I put the clothes basket away and, grabbing some fruit to eat on the way, left for the Jansoon home. My brown robe felt good against the cooler air of the day, and the walk was nice. I set my mind on the paintings, and refused to think about anything else.

As I came to the Square though it was hard to quell the emotions that welled up inside me. I took a deep breath and a good hold of myself with a bit of a lecture. I well knew my plan for the day. I didn't need to worry it over again. It would happen as it happened, when it happened. Right then things were fine. Take one thing at a time, I told myself, just one minute after another.

With that in mind I made it across the Square. I was soon at work at my easel putting the finishing colors to the two paintings. The playing children laughing out at me from the canvases did much to help me through that afternoon. By the time the Jansoon family came home I was done, and had the paintings set just right for the viewing.

There was much oohing and aahing and enough compliments to make me blush. It's always a funny time for me. I'm anxious about whether or not the client will be happy with what I've created, relieved that the work is done, embarrassed by the praise, worried that there was something I could have done differently, and excited by the client's excitement. It's fun. Sort of.

After the toasts I finished my glass of wine and slipped out of the celebration, and into another world. I hurried to get to the Square before sun-fade. The rest of my day was about to begin.

~~~ ~~ ~ ~~ ~~~

The sun was going down as Jahon rode toward the Square. His mind was full of thoughts of the frustrating day he had spent, trying to line up people and materials for a job east of town. It was the type of project that he normally wouldn't have taken on. But the woman who had been doing it had been called out of town unexpectedly, and he had agreed to help out.

Unfortunately, both of them had their minds on other things when they'd talked. And that day the miscommunications showed. Jahon had to sort out what had been done and what had not, what had been ordered and what was missing. Normally he would have realized the problem early on, taken a deep breath and a break. Then calmly laid out what needed to be done, and what he could do with it at that point. But he wasn't thinking that well, he was tired and edgy. He had just plowed ahead with results much as one might expect.

The previous night he had played his guitar till the early hours of the morning, when he'd finally put it down and gone to sleep. Soon after sunup Sinat had wakened him for a short visit and conversation. Sinat had been preoccupied and in a hurry. He said he couldn't tell Jahon what was up exactly, but would he please be in the Square at sun-fade to meet Neana.

Jahon knew Sinat well enough to trust him and to

realize that if he could have told him more he would have. But since Neana was involved he couldn't accept that, and he had pressed Sinat for more information. He was aware enough of what was going on that he didn't take the request lightly. Sinat was not one to exaggerate a situation. Or ask for action when none was needed.

Sinat realized maybe even more than Jahon did how he felt. But he knew the rules, and why, so he could just repeat what he had said. He told Jahon he was sorry, but would he please just trust him and be there. Then he left, and Jahon's day had started.

It hadn't helped any when later he ran into Binjer who told him he thought Jahon ought to bring Neana over to their place that night for a small get-together. Jahon snorted and asked him how he suggested he do that, kidnap her? She wasn't exactly pushing to be in his company lately. Binjer just said he thought Jahon should be able to work that out, and he was looking forward to seeing them that evening, but he couldn't stop to talk right then. With a friendly wave and smile he was off before Jahon could respond. There was not much Jahon could do but shrug and continue on to the job site. Where his day continued. But that part was over. Now he had to find out what Sinat had been talking about, and why he had made that insistent request.

The sun was touching the trees by the time Jahon got to the Square. The place was bustling with people, and the first person he ran into was one of Caljn's followers. He came very close to laying the man out on the tiles when the fellow started preaching at him. But a few short, sharp words got his point across, and the man quickly moved on. Jahon was in no mood for that kind of garbage right then.

He looked around the Square for Neana but didn't see her. Sinat had said he was to 'meet' her there, so did that mean she'd be waiting for him? He didn't know so walked on across the tiles, not paying much attention to the people around him, his anxiety building. He was too involved with his own worries to realize that the anxiety was not just within himself.

The sun was down and the light fading when he saw Sinat and Chanthan enter the Square, deep in discussion with each other. At the same time he noticed the lamps were being activated. He knew that could be Neana, she used to do that quite often. He quickly headed in that direction.

Then he saw Caljn. Standing by himself in a small raised area of the Square, his hands waving as he talked at the people. He seemed oblivious to the fact that few were paying him any attention. Jahon's frown deepened at the sight of the man, then he stopped short as he saw Caljn direct his attention to the woman coming toward him.

He saw Neana nod to Caljn as she activated a lamp beside him. Then another. Caljn stopped talking for a moment, then turned to look out across the Square. Neana lit the last lamp in the circle, quickly looked around, then quietly slid a small package to the ground behind him. Caljn slowly put his hand in his pocket, a strange look on his face. Neana, and all the others, forgotten.

Jahon didn't notice. When he saw Neana with Caljn he walked on by, his jaw set in a furious clench.

~~~ ~~ ~ ~~ ~~~

My mind was surprisingly blank as I made my way across the Square, lighting the lamps one by one, deliberately making my way toward Caljn. I was intent on my timing, carefully attending to my actions as I would a painting. I had gone through this so many times in my mind that it seemed more a copy, not real. The brown robe around my body felt light, an extension of my self. The sleeves pulled back some each time I raised my arm to reach a lamp, showing the remaining marks of the wounds on my wrists. But they didn't concern me then.

People flowed around me talking, laughing, thinking their way across the smooth tiles of the Square. There were many friends but I didn't greet them. I felt separate, alone. Maybe it showed since they kindly let me be. Most must have been aware, in a general manner, of the currents flowing around them, though they didn't know of the event soon to come. Except for the few who would be intimately involved. And even they didn't know exactly how the event would transpire. Or which event would win out. The many possibilities floated all around me, but I ignored them.

I saw Caljn. Self-involved with his inflated discourse, standing on the same raised platform where I had first seen him, so many months ago. The thin gray-blond hair on his head lifted and settled randomly with the breeze. His pale face reflected poorly the fading sunlight. He wasn't particularly interested in those around him, though he was supposedly voicing his words for them. I doubt that he noticed or cared that few were listening. As I approached he shifted his performance slightly, nodded briefly, paused his flow of words as I started to light the lamps around him.

But Caljn's interest in me at that moment was casual I'm sure. There may have been a brief thought of satisfaction that I was there to see his show. But maybe not. After all, he had told his followers to be in the Square. He expected it, and he considered me one of them. His attention right then was taken up with the "great plan". He looked out past me, across the people, to see those to whom he chose to direct his controlled excitement.

I barely acknowledged Caljn. My throat was tight but my hands were as steady as if I were brushing in the light myself. I activated the last lamp behind him. A passing breeze tried to distract me by lifting my hair from my shoulders. I ignored it and the dark brown hair settled back down. The breeze continued on. I quietly glanced around. No one was watching.

Almost without movement I set my small package on the tiles behind Caljn. As I turned away he slowly put his hand in his pocket. A shadowy excitement briefly colored his face, then faded away. No emotion was allowed to linger. My intense calmness continued as I moved from him. No thoughts.

Then my emotions gave a sharp tug as I saw Jahon striding quickly across the Square, moving away from me. I quickened my steps to catch up with him. But something pulled at me from behind. I stopped to look back, for just one moment, at Caljn. No one else seemed to notice him. No one else was near him. I could do no more.

Jahon whirled around as I caught up with him. His anger and frustration lashed out and his voice, though low, was not kind. "If you're so wanting to be with that man then don't let any of us stop you. Go on back, stay with him. Forget your friends." His hand snapped out toward Caljn and he turned abruptly to continue on his way. His usually friendly features were sharp with tired emotions, his dark brown eyes almost black.

I couldn't react to Jahon's outburst. I stood a moment, blinking, breathing deliberately. I took a step forward to follow after him, trying to get my thoughts going as well. What was it exactly that I wanted to say to him?

Then it happened. A flash / crack. Almost beyond light and sound. I had almost forgotten why I was there. In the moments before comprehension both Jahon and I turned with the others to stare at the spot where Caljn had stood, just moments before, hurling his rhetoric at the crowd. He was no more in this reality. It was over.

The crowd moved toward the space where Caljn had been. Except for me. I stood stiff, clenching my fists. My body was cold. I felt smaller than myself, without feeling. The people around me were full of questions. I had none.

Jahon looked briefly at where Caljn had been, then quickly at the sky before coming back to me. He had more of a comprehension than most of them, without consciously thinking about it. He was beside me as I turned to move away. He took my arm and pulled me with him to the edge of the group. There was soft, somewhat confused talk around us as people tried to take in what had happened, what they should do, if anything. I wanted to leave, get away. But Jahon somehow knew it was important that we be one of the crowd. He put his arm around my shoulder, carefully looking at the people filling up that area of the Square. I wondered if he could feel my cold through his light jacket. His anger was gone, the frustration changed. He was concentrating on what was, what might be, happening.

I could feel him beside me. A close friend quietly offering. But I couldn't share anything with him right then. I could hear voices around me, but I didn't listen. I turned inward, drifting through the days, the nights, the meetings. The words said, and those not said. To the night that I had set my decision before Starpeace, and before myself, for a final time. That night is very clear to me, even now.

Jahon's hand on my shoulder brought me back to the present. He gently drew me away from the excited crowd. I was numb, no feelings at all, just emptiness. I went with him without thought until we were through the Hall and on a path going away from the Square, away from the people.

Then I stopped. I turned back and stood, shaking, as the feelings came rushing in. I put my hands up to my face to slow the onrush, and maybe to hide. The sleeves of my robe pulled back. I was no longer numb, and I didn't know quite what to do with it all.

In the light of a nearby lamp Jahon stood looking down at me. His emotions weren't all that steady either. He gently pulled my hands into his, looking at my wrists, then up into my face. He waited until I met his eyes.

"You have much to tell me, Neana, but right this moment it doesn't matter. You're here with me and you're safe. We'll go on to Binjer and Tamoi's in a minute, but for now just take some deep, even breaths. You'll be OK." Jahon waited quietly while I calmed down, then he asked, "All right? Are you up for a walk?"

I nodded assent to both questions. I didn't trust myself to speak. I pulled to free my hands from his.

Jahon let go and we continued on down the path toward our friends' home. There were no words spoken, we just concentrated on the walk with the security of close friendship. It was almost dark but there was enough light to see our way. I both felt and didn't feel. The movement was good and gave my body an outlet for some of the emotions churning inside.

The silence between us was full but not stressful. The evening air enveloped us, and I held on to it for support. I was aware of Jahon walking sturdily beside me. But I didn't reach out either mentally or physically. I couldn't. I let all thoughts and emotions wash in and out of my mind without touching me. But I watched them come and go. Though we walked some distance, it seemed but a short time before we arrived.

Binjer, Tamoi and their family live past the outskirts of town in a large open meadow. The area is dotted here and there with trees and low houses. Across the fields to the north are the hills, and to the west the forest, with a small river connecting the two. Theirs is a small homestead which blends well into the land around it.

As we neared the house we could hear Binjer and the children out back, apparently saying farewell to the day with a lot of fanfare. There was no answer to Jahon's knock so he opened the door and we went in. It's a simple, comfortable house and one in which we are both at ease.

Before Jahon could call out, the side door opened and the lively crew entered. They left enough of their outdoor rambunctiousness behind them so it wasn't an overwhelming onslaught. We all shared greetings and hugs, and the children told Jahon and me their latest excitements. The blueberries they'd scouted out but weren't quite ready to pick yet, the new birds discovered flitting in the grasses behind the house, how big the baby snakes were getting - the ones that lived over behind the big rock. It had been awhile since I'd seen them so I had to be updated with their lives. And I certainly didn't mind, though I wasn't able to give much in return. I just listened with a smile.

At a break in the exchange Binjer shortened the visit with a few quiet words to his oldest daughter. She had enough of years and her parent's sensitivity to understand without questions. She soon had the younger children headed off toward the back of the house to wash up and get ready for a pre-bedtime story.

In the calm that followed Binjer smiled, "Tamoi should be back soon. She's walking a couple of our young friends home. As usual we lost track of the time and it was darkening before we realized it."

He looked from Jahon to me, "Would you like to relax in the baths before dinner? You can go ahead if you want or wait till Tamoi gets home. The children have already eaten but I'm going to go get our dinner started now. The vegetables are all washed so it shouldn't be long."

As I considered his suggestion Jahon said, "Why don't you go ahead and I'll help Binjer with dinner."

I agreed, and turned to make my way through the living room, down the few steps into the small bath area. I was still operating in a detached haze. Jahon and Binjer headed the other way to the kitchen.

I undressed and picked out a towel, then went into the bath. It's a simple room on the east side of the house with two low benches and a shallow pool through which one of the natural warm springs flows. There are mats on the floor and sliding windowed doors leading to a nicely flagged area outside.

I slowly lowered my tired self into the bath and let the warmth flow all around, in and out. I didn't think of the day, or the evening. I just gently set my thoughts aside and let my mind, my body and my emotions soak up whatever it could without resistance. It felt incredibly good.

When I finally felt myself coming back together I climbed out and picked up my towel. I felt like everything was in slow motion, that it was almost too much of an effort to towel dry. I draped the towel around my shoulders.

Through the windows I saw the moon was coming up. I slid open the doors and stepped out into the night to soak up some of its soft light. The cool evening breeze was refreshing after the warmth of the bath. Not the same as a sauna but it can be as renewing.

I sat on one of the benches on the flags and relaxed against the back. The hills in the distance seemed almost touchable. It was a special spot that Binjer and Tamoi had. Although I generally prefer the woods, I can enjoy the openness too. They had enough trees to be comfortable, yet not so many to obstruct the view.

It was so quiet and beautiful. And cold. At least to be dressed the way I was, or rather wasn't. My goosebumps were getting goosebumps.

I fled back to the warmth inside and let it surround me. A strong weariness hit me. So did hunger. I decided to lie down for a few minutes. Otherwise, I thought, I might not be able to stay awake through dinner. Tamoi must not have gotten home yet, or they decided against a bath.

I spread my towel on one of the mats and was soon fast asleep.

~~~ ~~ ~ ~~ ~~~

Several hours later Jahon came quietly into the bath area to find Neana. He stood there looking down at the familiar warm brown skin, her brown hair lying loose across her shoulders.

He had meant to reach down to waken her but he hesitated. It was as if he were seeing her for the first time. Not just the physical her, but all of her. It wasn't like he hadn't seen her without clothing before. They had shared swims and baths and saunas for years with friends. But . . .

He shook his head and knelt down, reaching out to shake her awake.

~~~ ~~ ~ ~~ ~~~

Something woke me and I opened my eyes to look directly into Jahon's eyes. The green and the brown were locked together for what seemed like a century. I blinked, startled. "Oh, hello." I sat up, shaking my head. "I must have dozed off."

I wasn't prepared to arise fresh from my dreams to find Jahon so close. Though what I should have needed to be prepared for I couldn't exactly say.

Jahon just stared at me a moment then sat back and laughed. "Dozed off indeed. The cook is in his kitchen pacing back and forth lamenting the demise of his dinner. And has been for almost three hours."

"Oh dear, did I really sleep that long? I only meant to take a short rest, why didn't you wake me earlier? Have they really waited dinner for me?" I jumped up, picked up my towel, and hurried into the dressing room.

Jahon followed, "Relax, do you think Binjer would really allow his dinner to die of old age? It's just finishing now so there's time. We had a snack earlier and have been sitting around talking. I thought maybe you might be getting hungry though."

"I certainly am." I pulled my robe over my head and reached back to pull my hair out. I stopped as Jahon reached for the small gold chains that hung around my neck and gently lifted them. I watched him as he looked at the two pendants resting on his hand.

"You always wear these?" It was almost more a statement than a question, as if he hadn't noticed them before. The one on the shorter chain was my symbol, my 'signature' on my paintings. I'd received it to celebrate my first real commission. The other, hanging below it, was for my 18th birthday. It was a design I had admired, it was Jahon's signature symbol. He'd had a goldsmith friend of his make them both as gifts for me. He let them fall back against my skin and I quickly moved to fasten the ties of my robe over them.

I turned to the shelf to reach a comb and said simply, "Yes, I do." Neither of us spoke as I quickly combed my hair. I tied the belt around my waist and sat to lace on my sandals.

~~~ ~~ ~ ~~ ~~~

Jahon stood there watching, fascinated, with her and with his feelings. It took an effort to bring himself together. Not tonight. There would be time enough for all that later. She had gone through enough for one day he reminded himself, and there was much else to get out of the way first.

Watching her face, as she finished and rose to leave, he remembered that there was even more to discuss than he'd first thought. Binjer, Tamoi and he had pieced together at least some of the story from what he knew, what Kasho had told them, and from what Tamoi had brought home from their neighbor's. The father of the children she had escorted home had been in the Square soon after sun-fade. He had passed on to Tamoi what he'd heard from the people still milling around the area.

Now it was up to Neana to fill it all in. He followed her through the door and up the steps into the house.

~~~ ~~ ~ ~~ ~~~

We came into the small eating area just as Tamoi was pouring the wine. Binjer was setting a steaming bowl of grain on the table.

Tamoi handed the bottle to Jahon and greeted me with a big hug. "Neana, it's so good to see you, it's been too long. How was your rest? Come, sit down while Binjer fusses with his dishes."

I laughed and settled myself on a pillow at the low table. Tamoi is as bustling and buxomly as I am quiet and small. We get along great.

"The bath and nap were both very refreshing. But I sincerely apologize for holding up dinner. You really should have eaten. I don't know how you could have waited so long."

"Actually, Binjer just got around to finishing dinner because he was waiting for the celery to grow a little more before he cut it up for the pot." Jahon settled in across the table. "If you look really close you can see the poor little things hiding among the other vegetables. Picked right from the cradle."

"Go ahead and joke. But just wait until your taste buds get around this special dish. You'll take back those unworthy words. Someday I will teach even you to appreciate the subtle nuances bestowed upon a meal by a truly great and talented chef." Binjer loftily set the bowl down on the table, then grinned at Jahon as he took his seat, "Besides which those poor peppers you brought were hardly weaned!"

Jahon defended, "You just don't know a gourmet pepper when you see one, they're supposed to be that size."

"Enough, enough," Tamoi laughed, "If we will admit to the great talent and knowledge of the two male chefs present, may we then eat before Neana slides under the table from hunger?"

I grinned as my stomach rumbled again, "It may be too late." I couldn't deny my obvious hunger. It smelled great.

"A toast first." We all groaned protests. "No, now, a short one at least." Binjer raised his glass, "To friends."

The ringing glasses echoed the smiles. Then we all turned our attention to the food. The bantering continued through dinner, an unspoken agreement having been made to save the serious talk for after.

I felt much better by the end of the meal. I leaned comfortably back, almost forgetting the day. Both the food and the conversation had done their part. And I knew it was time for me to do mine.

My eyes met Jahon's and I half smiled, then looked down. I felt a sudden moment of panic. What if they didn't understand? I knew better, but at the same time all my self-doubts came flooding back. I felt flushed. Maybe I should have skipped the wine considering the day I'd had. But it wasn't the wine. I rolled up my sleeves and loosened the top ties of my robe.

Binjer rose, "How about we retire to the other room with some tea?"

"Sounds good. If you want to get the tea started while we clear the table . . ." Jahon stood, picking up dishes, and followed Binjer into the kitchen.

Binjer glanced at Jahon then said in a low voice, "It's time to hear Neana's side of the story."

"Yes," Jahon replied, scraping plates into the compost bucket. "I'm just not sure I'm ready for it. I'm almost afraid to hear what she has to say. But we have to know, and she has to let it out." He stacked the dishes carefully beside the sink.

Binjer commented on the look on his friend's face, "You look wiped out. Is something else the matter?"

"I'm just tired," Jahon replied quickly. "Short night last night and long day today. On top of . . ." he gave a short wave toward the kitchen door. "Not a great combination," he finished almost under his breath, then reached to take a bowl from Tamoi.

The table was soon cleared and Tamoi insisted we leave the dishes till morning.

The lamps in the sitting room cast a soft glow. It isn't a large room. Nestled several steps down from the eating area it is for more intimate gatherings. A small woodstove stands in one corner, and next to it is what they call the meditation spot. A simple raised platform with a plain pedestal, usually holding a sculpture or other piece of artwork, or maybe a vase of flowers. Behind on the wall hang one or two paintings. The contents change often but the effect is almost always pleasing, and surprisingly comforting. All the members of the family take turns managing the spot. The youngest children have help and guidance from Tamoi or Binjer, but the older ones have free reign when it is their turn. I recognized Tamoi's artistry in the arrangement that night.

I sank down into one of the soft, low couches that combine with similar chairs and pillows to furnish the room. Drawing off my sandals I drew my legs up, and tried not to feel anxious.

Binjer and Jahon handed round full tea mugs, then they and Tamoi settled in. Not pushing, but patiently waiting. I knew what they waited for. It was time.

I looked down at my hands, my wrists. I took a deep breath and began. "I don't know if you'll understand, I hope you will, but . . . Well, I'd like to tell you, explain . . . everything, at least all that I can." I knew they would know what I was talking about.

As I hesitatingly began they watched me closely,

sending out all the love, friendship and understanding that they could. Unfortunately, as I sank back into that world of Caljn and the Power Movement I fell once again back away from my friends. I couldn't take in much of their support, at least not consciously.

I focused on a painting and told my story, my hands holding tight to each other for support. My meetings with Caljn. My meeting with Starpeace. My involvement with the Power Movement. The decisions I made. The actions I took. I told them everything that I could, matter of factly, leaving nothing out. My voice was calm, unemotional. But inside I felt it all over again, as I had gone through it, each step of the way. I doubted that my face was as calm as my voice, but I couldn't do anything about that. No one interrupted me. I just kept talking.

Then I was done. Ending with the lighting of the last lamp. And my last view of Caljn. When my part of the job was done. Just before Starpeace finished their part.

"So, he has been destroyed, and I helped to kill him." I said the words for the first time, slowly, quietly. I looked down at my hands, waiting, fearing my friends' judgment, worried about what they would think. That was so very important to me.

Jahon's look was a mixture of serious concern, painful knowledge, and deep caring. All suspended together in the momentary silence. Then his feelings snapped together and his body responded. "You damned little fool!" he exclaimed. In a few movements he was beside me, holding me in his arms, half squashing me. His reason stepped aside for his emotions.

I pulled away a little, startled, trying to get my composure. I was still trying to pull myself back out of Caljn's world. And I wasn't comfortable with the way my body was responding to Jahon.

"Why didn't you tell me before?" Jahon half shook, half hugged me.

Tamoi shared a look with Binjer. She wiped her eyes and blew her nose. "Oh Neana, how could you ever think we wouldn't understand? What kind of friends do you think we are?"

Binjer added, half seriously, "If I had known exactly what you had been up to I would have beat it out of you. Obviously, I should have anyway. Or helped Jahon to."

Since I had never known Binjer to strike, let alone beat anyone or anything, I took the comment as it was meant. Besides, he could not have beat me any more than I wanted to beat myself. I was seeing myself, and my actions, a little more clearly than I really wanted to.

Jahon was still beside me, and didn't seem inclined to let me go. The intensity of his look was making it hard for me to breathe. I thought his reaction was a little overdone. But I didn't know at that time just how well he knew Caljn and the Power Movement. I wasn't the only one who had kept past activities quiet.

I loosened myself a bit from Jahon's arms. And with a wry, tired smile, and not a few tears, I answered honestly. "I don't know. I guess I made a mistake. After you left yesterday," I nodded to Binjer, "I realized I had been wrong maybe. But I couldn't do anything about it then, it was too late, or at least that's how I felt. Not about what I had done, but about not telling anyone. I just didn't want to get anyone else involved. I was afraid of where it was leading. I guess I was afraid of what Caljn and his friends were doing. Or might do."

Jahon shook his head, saying, "It's no use going now into the 'If you'd only told me', but can't you see that none of us would want you to go in to any kind of danger alone? Think if the tables were turned, and it had been one of your friends in your place?' How would you have felt?" He didn't mean to lecture but he was intent on his concern, and his fears were very real. He had a feeling that the event was far from over. He knew the Power Movement too well to assume that.

"You couldn't keep your feelings from us you know, Neana," Tamoi told me. "We knew you were troubled, we just didn't know the reasons for it."

"I know, I know," I answered with a somewhat frustrated wave of my hand. They were no doubt right, but my reasons had been very real to me at the time. I just couldn't explain them coherently right then. I pulled away from Jahon and he let me go, settling back into the cushions beside me. He was looking at me in a rather strange way, but I wasn't up to analyzing it.

I sat quietly looking nowhere. I felt drained, and couldn't think of what else to say.

Tamoi started to speak, then realizing my state, and noticing that Jahon didn't look too fresh himself, she changed her words. "I think we all need to sleep on it. Tomorrow we can look at it afresh and see everything clearer." She stood and came over to me, reaching down a hand to pull me up to her for a sincere hug. "For now, Neana, I have no trouble with your part in Caljn's destruction."

Binjer agreed, hugging me himself, adding, "We love you the way you are, you're our friend. Caljn is over, as he should be." He started collecting the tea mugs, "No use you two going home tonight, there's not that much left of it. If you want to get some blankets out of the hall closet Jahon, I'll . . ."

"Oh!" I interrupted him, suddenly remembering. "I forgot all about Shahvid! He doesn't know where I am and I didn't leave him a note. And if he hears about Caljn . . ."

"It's OK," Jahon caught my arm and gave me a gentle hug. "Calm down. I left a message for Shahvid this afternoon telling him you were coming here with me and we'd maybe stay the night."

I looked at him blankly. How could he have known that? My thoughts spun and I couldn't catch them to make sense of anything. I responded automatically, "I *am* calm. I just think I ought to talk to Shahvid." But I was shaky. I felt like I'd run a hard race and just recovered my breath but not my muscles. And I was very tired.

Tamoi took charge, "If you want to use the dressing room first, Neana, I'll go find you a nightshirt. You can talk

with Shahvid tomorrow. It's pretty late to call him tonight.
The guys can get the beds ready. Do you want to stay in
here or we can move one of the children?" She headed me
out of the room with her words and left the sleeping
arrangements to Binjer and Jahon.

I really didn't care. If Shahvid knew where I was he
wouldn't worry. And there was no real reason to talk to
him right then. I wasn't feeling capable of carrying on much
of a conversation anyway. I quietly followed Tamoi down
the hall.

As Jahon headed for the blankets, he told Binjer,
"I'll arrange some of the cushions and pillows and we can
both stay in here."

Binjer agreed. On his way back from the kitchen he
stopped at the desk to write his oldest daughter a note, a
request to all of the children that they tend to themselves in
the morning as quietly as possible. He noted the time along
with a cartoon drawing of the adults dragging themselves
off to bed.

He stopped by the sitting room to see that Jahon
had what he needed. He exchanged a few words with his
friend. They knew each other well enough that a few words
were all that was needed. With a light heart Binjer checked
on his children, attached the note to a door, and wearily
fell into bed. A few minutes later Tamoi joined him and the
household drifted off to sleep.

When I first awoke I wasn't sure where I was. I felt as if I'd been spit out of a dream into a strange place. Then I opened my eyes to see Jahon sleeping not far away. Maybe I'd simply changed dreams. It wasn't an unpleasant one. I swam in the feeling for a moment. Then noticed the room. This wasn't a dream. I frowned and shook myself fully awake.

I had successfully denied and buried those feelings some nine years ago, and I wasn't about to let them out again. Jahon was a friend, a very kind friend, but that was all. Remember, I told myself sternly, you don't want to be Shahvid's little pest of a sister.

The thought of Shahvid pulled me firmly to the here and now. Somewhat reluctantly I withdrew from the blankets and got up, quietly so as to not awaken Jahon. A glance out the window told me it was midday, and from the quiet I guessed Binjer, Tamoi and the children must be out.

I headed toward the rear of the house to the toilet room. It was an interesting arrangement, with three seats at different heights to accommodate the varied sizes of the family members. Their's was an older unit that was accessible from outside for emptying, but it worked well, and was large enough for their often extended family. Ours at home was smaller and newer, and rather boring compared to their's. Of course, the liberal use of 'local' art work in decorating their room probably had something to do with the difference. Neither Shahvid nor I could have come up with anything close even if we had tried.

After washing and dressing I made my way to the kitchen. My dreams had been stressful and crowded. I didn't feel much rested, though I knew I slept. Maybe some food would help.

A note from Tamoi greeted me from the kitchen table. It confirmed that the family had gone out to the blueberry patch with a picnic lunch. Jahon and I were welcome to join them (she had drawn a small map on the note) or there were sandwiches and fruit waiting for us in the cool room. If we left before they returned they'd see us later. It was signed with a heart, a hand and a P.S. *Binjer and I both hope you had a successful night.*

I wasn't real sure what she meant by that but food was my top interest right then. I found the lunch set aside for us and returned to the kitchen. After arranging the food on the table I went to see if Jahon was up.

He was sitting in the middle of the pillows and blankets, his chin propped on an arm, staring out the window. He didn't notice me at the doorway. I suddenly felt shy. It was several moments before I spoke.

"Good morning."

Jahon looked up and smiled, "Good morning, or rather Good Afternoon. It looks like the day is well on its way, as do you. Did you sleep well?"

His sitting there so comfortably on the bed was making me uncomfortable. But then he got up to dress and I wanted him to sit back down. Oh for heavens sake, I told myself, this was ridiculous. I quickly began rearranging the pillows and folding the bedding.

"Well enough, and you?" I answered him. "No, no, I can get these, go ahead and get dressed, lunch is on the table when you're ready." I felt the immediate need for some distance between us.

His eyebrows raised a bit but when I refused to meet his look he finished dressing and went off to wash up, leaving me to straighten the room. And my emotions. I accomplished both quickly and without unnecessary thought.

"I want to talk with Shahvid," I told Jahon as we sat at the kitchen table to eat, "as soon as I can. I don't know what he knows or has heard, about Caljn and all, and I just won't feel right till I've talked to him, told him what I told you last night." I distractedly turned my sandwich around, again, "Do you think he'll understand?"

Jahon swallowed his bite of sandwich, "You're going to make that poor thing dizzy, Neana."

I didn't answer. I looked out the window, resting my chin on my hand. I didn't know what I'd do if Shahvid rejected what I had done. Although a tolerant man, he could be stonily firm when he disagreed with my conduct. And none of my past actions could compare even closely with this one.

"Look here," Jahon put his sandwich down and waited for my eyes to meet his. "Neana, there are a great number of people who love you, and you're not giving any of them credit for it. Let go of your fears! Do you really think Shahvid is going to turn you away just because you did something that you felt was right? I don't think he's that kind of person, and if you'd just stop to think about it, neither do you."

I listened to him intently without wavering. He asked, "What *is* the problem? What are you afraid of?"

I clenched my hands in my lap, my eyes going back to the window. I didn't think I could answer his questions. It would have been hard enough to myself, but out loud to Jahon? I wasn't even sure I knew the answers. But he was waiting.

"I'm not sure," I finally said. "I guess I'm afraid my life these last months has been wrong somehow. Yet I know I had to do what I did, that it was the right thing to do. It's just, well maybe I don't understand it after all. It seemed so straightforward before, but now, trying to tell and explain everything, it feels mixed up. Maybe I just don't know how to get on with my life."

I looked down at my bowl of fruit, the tears too close. I took a breath. "I sometimes think I've forgotten how to be happy, and I don't want to be around other people when I'm like that. And maybe I'm afraid I've lost the people that mean the most to me." There, I had said it, and it was the truth.

Jahon moved to the chair next to mine, put his arm around me and pulled me to him. I didn't move away this time but buried my face in his shirt and let the tears come. He held me, quietly, until the storm lessened and I loosened my grip on him. I wasn't happy about breaking down like that but I couldn't help it.

Jahon pulled back to look at my face, "Neana, you haven't been listening to what we've been saying to you. You haven't lost any friends. We're all still here. If you'll just let us help you, we can work this out together. I don't think it's as bad as you think. You've been so close to it that you haven't been able to step back and see the whole picture. If you did, you'd see a lot of people you know right there beside you, the whole way."

I pulled away to wipe my eyes and blow my nose. What Jahon said made sense, but I was having trouble pulling my thoughts in line. I wasn't sure if being so close to him was making things better or worse. I thought worse. I had to get myself regrouped.

"Look, do you think you could just set it aside for a bit and eat? I think you'll feel better if you do. Then we can take the whole thing, one piece at a time, and look at it. Nothing is so big that it can't be broken down into manageable pieces. There are parts of it that you don't know, and it will probably help when you do." Jahon calmly assured me, "You don't have to worry about Shahvid. He will understand. Even more than you think."

"Probably," I agreed and got up to wash my face with cold water. He made it all sound so reasonable and calm. I could probably have agreed with him more if I hadn't just the day before helped to kill a man. I just didn't feel reasonable and calm right then. I hadn't realized how much I had counted on my life dropping back to normal when the event with Caljn was over. It hadn't happened. And on top of that this bit of stress I was feeling with Jahon. Tranquility seemed far away.

Jahon moved back to his seat and when I sat back down he continued, "Look, I have some work I should attend to this afternoon, but why don't we plan to meet tonight at my place for a long talk?"

~~~ ~~ ~ ~~ ~~~

Jahon thought fast while he ate and talked. Caljn's death was not a minor matter. He wanted to talk with Sinat and Shahvid as soon as possible, but that would have to wait until after Neana had told her story to Shahvid. He also didn't want Neana there for the meeting. He knew she'd balk at that, to put it mildly, but he didn't think she had thought of the current danger. And he didn't want to dump that on her. Besides which, she apparently didn't know about his and Shahvid's association with Starpeace. And he didn't quite know how to bring it up. Not after having lectured her about having kept important matters to herself. Of course, the situations were quite different. But she may not see it that way.

If he could just keep her out of circulation until he had a chance to find out what exactly was going on with the Power Movement people, what they were thinking, or doing, about Caljn's death. What they might know, or suspect. But he also had to be on that job site in the afternoon. He had promised. And if he told Neana about his concerns she'd no doubt just tell him she could take care of herself, and take off. Maybe she could, but he certainly wasn't going to chance it. Not now that he knew. Damn.

Why hadn't Sinat told him? If only he had known before what exactly had been going on. But none of them were involved in every situation, except Chanthan and

Sinat. He and Shahvid had been very involved in the last one. So had Caljn. His breath tightened for a moment, remembering that event. He and Shahvid should have been involved in this one too. At least he now knew that Neana hadn't been involved with Caljn, at least not the way he had feared. In spite of the rest, that thought made his spirits rise. But that was for later. He brought himself firmly back to the kitchen.

~~~ ~~ ~ ~~ ~~~

Out loud Jahon continued, "You could spend the afternoon here and I could pick you up on my way home. Or better yet, come with me now and stay at my place. I'm going to be out on the job for a while but you could work in the shop or just take it easy inside with Skaduter."

I frowned at him, puzzled. Maybe I wasn't thinking very clearly right then, but why would he think I wouldn't just go home? To him I said, "Well, thanks, but I think I'll just go home from here. I'd like to talk with Shahvid as soon as I can, though I don't know what he's up to today. But if he's not around I have some other errands to take care of."

Actually, I didn't know what I wanted to do. For some time my plans hadn't carried me any farther than the previous night. Now that it was over it was hard to think about everyday things.

"Maybe I just need time to organize my thoughts and feelings about the whole thing. I'm sorry about my tears, I didn't mean to do that." I finished my sandwich and started clearing the table.

After a moment I added, "I don't know about tonight. It depends on whether Shahvid's home this afternoon or not. How about if I give you a call later?" I didn't want to tell him that I wasn't sure I was up to spending the evening with him. My feelings seemed a little too crazy. Maybe after I talked with Shahvid my mind and my emotions would smooth out. That pending conversation was hanging heavy over me, in spite of what Jahon had said.

"Besides," I continued instead, "I probably ought

to get out around town, to find out what's going on, what's being said." I didn't mention my concern about Valjar and the others. I didn't think things were over and done with just because Caljn was gone. His friends' reactions to his death could backfire in actions that I frankly didn't want to even consider. It all depended on how they viewed the event.

Would they believe that Caljn had killed himself, by accident or on purpose? I fervently hoped so. And then there was still Caljn's weapon system. How much did the others know about it? Had he been holding the only handpiece? Questions that could drive one crazy, but they had to be asked. Or, more importantly, answered. I knew I should leave that area to Starpeace. I had planned to. But it turned out it wasn't that easy, to just drop it all and go back to my life.

I realized Jahon was watching me so I tried to wipe my concerns off my face. I gathered up the few dishes and started washing. I searched my mind wildly for a neutral, safe subject.

Jahon picked up a towel and we did the dishes in silence. Not a comfortable one. It was as if we were from two completely different cultures, neither quite able to grasp the other's intent and direction.

But that wasn't Jahon's way. Leaning against the counter he put his hands on my shoulders and turned me toward him, "Why not just give yourself some time. And give your friends a chance. I can tell you're off on your own again, shutting everyone else out. If that's what you really want then we all have to accept it. But I wonder if it is, or has that just become a habit? Do you really want to go it alone right now?"

I didn't say anything, and he waited. I didn't pull away, but I didn't come any closer either. He let his hands fall. "You can choose whomever you want to talk it out with, but I think you ought to do that. As I said, you don't have the whole picture. Probably none of us do, but together we can put it all together.

"I don't mean to push Neana, but I don't like seeing what you're doing to yourself," Jahon told me. "You shared with us what you've been doing, what you've gone through. But you haven't let us share back with you from our side. I don't think you've listened to what Binjer and Tamoi and I have tried to tell you."

I met his eyes squarely, and with a deep breath, answered, "I have listened. I know I've been a fool. But I'm not very happy with myself right now, and I don't think it's right to share that kind of me."

Inside I was shaking but I held my composure, not moving away or shifting my gaze. "I don't know if I should have told you and Binjer and Tamoi what I did. I went into this whole affair on my own knowing I didn't want to drag anyone I cared for with me." My voice stuck and I looked away, clearing my throat.

"If I am honest with myself I guess I have to admit that no, deep down, I don't want to go any farther alone. Sometimes it's just very hard to be that honest."

"Being completely honest with ourselves is something we all have trouble with Neana, it's not just you." He touched my chin to bring my eyes back to his. I half held my breath. There was just too much going on inside me right then.

Smiling gently Jahon offered, "I think there are things that both of us are having trouble with right now. How about a truce, an agreement, between friends. To be as honest as we comfortably can, to not push - either toward or away."

I knew he was talking about more than just the affair with Caljn. It wasn't an easy discussion. I managed a wry smile, agreed, let some hard-shelled feelings go, and put out my hand to shake on it. Not long ago a hug would have come naturally. But this was now, and things had changed. I felt a vulnerability that I wasn't used to.

Taking advantage of the mood, Jahon tried, "What would you think of just laying low for now? At least till you've talked it over with Shahvid?"

I shrugged and nodded, "You're probably right, at least for today. Actually, I'm really not up for dealing with any of that crowd right now. I'd rather thought I wouldn't have to ever see any of them again. But now I think that wouldn't be the best move. Of course, I won't be seeing Caljn at any rate."

My spirits had taken a wild swoop upward. All of a sudden my thoughts were acting as they should. I no longer felt alone. The shift was so fast and unexpected that I felt a little giddy. My thoughts ran ahead, planning. I was so caught up in this pleasant organized chaos that Jahon's next words, and serious tone, caught me by surprise.

"How do you feel about that Neana? About Caljn?" he asked me, watching my face intently.

I didn't answer for a moment, thinking of what he asked. Then he looked away, made a gesture sort of a dismissal and started to say something more. I answered him honestly.

"Why, I don't know. I mean, I know how I feel about having been involved in killing him. I know there's no justification for killing so I should feel bad about it. But I can't honestly say I do. It's hard to explain. I guess I feel depressed about the whole thing, that it had to happen at all. But it was Caljn's choice to be who he was and he didn't belong here. He didn't even want to be here I'm pretty sure. But about him as a person . . ." I shook my head, frowning, trying to express what I felt.

"He was almost not a person, Jahon," I continued. "How could you be a part of the human race and think the way he did? I know it's an awful thing to admit, but I really don't care that he's been killed. Maybe that's why I'm having so much trouble with it all. I know what I think I *should* feel but it's not the way I *do* feel. I don't know. I guess I'm having trouble putting it in words."

Jahon grinned rather wryly, "I wasn't questioning your ethics, I'm comfortable with them as they are. I was just wondering. Do you know what you want to do then? Today that is."

"Oh, well, I think I'll just go home and stay there for the afternoon whether Shahvid is around or not. Would you like to stop by when you're done with your job? You could plan on dinner with us." I thought a moment. "We should leave Binjer and Tamoi a note, though I'm not sure what to say."

"That sounds like a good plan. I'll write the note," Jahon said. "Binjer mentioned that they had plans for tonight so they won't be expecting to see us. I'm sure they know that we'll be talking to them soon. Thanks," Jahon took the pencil I handed him and used the back of Tamoi's note for his.

He finished writing, thought a moment, then said, "I'd like to ask Shahvid something about this job I'm involved in. If you want to come with me I have to pick up a couple of things from my shop then we can swing by your place. If you wouldn't mind the walk. I could then pick up a vehicle from the garage near you."

I couldn't think of any reason not to agree. "That sounds fine."

We headed out and our conversation soon found a comfortable groove to travel in. It was late afternoon by the time we reached the house.

When we arrived Shahvid was at work in his study. Jahon went in to talk with him and I went to the kitchen to make a pot of tea. It was past time for my talk with my brother. I sincerely hoped Jahon was right, that Shahvid would understand. In spite of all that had been said my self-confidence was low.

After Jahon left, Shahvid came out and greeted me with a big, brotherly hug. My misgivings flew off. This was my brother. I had forgotten. I should have discussed things with him long ago. We settled down to our long overdue talk.

By the time Jahon returned that evening we had brought ourselves back together, and shared what we had needed to share. He took my involvement with Caljn, the Power Movement and Starpeace fairly calmly. Not that he didn't take me strongly to task about going it alone. He tends to feel I'm still under his wing. Maybe I am in a way. Besides, when he told me about Careen I felt much the same way. Just because it was a good move didn't mean he wasn't feeling it. I tried to be supportive without showing my relief. It was, I was sure, a positive split.

When we heard Jahon at the door, Shahvid had one last thing to say to me. "You know Neana, there's something I think I've learned over these past years. It is just as important, maybe even more important, to share the bad times and the bad feelings as it is to share the good. They are one and the same when you're dealing with someone you truly love."

Shahvid went out to greet Jahon but I stayed behind. I needed a few minutes to digest what he had said.

~~~ ~~ ~ ~~ ~~~

Jahon had hurried out to the job site after leaving Shahvid and Neana, concerned about being late. But everyone was doing fine and he had spent the next several hours working on special problems. He felt much better than he had the day before so things went smoothly. Just as he was about to leave a message arrived that the woman whom he was filling in for would be back Monday.

He made sure everyone knew what the schedule and plans were, then he made his farewells, wishing them all a good Sunday. He gathered his tools, settled himself in the vehicle and drove in the direction of the Square.

His mind and attention had been focused solely on the job all afternoon, but now it was free to travel back to Neana. Which it did with no trouble. He wanted to talk with Sinat soon. So how best to get in touch with him? And what would he have to say? On impulse he pulled off the road and parked the car. He was near the Square so decided to take a few minutes to wander around, see if he could hear anything of importance. None of the people he had been with that afternoon had mentioned anything about Caljn. But they were involved in their work and none of them were the type to gossip. Even if they had anything to offer they couldn't have known that he was interested or involved.

There were a good number of people walking

through and across the Square. A typical active but not overbusy day. He walked around, sharing greetings here and there. Not obviously aiming toward that spot, but ending up where he had seen Caljn the previous night. He stood a moment looking at the raised area. He took a deep breath and raised his head, surveying the people going by. He soon realized the futility of his plan. There was nothing to be learned there. Most of the people of the town were not meddlers or gossips. They weren't apt to get involved in things that weren't their affair. Unless, of course, they could help in some way. He turned and walked back the way he had come.

Sushati was entering the Square just as Jahon was leaving. He called to her and waved. As she headed toward him with a smile, he couldn't help but admire the picture she made. Her light colored caftan was a pleasing contrast to her beautiful dark skin.

"Jahon, how good to see you," she held out her arms for a hug. "It's been too long since you've visited, how are you?"

"Just fine, Sushati, and you? You're looking as great as ever. I can never figure out how you can be so active and look so cool in these hot days."

She laughed at him, "I'm doing well and greeting many new little people right now. Apparently a lot of babies prefer this time of year to be born. I can't say as I blame them either, isn't it lovely today?"

"If I admitted that I hadn't really noticed you'd probably leave me in a huff." Jahon did feel a little sheepish about having been so unaware of the day. "My mind's been otherwise occupied these last few days I guess. Speaking of which, I'd like to talk to you and Sinat as soon as we, and Shahvid, can get together. We have quite a bit to discuss. I'm on my way right now to his house and will probably be there till late. I should be home tomorrow morning though. You could leave a message either place."

Sushati didn't pretend not to understand, nor was she surprised. She nodded agreement, "I'll check with Sinat.

I'm on my way home right now and I think he will be home soon. How is Neana?" Sinat had seen her safely leave the Square Friday night with Jahon, but still, Sushati was concerned for her.

How was Neana? Jahon wished he could say she was just fine, thank you. But he wasn't sure she was. He shrugged, "On the surface, OK, but inside I'm not so sure." He paused, "I should have been told, Sushati."

Sushati understood but shook her head, smiling, gently, "She is her own person, Jahon. It was her decision."

Jahon sighed and smiled back, "You're right of course, but you know I can't really agree. I do know Neana though, and I don't blame you or Sinat. I just wish I had known. I do appreciate his visit Friday morning, even though at the time I maybe didn't come across that way."

Sushati smiled. Sinat had told her of the meeting. "He wasn't at his best right then either you know." Her smile faded, "It was a long day for many people."

Jahon answered her with another hug. He realized that he couldn't know what all they had been going through with this affair. "I won't keep you from him any longer. I have a feeling you two haven't been together much lately."

Sushati was one of the best birth helpers in town, and spent much time with the families in addition to the birthing time. And on top of that, Caijn. He knew she would have been just as involved as Sinat. He added, "But I have questions, and worries, and so will Shahvid."

Sushati assured him, "I *do* understand and so will Sinat. We will of course make time to talk with you. Please don't ever question our friendship, Jahon, no matter how busy we seem, or what else is going on. But I do wish the talk would include Neana."

"Thank you, and I don't. As far as Neana, I'm sure she will be included later. I want very much for you to meet. But I think now is not the time, not yet. Neana is a strong, independent woman, and I respect her for that. But . . ." Jahon hesitated, it was hard to put it into words.

Sushati interrupted, "I know, I think I understand.

I'll trust you to do what you feel is best and that will be fine with me. One of us will give you a call tonight. Maybe we can meet tomorrow morning. Meantime, take care of yourself, and Neana, and give Shahvid my love."

Another hug and they were on their respective ways, both of them with higher spirits. They were friends who didn't see each other often but that did not diminish their closeness. Their paths crossed whenever it was needed.

It was raining Sunday morning as Jahon and Shahvid met in the Square to continue together to Sinat and Sushati's. They didn't say much as they walked along, both lost in their own thoughts, and somewhat weary from another short night.

The three of them had talked till well after midnight. Neana found out about Jahon and Shahvid's involvement with Starpeace when Sinat called, and it became obvious they knew each other well. It was a bit rocky for a time but after things settled out they were able to add some background on the Power Movement, and Caljn, to Neana's story.

They discussed the group's actions and beliefs, and how Neana had gotten so close to the center. No one else had been able to do that. That it had obviously been Caljn's strong attraction to Neana that had made it possible was a little hard for them to accept, each for their own reasons. Little had been said, however, of the possible other dangers. Jahon and Shahvid wanted to find out more before they said anything. And Neana didn't want to worry them. They finally called it a night, and each went their own way once again.

~~~ ~~ ~ ~~ ~~~

I was wakened suddenly by a loud knocking at the door. I jumped out of bed, quickly threw on a robe and tried to bring myself together as I hurried to answer. I briefly noted the rain, and wondered where Shahvid was. The knocker pounded loudly again just as I reached the door making me wince and open it with a frown.

Later I realized that it was good I had been still half in my dream world and operating automatically. Otherwise, I might have been tempted to just shut the door in Valjar's face.

But instead I said a surprised hello, opened the door and invited him in out of the rain. I didn't stop to think what I should or shouldn't say, I just fell back on politeness.

"Can I take your jacket?" I asked him as he stepped inside just barely far enough for me to shut the door behind him. "Would you like some hot tea? It's rather cold out there today." I sounded rather stilted but it was the best I could do, considering the visitor.

Valjar declined with a short no, not smiling, not looking around. He just stared at me, his blue-gray eyes as unfriendly as ever. Rain drops slipped off his black leather coat making a damp area around his feet.

I tried not to see the hatred there and simply asked, "What can I do for you?"

"Nothing." He half growled, "Some of our people thought you should be informed about the services for Caljn." It was obvious he didn't think so. I wondered why he had come. "They start in an hour, at The Church. You are expected." He paused and I made myself stay still.

Valjar continued. He hadn't moved at all. "I wanted to say a few words to you while no one else was around. Your sister-in-law informed me where to find you, and that your brother was out."

I didn't comment, just waited. Alert but, with great effort, calm.

Another pause. His eyes didn't leave my face. He seemed somewhat disconcerted with my reaction, or lack of it. He abruptly said, "Caljn didn't destroy himself like the people are saying. And I'm not going to quit till I've found out who was responsible."

"I can understand that." I told him. " And I'm sorry Valjar." I *was* sorry. The man was obviously hurting.

My words seemed to take some of the threat and power out of his own. He stood a moment then turned without another word and stomped angrily out of the house, slamming the door behind him.

I stood where I was until I heard his vehicle roar off. Then my legs gave way and I sank to the bench by the door, shaking. I may have felt sorry for him but I couldn't ignore the threat. He was not someone to be trusted, and he had no love for me I knew.

In a few minutes I made my way to the kitchen, and another wave of shakes overtook me as I saw the note on the table in Shahvid's large, plain handwriting.

'*Jahon and I are off to visit Sinat and Sushati. Sorry Neana but we both feel the need to talk with them alone. We hope you'll understand. We'll have a good talk when we get back. Please stay around the house till then (big brother request, but sincere). I just don't feel comfortable with this whole affair.   Love, Shahvid. P.S. Hope you had a good night and are well rested.*'

Thank heavens Valjar hadn't accepted my invitation to tea in the kitchen. I sat down to think. Big brother or not I knew what I had to do and I hadn't much time.

I hurriedly ate, washed and dressed, and was soon on my way to the Church of the Final God. I tried to concentrate on the feeling of walking in the rain, something I usually enjoyed, and to not think of what was ahead. It wasn't easy.

~~~ ~~ ~ ~~ ~~~

Kasho woke to the pleasant sound of raindrops. She lay in bed listening, and thinking. Her contact had told her about the services for Caljn scheduled that day at their church. It seemed rather short notice, but he hadn't given any indication of anything ominous or wrong, although she thought that particular church's view about death and dying pretty ominous in itself. And what she'd heard about their services for the departed souls would make anyone not want to die and move on. She was glad she didn't need to attend. Having someone you cared for die was pretty sad for those left here, but there was no reason to be morbid about it. But for some reason many of that church's members believed that death was pretty much the end of you. That *would* be a depressing thought. She certainly couldn't understand why anyone would want to believe that.

She had considered letting Jahon know about the services but hadn't thought it that important. Surely Neana was out of it all now. But that morning she felt uneasy. She couldn't figure out why but knew better than to ignore her feelings. She just wasn't sure what to do about it.

She thought of going to Shahvid but hesitated. Last Thursday with him had been pretty emotional, almost all of it inside, and she wasn't sure about seeing him again yet. He and Careen were still married, and they had to work things out one way or the other. She had decided late that night to stay away from him until it was all settled. Then, well, then she'd just have to see.

The rain was echoing her falling spirits. Darn it all, she felt like going over to talk with Shahvid. But maybe she'd head to Jahon's instead. She probably should go straight to Neana, but she didn't know for sure where Neana stood as far as her involvement. It had been some time since they'd had a close conversation. Or much of any conversation for that matter.

She threw off the covers and jumped out of bed. This wasn't getting her anywhere. She decided she would just get ready and go, and decide on the way. She quickly dressed and pulled a comb through her light brown curly hair, tying it back with a ribbon.

There were a number of people in the Square in spite of the rain. It wasn't stormy or particularly cold and most people simply fit themselves into the rain and went about their affairs. Kasho turned to watch a youngster as he tried to step in every puddle while not letting go of his father's hand. She was laughing at his gymnastics and almost ran into a woman standing in the middle of the tiles, staring in the opposite direction. She started to apologize and was startled to have Careen's cold blue eyes turn toward her.

Careen barely acknowledged Kasho and rudely turned away, hurrying off across the Square.

Kasho turned to stare after her and as she did she caught a glimpse of two familiar figures heading off to the right, where Careen had been staring. It was Jahon and Shahvid. Even at that distance and through the rain Kasho couldn't mistake her friends.

She thought of trying to catch up to them, but decided not. It looked like they were intent on an errand and she didn't want to butt in.

So now what? For some reason her run-in with Careen had made her feel even more uneasy. Though she had to admit she shouldn't have been surprised at seeing her, the woman had certainly been in her thoughts a lot lately. Good reminder to watch what you kept in your mind.

Well, she wasn't going to get Shahvid or Jahon that morning so she decided she might as well go talk to Neana. She would just play it by ear when she got there. She turned and walked briskly away from the Square.

Kasho was a distance from Shahvid's house, about to cross the road, when she saw the car. It was sleek, black, and noisier than necessary. It was also traveling too fast, a rare occurrence in that area.

As it passed, Kasho stood staring after it, the wind and the rain forgotten. What in heaven's name was Valjar doing in these parts? She didn't like the possibilities.

Turning, she continued along the road to Shahvid's house. It was faster than the foot path and there was little traffic. Nature seemed to sense her urgency and whipped up the wind to match her pace.

There was no reason to think Valjar's destination was the same as hers, she told herself again and again as she hurried along. But once the possibility had come to mind she couldn't shake it loose. She bent her head against the rain, walking faster, and trying not to worry.

When she finally reached the path Kasho paused a moment to catch her breath, then walked quickly up to the house. There was no answer to her knock. She opened the door and walked in, calling out as she did so.

Still no answer. The house seemed unusually quiet. Oh stop it, she told herself. Neana was no doubt just out on an errand. Nothing more.

She got out of her wet coat and boots, then walked back to Neana's rooms to knock at her door. She really didn't expect an answer, she didn't feel anyone around. Kasho called out again, waited, then walked back up to the kitchen.

She could have used a friendly face right then, and a cup of hot tea. She wasn't a nervous person and the fears popping into her mind were beginning to bug her. She was feeling chilled and didn't want to go back out into the rain.

And the prospect of just going home, alone, didn't appeal to her. She usually didn't mind being alone, but that day was different.

Instead she decided to brew some tea and sit down to think about it. It wouldn't do any good to rush off without knowing where she wanted to go. When she entered the kitchen she saw Shahvid's note, and next to it Neana's smaller one.

'Had to take a trip out, not sure when I'll be back so don't worry if I'm late. Neana'.

Kasho sat at the table, chin in hand, and stared at the two notes. The feelings of friendship, love and worry almost overwhelmed her. She knew from what Jahon had said that notes like that from Neana had become common these last months. But when she had heard of Caljn's death she had thought, hoped, that Neana's meetings with those people would have ended.

She thought she had a good idea about Neana's interest in Caljn and the Power Movement. She had never seriously thought that her involvement was philosophical, or romantic. Kasho snorted to herself, romantic indeed, there was nothing at all romantic about any of those people. Besides, she thought she knew her friend well enough to know where her heart was, and it certainly wasn't aimed in that direction. At least it didn't used to be.

So what *was* going on? Her thoughts went off in directions that she didn't like, with possibilities she just couldn't consider. She felt frustrated and uneasy. Maybe she shouldn't have just let things go when Neana had started avoiding her. Maybe she should have confronted her and insisted on some answers. But Jahon had tried that, and it hadn't worked. She had felt she had to let Neana live her life her own way. She trusted her to ask for help if she wanted, or needed, it. But maybe she had been wrong.

"Oh, damn, and damn, and damn!" Kasho said out loud. It wasn't just her own feelings, it was also the thought of how Shahvid and Jahon were going to feel when they came home to read Neana's note. She had talked often enough to Jahon about Neana's activities to know what his reaction was going to be, and she wasn't looking forward to it. She also knew well how Shahvid felt about his sister.

She took a deep breath, sat up and brought herself together, reigning in her runaway thoughts. She was letting her emotions carry away her imagination. Enough of that. As soon as she calmed down she realized where Neana probably was. She had gone to the Church. To the services for Caljn. Nothing more, nothing less. But what about Valjar? Where did he fit in? *Had* he been here? Was she right about Neana's involvement?

Kasho sat, lost in thought, the tea unmade. Shahvid and Jahon came in an hour later to find her still sitting there.

Kasho stood up to greet them, "Hi, welcome home. I walked over for a visit and didn't feel like going right back out into the rain when I found no one home, hope it's OK."

"Don't be silly, of course it's OK, it's good to see you. Why didn't you make yourself some tea or something?" Shahvid gave her a sort of half hug as he went by to heat up some water, "It's a great day to stay inside."

After their last meeting he had made the decision to keep his distance from her until he and Careen had things settled. But to be honest he didn't much care for it. He was so happy to see her that he temporarily forgot about Neana, and the meeting he and Jahon had just come from.

Jahon hadn't forgotten. After greeting Kasho he saw the note she had half hidden with her hand. He slipped it out and read it without comment.

Kasho watched his face wishing she could think of something positive to say. Shahvid turned back to them with a comment, but stopped when Jahon silently handed the note to him.

"Damn, why couldn't she just stay home for *one* day? Why did she have to go out?" He was angry. For a few minutes his world was happy with no problems, and now back to this. He knew he was being unreasonable but it was how he felt right then. He threw the note on the table without looking at either Jahon or Kasho.

Jahon stood staring out the window at the rain. Kasho waited a few moments for the immediate storm to pass before speaking. She wasn't sure she should tell them about Valjar, though there were probably enough problems around already caused by not communicating. But she could help with the immediate question of where Neana was, and hopefully calm them both down.

"I think I know where Neana is, and I don't think there's any need to get so worked up, or worried. There are services today for Caljn at his church, and I suspect Neana decided she should attend. She might be expected to by those around Caljn. I've been thinking about it. I know I don't know all of what's going on, but I'd think it would be best that she did go and not seem to drop out, bam, just like that the minute Caljn died."

Shahvid looked at her with some surprise. She probably didn't know all that was going on but had apparently guessed an awful lot. He seemed to be lately often surprised by her.

"What else?" Jahon's question broke into Shahvid's thoughts. At Kasho's questioning look Jahon continued, "You've been just sitting here for some time without even making a cup of tea. There's something more that's bothering you, what is it Kasho?"

He wasn't being unkind but his thoughts were on one path only right then, Neana's safety. Their conversation with Sinat and Sushati had done nothing to ease his mind in that direction, quite the contrary.

Kasho frowned at him wondering how he would know how long she'd been there.

"Your rain coat is dry," Jahon told her wryly.

Kasho raised her eyes to the ceiling. Oh well. "Yes, there is something else, but I'm not real sure how it fits in and I don't want to raise false fears. Is the tea ready? Good, if you'll both just sit down I'll tell you, and we can think it out together."

Jahon agreed and pulled out a chair. Shahvid set the mugs of hot tea on the table, and the cookie crock, then sat down across from Jahon. Kasho joined them.

She proceeded to tell them about seeing Valjar on her way over. "You see, it's not much, but it just didn't strike me well. I doubt that this area is one of Valjar's normal haunts."

Jahon thought a moment then got up decisively, "I'm going over to the church."

But before he could get more than a few steps away from the table Kasho got up and grabbed his arm, "No, Jahon, think about it! What would that do but cause a scene and make Neana stand out? Your feelings about Caljn and that group are too well known."

That stopped him. He frowned at her. He had been careful not to talk the Power Movement these last months. He hadn't wanted to bring out Neana's involvement. Of course, he guessed that anyone who knew him well knew his views about life and misdirected power, and people like Caljn, but . . .

"Come sit down. There's one other thing." Kasho gestured toward the table.

Jahon stood a moment, then sat back down.

"I know you're not going to like this, but whatever you think about him, I saw Rafnon when I was in the Square." She decided not to mention seeing them there too, and didn't feel like bringing Careen's name up either. "I'm pretty sure he will be going to the church, and I don't think he'd let anything happen to Neana."

Shahvid didn't look at Jahon, "Actually, Sinat did say that Rafnon would be going to the services." He didn't mention what Jahon's response to that had been. "We spent the morning talking with Sinat and Sushati. I have a feeling you probably know what we talked about."

Kasho didn't comment on that, she just smiled. Then she added, "You know, there is also the fact that Neana *is* quite capable of taking care of herself."

"We're talking about the Power Movement, Kasho, not a walk in the woods," Jahon replied, almost angrily.

Kasho understood, she didn't press her point.

Shahvid watched Kasho and made a decision. That morning when her name had come up he had said he didn't think they should get her any more involved in the affair. It wasn't a matter of trust, but concern about the possible danger. Jahon disagreed but had left it up to him. Now Shahvid was seeing it differently. "Kasho, I'd like to fill you in on what's going on, the parts you may not know. If you want that is. I don't think just because Caljn is gone the danger is over. On one hand I don't want to involve you, but on the other you're obviously already involved." He didn't add that also he just wanted very much to share it with her.

Jahon wondered if his feelings for Neana were as obvious as Shahvid's for Kasho. If so, he'd better be careful, especially around Neana. He wasn't even that sure of them himself.

He quietly left the discussion to the two of them, taking his thoughts elsewhere. As Shahvid and Kasho shared their information Jahon concentrated on what he'd learned that morning. Putting it together with what Neana had told them. He knew that his closeness to the people involved made it hard to see the right path. He also knew how important it was to not spend time down a wrong one, not right then. He was afraid the Power Movement would not give them time to sit around and think things over.

Jahon abruptly interrupted, "Do you know what time the services should be done?"

Kasho and Shahvid stared at him a moment. They had been so wrapped up in their talk that they'd almost forgotten Jahon was there.

"Um, well, let's see," Kasho tried to come up with a time based on what she knew. It was easy to see where Jahon was headed and she wasn't sure she agreed, but, "I'd say four o'clock maybe. But then there will be a dinner somewhere, and then they'll go back to the church for an evening service. Probably from say seven to ten. It's a pretty long, drawn out affair and a real downer. Have you ever been to one? Know what they believe about death?"

But Jahon wasn't to be put off track. He looked at the clock, "I'm going to walk over that direction." As both Kasho and Shahvid started to speak he held up his hand and shook his head at them. "No, don't worry, I'm not going to make a scene or anything. I agree about not putting Neana in the spotlight any more than she is. But I've been sitting all day and I have to get out and do something. Seems like all I've been doing lately is sitting and talking. A walk will do me good."

When they just looked at him without comment he added, "OK, and I want to make sure she's all right. I won't pretend to put any trust in Rafnon, or anyone else for that matter. It's just too uncertain as to what those people might know. Or suspect. And we know only too well what they're capable of doing. I'll play it by ear, but I promise to be inconspicuous. And I'd rather go alone."

Shahvid knew there was no use arguing, besides he agreed. He had to admit he too was worried. "Come back here when you're done then, OK? We'll be here waiting." He directed the first at Jahon and the second, with a questioning look, to Kasho.

She smiled her assent. To hell with her decision, and quite frankly, the hell with Careen.

Jahon thought a moment, then, "Probably. If not, I'll call." If he did manage to make contact with Neana he wasn't sure what would happen, what her reaction would be. Or his for that matter.

He made a quick trip down the hall, his bladder yelling about all the tea he'd downed that day. Then he slipped into his long raincoat and was on his way. The rain had lessened somewhat but the day seemed to be reflecting his mood, cold and gray.

~~~ ~~ ~ ~~ ~~~

I sat in the back of the church trying to keep my spirit apart from those around me. The man up front had been going on for what seemed like forever, saying ridiculous things about Caljn. It appeared he had never met him nor knew anything about him. They were just words he was preaching, nothing about the man who had died.

I suppose I shouldn't have gone to the service alone. But I had to be there. And who could I have gotten to go with me? I couldn't see Jahon or Shahvid sitting through it. I almost snorted out loud at the thought. Kasho probably would have gone with me, but it had been awhile since we'd been together much. I hadn't even thought to ask her, besides which I'd have had to go through the whole story first. No, if I had asked, Kasho would have come without questions. It just hadn't occurred to me to ask anyone. But then, I hadn't known how bad it was going to be.

The music was awful but it matched the mood of the people there, despondent and hopeless. I felt the old depression washing over me.

No one had paid any attention to me as I slipped in at the last minute. Well, not too many. I had seen Careen craning her neck around, looking at the last arrivals. I didn't care for the speculative narrowing of her eyes as she saw me. I had nodded briefly and turned away before she could make any response.

I had also nodded briefly, but with a large question mark in my mind, at Rafnon when he had also slipped in at the last minute. He had sat far away from me on the other side, his only response to my nod being a frown.

And Valjar of course. He had been standing at the door greeting people as they walked in. I had felt his cold stare as I walked by and had to consciously keep from shivering. Corny, but it was how I had felt. I also felt I was overreacting and told myself to get it together. Not that it helped a great deal but arguing with myself kept me occupied for a time.

I felt sorry for Valjar. My comment to him at the house had been sincere. I knew he was very attached to Caljn, and to say good-bye to a close friend in this manner was such a shame. It didn't give you any support, any hope, nothing to fall back on. But I also knew it fit him, and it fitted the man Caljn had been, still was no doubt.

Caljn. I felt strangely detached from his death, the killing. If anything my feelings were of relief that he was gone. There just hadn't seemed to be any hope for him here. I couldn't see much for Valjar either, or the rest of that inner group. But somehow I could feel sorry for them. Maybe it was because Caljn hadn't seemed to have any feelings. And Valjar, though thoroughly messed up and distorted, did.

The service appeared to be drawing to a close. There had been talk about a meal after for friends of the 'deceased', as they called Caljn, at some hall. And then another service that evening. Guess they felt you were supposed to prove your friendship by sitting through all that.

But I knew I couldn't take any more. I didn't care what Valjar or anyone else thought, I was going home. I was enough in touch with myself, and cared enough about myself, to know that I needed to be with friends. Soon. And if these past months had taught me anything it was to trust and follow those feelings.

I didn't try to think of who I needed or where they would be, I just had faith that they would be there. As soon as the service ground to a close I slipped out as quickly, and as unobtrusively, as possible.

It was still raining lightly as I quickly walked away from the church, and from the people, toward the Square. I didn't stop to notice anyone, or see if anyone noticed me. I didn't care. My spirit felt as cold and gray as the rain and I hurried to find help and warmth.

As I neared the Square I could see the warm glow of the lamps, and the feeling that it was going to be OK came over me. I slowed my pace and felt my fast breathing. I hadn't realized how fast I'd been walking. My eyes were on the wet tiles as I bent my head to keep the rain out of my face. I would have run right into Jahon if he hadn't reached out to catch me first.

I knew who it was before I looked up, briefly, then buried myself in his arms, not the least mindful of the people around us. And the people politely made a detour around as they hurried by. Jahon just stood there holding me. Neither of us spoke.

Several minutes later I pulled back and without words we clasped hands and walked back to Shahvid's in the rain, together. It turned into a beautiful rain, cool and refreshing for the earth, and for us, and full of sudden color.

Shahvid and Kasho were still in the kitchen talking when we arrived. We slipped out of our wet gear and joined them. Not much was said other than greetings but my hugs to both of them were extra special. It felt so good to be back.

"I've started the sauna," Shahvid said. "It should be about ready, if you're interested. We can come up with something to eat after."

"Sounds good to me," Jahon replied, "*If* you let me be in charge of the food. Your aversion to cooking is not the kind of meal I need tonight."

We all laughed, agreed, and headed for the sauna. The rain had lessened but it was still cool and the hot sauna room felt good. We soaked up the heat and the feelings of friendship and love. Talk was general, loose and light.

After several rounds of heating up and cooling off, we dressed and ran back into the kitchen through the drizzle, thoroughly warmed and refreshed.

Kasho helped Jahon fix a simple dinner, while Shahvid and I set the table and generally harassed them. Jahon enjoyed cooking for friends, and both Shahvid and I were more than happy to leave him to it. The conversation was light and lighthearted, the sound of the rain offering a fitting background music to the sudden cheerfulness. I could hardly believe it had been only hours before that I had been sitting in that church so depressed.

"Did you know your cooking unit needs charging? It's a little low on heat," Jahon informed the room, his back to us as he stirred the vegetables.

Shahvid laughed at him, "A good chef doesn't blame his tools you know! But seriously, maybe I ought to get Toler to take a look at it, I'm sure it was charged up a week or so ago. Oh, maybe not now that I think on it, it may have been longer. I'll hook it up next sunny day and see how it goes. Try to remind me, Neana."

I agreed, "There should be an intense charging day coming up soon, hasn't been one for a while. I'd like to take all our wands and hand chargers out to the Wild Tree spot when it comes. Want to plan on going Kasho? Or we could go somewhere else."

"No, I like the Wild Tree, it's not so busy. And if we go early there will be even fewer people. Want us to take yours with us Jahon?" Kasho offered.

"Depends on the day I guess. I'll let you know. I mean whether you can take them or I will. Or is this a women only party? Shahvid and I invited?" Jahon set dinner on the table and joined the group. Crazy that he'd want to go along, but right then he felt pretty crazy.

"Of course you two can go. It'll cramp our usual wild style, but I guess we could handle that for once, eh Neana?" Kasho teased with a laugh. It was almost like the old days, but at a higher intensity that was close to scary.

The bantering continued through the meal. After

dinner and the dishes were done, Shahvid suggested we take our tea into his study. The living area of the house had been Careen's as far as decor and it didn't seem to fit Shahvid or me. Neither of us had used it much, being much more comfortable in our own rooms which were furnished to accommodate a small party of friends.

Shahvid's study was on the same side of the house as my rooms and had several large windows looking out on the grounds. A large work desk, a smaller computer desk and several file cabinets fit comfortably in the room. Along with a small couch and several comfortable chairs and piles of pillows. Most of the furnishings had been made by the people in the room so we all felt quite at home. The wood pieces being the work of Shahvid, Jahon or myself (and most of the furnishings were of wood), and many of the cushions, pillows, curtains and rugs were made of Kasho's weavings.

Jahon stopped at a small bookcase as we went in. Most people don't keep many books for themselves, preferring to share at the library. The books one finds in a home are usually of a specific nature along the lines of special interest to the owner, and ones used often. Many of Jahon and Shahvid's books were shared so often between the two of them that the label of ownership had no meaning.

Jahon picked one out. "Going to be needing this?" he asked Shahvid, showing him the title. At Shahvid's response to the negative, "Good, I think there's some information in here that might be of use to the woman who is in charge of that construction east of town. When I filled in for her there were a couple things that didn't look quite right to me, but I wasn't sure about it. I'll take it along with me tomorrow." He set it on a shelf by the door and settled into a chair.

Everyone was quiet for a moment, then I spoke, "I went to the church services for Caljn this afternoon, as I guess you already know."

Shahvid answered, "We weren't sure, but Kasho guessed that's where you were."

Kasho told me briefly of her uneasiness that morning, her trip over, and seeing Valjar.

I didn't say anything for a moment. We had slipped easily back into our friendship and I was happy for that. And I gathered that Kasho knew what was going on.

Neither Shahvid nor Jahon said anything but Kasho had no problem asking the question. "Why did you go, Neana? *Was* Valjar here? He sure gave me the willies when I saw him on the road so close by." Kasho shivered.

"Yes, it was because of Valjar and his visit to me this morning that I went," I answered. They all looked at me startled. I then proceeded to tell them about my encounter with Valjar.

"The willies is an understatement, he is a strange character. But I decided it was best to go. I didn't think it would be that hard. Actually, I guess I didn't think ahead at all, I just decided I should go and I did. I wouldn't do it again, not alone. And I wouldn't ask anyone I cared for to go either. It was such a depressing experience. I ended up feeling even more sorry for Valjar and those who were Caljn's friends. It was such a different event than deaths I've been involved with before."

I was silent, thinking of it. The feelings that had enveloped me at the church flooded back too readily.

"Most things aren't so bad when you share them." Jahon's reminder brought me back to the room.

I had to smile at his words, at myself. I had become too used to keeping to myself. I told them of the service, and my feelings about it. I felt better just putting the feelings into words, among friends. I didn't mention Rafnon, or Careen. No use opening up old wounds even a little. Maybe I would talk that over with Kasho later. I didn't think she would mind.

It was funny how it felt that Shahvid and Careen's marriage was long in the past when it was hardly a week since Careen had moved out. And I didn't even know for positive that the split was final, though I had a pretty good idea. After all, marriage was a state of mind. Thinking that way, I wondered how long it had been since Shahvid and Careen had really been married.

I brought myself back to the conversation in the room. Jahon and Shahvid were discussing what they had learned that morning about Valjar. I had forgotten about their meeting. Jahon was saying,

"I know they don't think he's much of a danger but I disagree. He seems pretty unstable and if he thinks Neana was involved in Caljn's death then he needs to be watched carefully. I don't know about the others. Sinat seemed to think they would be lost without Caljn and weren't much for thinking on their own. What do you think, Neana?"

"I guess I'd agree with Sinat. He and Chanthan seem to know that whole group pretty well. I don't think I added much to their knowledge that night, except for the actual attack plan that is, and some details about their weapon." I considered a moment, then said, "As for Valjar, I think it's more just my feelings about him than an actual danger. And I think his hatred of me is from a purely jealous point of view. He seemed to dislike anyone being near to Caljn, and he hated me most for some reason. I don't know why since I wasn't *that* close to Caljn. Just rubbed him wrong I guess."

"I don't know, Neana. He did rather pointedly say to you about not believing Caljn destroyed himself." Kasho stopped, then added, "Do you think he'd go to the council with it?"

The town council is a group of ten people who hear and decide on any dispute or problem, ranging from a simple fair trade question to more serious theft or battery. The spirit of the council is well understood so almost everyone abides by their decisions, even if they disagree.

The members of the council are of two groups. The first being more or less permanent. They are people who have a special interest and talent in that area. Any vacancy is filled by agreement of the others. Anyone interested can submit their name, or recommend someone else they think would be good. If there are any feelings that someone in the group is not doing their best then it is brought up for discussion, and the problem resolved. It is a responsible job like any other responsible job, and carries no special honors.

The other five members of the council are people from the community, who serve on a rotating schedule for six months at a time. The qualifications are that you be at least fourteen years of age and have lived in the community for at least five years. No one *has* to serve on the council but almost everyone does when their name comes up. There are arrangements made to include those who are not able mentally to contribute in the normal fashion, thereby leaving no one out, except by their own choice. It is a system that works well.

Having Caljn's death brought up before the Council would have been a very ticklish situation. Not that we didn't all trust and respect the Council. They would have taken care not to put anyone in needless danger. But still, I didn't think it would be good to have the whole thing out in the open. Not right then. The possible danger from Caljn's inner circle friends was very real.

"No, it hasn't been brought up to the council. Sinat's a member you know," Jahon reminded, "and he didn't think any of the Power Movement people would approach the council even if they did question Caljn's death. And we don't know that any of them, other than Valjar, do. Besides, I can't imagine them taking a chance on having their own operations exposed."

I agreed, "No, I doubt that it will go there. The inner group wouldn't want anything to do with the council. They would know who's on it after all. They aren't the kind of people to be involved in the community that way, and the council is very much a part of our community." I was silent a moment. "No matter how much I look at it, and from which way, I just can't understand their direction. It's this very community that they tried, or are trying, to destroy. But why? It just doesn't make any sense."

"No, it doesn't seem to be a matter of sense at all," Shahvid agreed, "but it's not new you know. Starpeace has been around for a long, long time, working to counteract those types of people. But look at the old civilization. Back then more people than not were working to destroy their communities. And the whole earth for that matter. Sure it gets depressing now thinking about people like Caljn and Valjar, and those scientists, but think of what it must have been like living back then. If you had been trying to live as a part of earth and nature as we do, well, can you imagine it?" Shahvid shook his head.

"Not really," Jahon said. "From what we know of things back then, the way people chose to live, the way they raped their own earth, and each other. Their *greed*. It's really beyond imagining."

"And not something I care to think about quite frankly." Kasho said. "But, you're right Shahvid, it does bring our own problems back into perspective. Sounds like the thing to do is just to get on with our lives, Neana included, and try not to give their game any more impetus by thinking too much about it. Caljn is gone, and I don't think there is anything we can do to help the others. They have to get it together themselves. Though there's always hope that this whole affair will get through to some of them." She yawned, "I guess I better get on my way or you'll soon have an unwanted house guest asleep on your floor!"

Shahvid laughed at her, "You're as welcome as any of us to sleep here, and we *do* have places other than the floor. But I certainly agree with getting on with our lives. That group has gotten too much of too many people's attention already." He added, "As long as we don't ignore something we shouldn't. And as far as sleep, neither of you has to go home tonight, you know that."

"Thanks, but I think I will head home, the walk will clear my brain and it sounds like the rain has let up." Kasho got up to go.

Jahon agreed. "I'll walk with you to the Square. I want to check a couple of things in the Hall listings before I go home. But," he added, "I don't think we should forget Valjar. Not as long as he might be a threat to Neana."

Jahon followed Kasho out to the entryway to gather together their rain gear. I went to get sweaters for them since it had cooled with the night. I didn't reply to Jahon's comment about not forgetting about Valjar, but there certainly was not much chance that I would. Not any time soon. No matter how much I would have liked to.

After hugs and farewells all around, Jahon and Kasho left. Shahvid and I talked lightly of our friends, and the enjoyable evening, as we picked up the mugs and carried them to the kitchen. Then we said our goodnights, and went off to our rooms. It wasn't long before the house was quiet, and I was asleep. It had been a long day.

And it was an even longer week. At least it seemed that way to me. I didn't have any immediate jobs lined up, except to varnish and frame the Jansoon paintings, so I spent the week getting caught up on errands and small projects. I had put off so many things, and people, during my involvement with Caljn. It felt good to be back in touch, and to be once again enjoying life.

I hadn't seen much of Jahon, Shahvid or Kasho all that week. It seemed everyone was busy getting 'caught up' for some reason. My contacts with other friends were short but nice. Those who were close enough to have noticed my 'absence' the last months made subtle but sincere comments to let me know they welcomed me back. It felt good. I was able to let go of my thoughts of Caljn. Almost.

The cause of that 'almost', and the long week, was Valjar. I was constantly running into him. He seemed to be everywhere I was. Maybe that was overstating it, but by the end of the week I was becoming unnerved by the frequency.

He never spoke, though I always nodded or smiled politely. He just stared at me. And it wasn't a friendly look. I tried to ignore it, not make too much out of the meetings. Whenever he came to mind I just let the thoughts go on through without stopping. I didn't want to create a situation that wasn't there by thinking too much about it.

But here it was Friday, barely afternoon, and I had seen him twice already. I tried very hard to put him from my mind. The paintings were framed and hung, and I felt good about the work. It was time to start thinking about my next project.

"Damn!" I said to myself. It was too much. There was Valjar again. I saw him just as I was entering the Square. I turned abruptly to leave, and ran right into a woman walking toward me. "Oh, excuse me, I'm sorry," I quickly apologized.

Sushati waved off the apology, "It's OK, I'm fine. I was just coming over to talk to you, and wondering how to introduce myself. But I think it is taken care of." She laughed, "Anyone who dances as well as we just did shouldn't need an introduction."

She touched my arm in a friendly fashion and led me away from the area, making a half wave back toward Valjar, who was standing watching us, "Could I interest you in a more private conversation? Possibly a cup of tea and biscuits? I understand the Tea and Talk has a new Fresh Corn Biscuit they are trying out on any takers."

I knew who Sushati was of course, so I agreed and fell in step beside her, not looking back. It was apparent that she had seen my reaction to Valjar, and she would have an idea of its reason. Though we had never met I felt like I knew her quite well already. I mentioned that to her.

Sushati laughed, "I feel that way too, and I think it is high time we met formally." She held out her hand and we shook, half seriously, then continued on our way to the Tea and Talk.

It isn't a large place, but comfortable and filled with small tables and booths. Its purpose is as its name states - a place to have a cup of tea, a biscuit and a quiet talk with a friend or two. It isn't a place for large gatherings, and the tables are spaced far enough apart for a nice amount of privacy. The lighting is arranged for a soft, intimate kind of feeling, both the natural lighting of day and the lamps at night.

Sushati and I made our choices of tea and biscuit, then settled down at a table in a quiet corner, waving greetings to several people in the room on our way.

Sushati jumped right in, no use pretending we didn't both know what was going on, "Has Valjar been bothering you?"

It seemed quite natural to talk it over with Sushati, so I told her about the week's 'chance' meetings with him. It was so nice to talk to someone who knew well the related events, and who took the whole thing calmly and seriously, but not emotionally.

"I've been trying to not give it too much weight, but I've never seen him so often. And I can't deny his attitude, though maybe it's not all that different from before." I thought a moment. "Maybe he stands out so much because of the absence of Caljn. Valjar was always in his shadow before, as were the others. Also, it could be I'm just more aware of him now."

"It's not just you," Sushati assured me. "As you may guess, we've been keeping a close eye on what is going on. The rest of that group is keeping pretty quiet right now. But," Sushati mused, "what could Valjar be up to?"

We talked for a while about possible meanings and intents, possible dangers, possible actions. Then Sushati asked me if I'd mentioned Valjar's attentions to Jahon or Shahvid.

I tried to explain, "No. I don't want them to react to something that isn't there. I'd like to get the whole picture first, figure out what's really going on. It's not that they aren't both reasonable men. Shahvid is one of the calmer people I know, and Jahon usually thinks things over well before he acts. But," I hesitated, trying to find the right words, "well, either one of them is quite bullheaded once they decide on something. And right now I don't want them to do anything."

Sushati grinned, "I think I know what you mean. And I think you are right that they would respond. Maybe not the way you might want them to, but I don't believe they would be totally unreasonable. But," she added, "they will want to know what is going on. And you can't blame them. If the situation was reversed, and it was one of them or Sinat in your position, I don't think we would be very happy about being left out."

I thought about it a minute, then had to agree. "And if you think of it that way, I don't know how rational or objective we'd be either." I smiled at Sushati, "Thank you. I guess I will talk it over with them. If they get out of hand I'll just call in reinforcements!"

Sushati agreed with a laugh, "Just give me a call! But I have no doubt that you can handle them both just fine. Seriously, I know we haven't come to any conclusions, but I do think your uneasiness is quite justified. I didn't care for Valjar's manner, and I have never seen him out and among the people so much before."

We both sat a few moments thinking while we finished our tea. Sushati spoke, "I would like to talk this over with Sinat and Chanthan. This affair is not over yet, and we need to be knowing what is going on. Maybe we should all get together and share our thoughts. What do you think?"

"My honest first reaction is no, I'll just handle it myself. But," I admitted wryly, "I am learning. It's a good idea and it would be nice *not* to handle him by myself." Then I added, "But I do feel a bit, well, do you think it's important enough to involve Chanthan?"

Sushati smiled but didn't comment other than to say yes, she did think it was. We parted as established friends with the agreement to be in touch sometime that weekend. I continued on home with good feelings, about our meeting and our talk.

When I arrived home Shahvid was sitting in the kitchen finishing his dinner. I quickly set my things in my room and joined him. We exchanged greetings as I fixed myself something to eat.

As I sat down to the table I started to tell Shahvid of my meeting with Sushati. But then I noticed his manner, and instead asked, "Long day?"

Shahvid smiled, then sighed, "Yes, you could say that." He set his plate aside and leaned back in his chair. "Last night Careen and I got together for a talk, a long one. There's no reason to go into all of it, but it's final, she agreed that our marriage is over. We decided how to divide up our material goods, and it was well after midnight by the time we were done. But I'm glad we did it then. It wasn't that hard. It made the fact that we'd been living separate lives really stand out.

"Jahon and Binjer came over today and helped me move all her things. She's living with her Aunt for now. The living room is pretty bare, and of course her rooms, a few other things here and there. But I don't think there's much, if anything, that you'll miss."

I went over to him and gave him a big hug, "I'm sorry Shahvid. But I'm glad that it's over. It's good that Jahon and Binjer could help. I assume you would have asked if I could have been of assistance so I won't apologize for not being here. But I am sorry I wasn't around at least for support."

"You're here now, and there was nothing much you could have done today." Shahvid gave me a grin, "Except distract my help."

I ignored that and sat back down to finish my dinner. "Is it OK with you now then? Do you feel like doing anything special tonight or would you rather be alone?"

"I'm fine. If anything I feel relief. Maybe I even feel a bit of excitement, or expectancy, at a new life." Shahvid grinned, "Of course, that could just be because I'm tired. Our friend Jahon was as early a bird as yourself this morning, you just missed him. He was the one who recruited Binjer who brought the moving van. Actually, we had rather a good time of it, and a good swim after, so don't feel too sorry for me."

"Don't worry, I won't! A good swim sounds good, I could use one." It was inviting. But I didn't feel much like going out again that night. I didn't feel up to another 'chance' encounter with Valjar.

"Could you live with a quick wash up instead? We're due for some company any minute. I tried to catch you at the Jansoon's to tell you but you'd left already, and I didn't know where you were headed from there." Shahvid explained dryly, "Jahon and Binjer decided that the day's event called for a celebration. They told me it was OK if I didn't feel it was reason for a party, but they, honest friends that they are, did. So they will be here soon with Tamoi and Kasho. Since we didn't know where you were they decided the event should be held here so as to catch you easier - their words. They were both in a rather strange mood."

I laughed. Why did I bother to worry about Shahvid when he had friends like that! "Well, how could I refuse such an invitation. Is there any furniture left? Or do we need to move some around?"

"Oh, they took care of that too. If you had gone into your studio you'd have found it pretty bare, and my study too. But all for the cause and the party!"

Shahvid felt strangely lighthearted all of a sudden. About Careen, about the party, about our renewed friendship. He had been a bit down sitting there by himself, thinking. But he really was looking forward to the night's get-together. All he had to do was let himself go and enjoy it. The party would be good for everyone. The Caljn affair was too much on all of our minds.

"There will be only the six of us," Shahvid continued. "Binjer said the children were all visiting friends for several days, one of their fellow-parent children swaps."

"Well, I'll trust the arrangements. It's not exactly a picky group anyway. I'll go get cleaned up and changed then. Sounds like someone coming up the bike lane now." I put my dishes in the sink and hurried off to my rooms, more excited than I'd been in quite awhile. I didn't bother to question why, I just enjoyed the feeling.

They were all there in the living room by the time I was done with my quick shower and dressing. I was greeted with remarks along the line of 'you needn't have spent so much time getting all spiffed up just for us', and so on. Since my hair was still damp, and I had on clothes they'd all seen many times before, I took the comments as given - in jest - with like returned.

Only Jahon didn't say much, just smiled. He seemed oddly at a loss for words. Of course, with Binjer around that was no problem. He easily made up for any lack, as jovially as ever.

We spent some time just getting caught up with each other's lives. Binjer and Tamoi with the children (their own three plus three more at present), their school activities and plans, their garden and orchard.

Kasho with her quest for a new home - something more suited to her work and with a larger garden. (There was a couple interested in her present house who would fit it well, so she was quite anxious to find another). Her weavings, what she was working on, her plans after that.

Jahon with the jobs just finished, his work on his parents' homestead (mending fences mostly it seemed - the goats apparently thought they were there just for them to climb on), and his indecision as to what to go on to next (several options but none hit him very strongly right then).

Shahvid with his work on a remodel (children grown and parents getting into new interests), his drawings of several buildings (one a home, another a small shop), and his thoughts on a new greenhouse/sauna design.

And myself. I didn't say much. I just enjoyed hearing of the others' lives and plans, and the discussions. After my talk with Sushati, and my week's invasion by Valjar, I realized that my life was still wrapped up with Caljn's Power Movement people, and *their* plans. I didn't want to bring that up, didn't want to dampen the party.

Instead I suggested that ı go round up something to eat, and hadn't Kasho mentioned some new wine of Dainon's she'd picked up on her way here? The talk turned to the wine, and Dainon, and what other 'specialties' had (at the last minute) been found to bring along to the celebration. And they all ended up in the kitchen with me. But in spite of the help the wine was poured, the food laid out, and water heated for fresh tea. We settled around the small table.

"So Neana, any more trouble with Valjar?" Tamoi startled me with the question. "Kasho said he's been seen around a lot this week. I was hoping you hadn't run into him again, after what happened Sunday."

I hesitated, not realizing I was frowning, trying to decide what to say.

Binjer added into the silence, "Of course, if you don't want to talk about it that's OK. But we've been thinking a lot about this affair, and wondering how things were going."

I looked at him in surprise, "I didn't think any of you would want to talk about it tonight."

"Neana!" Tamoi chided me, "It's part of your life

right now isn't it? Give us a break, of course we want to talk about it! Why wouldn't we?"

I smiled sheepishly, "I don't know. It just didn't seem to fit in." Then I remembered the reason for the party and laughed at myself. No mamby-pamby friends these. They'd tread lightly if they thought you needed it, but if not it was full, honest, steam ahead. And why not? I'd just been too long away from them.

"Well, actually, it's been kind of a long week in that area." I went on to tell them all about Valjar, and his constant appearances, and how it was bothering me. Though after one look at Jahon I avoided meeting his eye again. He wasn't taking it well, and it unsettled me. I told them of my meeting with Sushati (well, the gist of the important parts) and our final decision to get the group together to talk it over.

"I'm glad you and she finally met," Shahvid said when I had finished, "and I agree with the meeting idea. I don't like the direction this may be going."

The others agreed. A lively discussion followed, but in the end they came up with much the same as Sushati and I had. Not much.

"Look, this isn't getting us anywhere, except to maybe make Neana paranoid about going out at all," Kasho finally said. "We need more real information. Like are any of the others doing anything? Is Valjar on his own as we think?" She thought a moment, "Maybe I can dig up something more if you give me a few days."

Shahvid was uneasy with that but he didn't comment. Kasho had explained to him last Sunday about her role as one of three minor links between the Power Movement and Starpeace. It wasn't something he could help with, except support if needed. And she knew that. He added, "Besides, Chanthan and the others may already have some more information. I'd be surprised if they didn't."

Binjer said, "Well, we'll leave the talks to you all, but be sure to let us know what's going on, and if we can help in any way." No one expected Binjer and Tamoi to be involved in the discussions with Starpeace.

"But we *will* keep our ears and eyes open of course," Tamoi added. "And speaking of those, mine are going shut. It's time we were on the road home, Bin."

We all agreed. It had been a great evening but it was late. The group sorted out and washed dishes, sharing comments and plans. Respective belongings were organized and gathered together, farewells were made, and Binjer and Tamoi soon rode off. The moon light made their bike lamps hardly necessary.

Shahvid suggested to Kasho, "How about if I ride with you to home, it's such a beautiful night." The offer was accepted and they soon followed Binjer and Tamoi down the path.

Jahon and I were left standing in the night looking after the departing couples. "I think we were just quite straightforwardly deserted," Jahon remarked rather dryly.

I laughed, "I think you're right, without thought and quite happily too it appears." I stood there grinning, thinking of Kasho and Shahvid, and not looking at Jahon.

But he was looking at me, and he didn't seem to be thinking of the others. He made a comment about wanting to share something with me.

And he did. Tentatively at first, then he let all his feelings loose. They meshed with mine. We missed the moon going down, and if Shahvid returned before morning we didn't hear him. Or care.

Jahon was up and off early Saturday morning. I snuggled back into the blankets. I wasn't ready to come down out of the clouds yet. I went back to sleep with the kind of thoughts and feelings that I couldn't have verbalized if I had wanted to, and I didn't. Some things weren't meant to be spoken.

~~~ ~~ ~ ~~ ~~~

Jahon pedaled down the path toward Sinat's. He had wakened that morning with several ideas (not counting the immediate ones) and was anxious to put them into action. It was a beautiful morning to match the beautiful night, and he let his feelings come and go as he slipped through the air. Even thoughts of Valjar couldn't disturb him.

When he neared his destination he had to make an effort to calm his emotions down to a more public level. He parked his bike and bounded up the stairs to the side door. He knocked gently, hoping Sinat was up but not wanting to waken him or Sushati if not. After a few moments Sinat opened the door, and with greetings invited him into the kitchen.

"Sushati is sleeping and I was just making something to eat. Water is hot there if you want to make yourself some tea. Toast?" Sinat sliced some more bread.

"Sounds great, thank you." Jahon poured the water over the leaves, "Glad I caught you up. There are a couple of things I want to ask you, just between us." He was intent on his thoughts and didn't waste any time. "I was with Neana last night and found out about Valjar's attentions toward her, do you know of that?"

Sinat nodded. Sushati had told him about her talk with Neana. Besides, they had been watching Valjar, as well as the others. "Sushati said she and Neana decided on a meeting to discuss it. She's left a message for Chanthan to give her a call to set it up." He tried not to speculate about Jahon's intensity, but he couldn't help but feel some of the happiness. He grinned to himself. But to Jahon he said, "But I take it you didn't want to wait for the meeting."

Jahon explained, "The meeting is fine, but no, I don't want to wait. I had a couple of ideas and I want to know what you honestly think. How much of a danger is Valjar? To Neana that is. I just don't know that much about the man, except that he was quite close to Caljn."

Sinat took some time to think while he set breakfast on the table and sat down. He realized how serious Jahon was. Not that he blamed him. "I've been thinking it over since Sushati told me about his watching Neana this past week, and about his visit to her Sunday. I had thought that Neana would be out of it after Caljn's death. It is what we had planned you know. But now . . ." He didn't want to fan Jahon's fears unnecessarily, but he had been asked for his honest opinion, and that was what he would give. He knew that Jahon would do the same for him.

"Now I think it would be best if Neana kept out of circulation for a while. Although Caljn was the leader of the group, the others who were closest to him are capable of, and have been responsible for, some pretty nasty affairs. As you well know. Even though there is no indication, I think we would be wise to assume that they might suspect Neana's involvement in Caljn's death.

"I'd like to hear what Chanthan thinks though. I haven't talked to him since Sunday night and we didn't have any new information then. Just Rafnon's report about the services for Caljn, and I didn't think there was anything there to tell you about." During their talk Sunday morning, Sinat had agreed to let Jahon and Shahvid know if anything of importance came up. "My feelings right now as to Neana's danger are not very clear, but I am quite uneasy about it."

Jahon nodded, "I think I know what you mean, no one seems to know anything specific but that doesn't mean there isn't a danger. The feeling is there, and I have no intention of ignoring it."

The two of them talked for a time about Caljn's group, then about several other ideas Jahon had. He took his leave with the agreement that Sinat or Sushati would get the meeting going as soon as possible. Jahon continued on home, deep in thought, trying to put his plans in working order.

~~~ ~~ ~ ~~ ~~~

Shahvid answered the phone and, after hearing the voice on the other end, answered with a wide grin, "Well, good morning yourself."

Silence. Jahon didn't know what to say exactly. For some reason he had not expected to hear Shahvid's voice.

After a moment Shahvid laughed out loud, he couldn't help it. He had noticed Jahon's bike still in the shed when he had returned last night, and was up in time that morning to see him pedal down the path. He felt so good about it he had to tease his friend a bit. Especially since Jahon was apparently unsure of his reaction. "I won't ask if you had a good night, but I'm glad to hear you're still around. May I assume we'll be seeing more of you?"

Jahon snorted, found his voice and an appropriate comment or two. The uneasy moment was over and the two bantered back and forth, half in jest, half serious. But in a few minutes they managed to convey their feelings about the matter to each other. And the happiness was mutual. Jahon finally asked, "Is Neana up yet? I'd like to talk with her. *If* you allow."

Shahvid started to comment but then I came down the hall. So instead he just handed the receiver to me with a grin and a quick, brotherly kiss on the cheek. He disappeared into the kitchen, leaving me staring suspiciously after him.

I looked down at the receiver, then put it to my ear and said, "Hello?" I couldn't help the blush that came when Jahon answered back. Traces of it were still there when, several minutes later, I went into the kitchen to face Shahvid.

It wasn't as if I hadn't spent a night with a man before. Through the years I had been in and out of several fairly close relationships. But this was different, this wasn't just any man, it was Jahon. And he was Shahvid's closest friend. "Good morning," I tried, with a sort of half smile.

"And a great morning to you," Shahvid answered with a very full smile. He didn't mean to push, he supposed it really wasn't any of his business, but it was the way he felt. This on top of the direction his own life was going was almost too much. He got up, gave me a big hug and said simply, "I'm glad, in case you're wondering."

I just hugged him back and smiled, then went out to the garden to pick some berries for breakfast. The day fit my mood - beautiful.

When I finished eating I sat drinking my tea and considering the day. Sushati hadn't called yet about the meeting. And Jahon had said he had several things to take care of during the day, but would plan to see me that night, meeting or no. It was too nice to stay indoors. I could have done some work in the garden, or the yard, there was plenty to be done.

Then another idea came to mind. I decided I would take the day and do something I hadn't done in quite awhile. Sit in the Square with my pad and pencils and do sketches for people. Just for fun. It was just what the day needed. With a light heart I went to gather my supplies.

I stopped by Shahvid's study to let him know where I'd be. He didn't particularly like the idea.

"Shahvid, I'm not going to hide out or be afraid to be in public just because a person is around who doesn't like me." At his look I added, "I've been out and around all week, and I'm certainly safe enough in the Square for that matter."

"Well, I guess I can't come up with any good argument why you shouldn't," Shahvid agreed, "but I'm still uneasy about this thing with Valjar. Just stay alert, and I'll come by later to see how you're doing."

My answer to that was to put my hands on his desk and lean over to look him square in the eye, "Shahvid, I'm not a child anymore. I am quite capable of going out by myself, and taking care of myself." I stood up and with a smile patted him on the head, "I've been doing it for some time now you know."

Shahvid just shook his head, "Well, have a good time then and I'll see you later. I'm going to be working at my desk today so I'll be here if Sushati calls."

I smiled back and started out the door when I remembered, "Jahon is planning to be here for dinner so I'll put some rice and beans in the solar oven. Would you check on them later?"

Shahvid agreed, with an extra grin which I ignored. I waved good-bye and left him with his drawings.

It was midday by the time I made it to the Square. So before I got started I found a shady spot to sit and eat my lunch. I watched the people and waved greetings, chatting with some, smiling at others. I was glad to see no sign of Valjar or any of the other members of that group.

When I got my tools out and began drawing I had no lack of models or audience. And no other thoughts intruded on my fun. I sent person after person away with a drawing and a smile. It would have been hard to decide which was the more important to the crowd. I didn't care, I freely shared both, and they were equally important to me. I caught a glimpse of Shahvid late in the afternoon, in spite of what I had said. But he apparently assured himself that I was safe and disappeared without speaking to me. Since I was surrounded at the time by friendly people he could hardly worry about me.

~~~ ~~ ~ ~~ ~~~

Careen walked onto the Square and couldn't help but notice Neana. A rush of anger came over her at the crowd around the woman. Careen was nursing the idea that Neana was responsible for her breakup with Shahvid, though even her Aunt told her that was ridiculous, that most everyone was aware that she hadn't been living as Shahvid's wife for some time anyway. But Careen had needed to blame someone, since she chose not, or wasn't yet able, to look at herself. It wasn't easy to work Shahvid into the role of a 'guilty' party, so she chose Neana instead. She had never liked her so it was an easy decision.

Unfortunately Careen never looked very deep into anything, she just reacted. She knew that for some reason Valjar had it in for Neana. She felt that somehow he could cause more trouble for her former sister-in-law than she could. Besides, Valjar had some high connection with The Church and Careen was impressed by that. Once again she headed in the direction of Valjar's house to relay to him her information about Neana's activities. She didn't care why he wanted to know and hadn't asked.

But just as she was leaving the Square she ran into Rafnon. Her feelings about him were mixed. The affair with him had been fine as long as he was also seeing Neana, even though she had sometimes had the feeling he was using her instead of her using him. But when he had stopped seeing her after Neana had ended their relationship, Careen had felt that she came out on the bottom. It wasn't a feeling she liked.

However, she thought now, Rafnon hadn't been happy with Neana either. And he had never really hit it off with Shahvid or Jahon, so maybe he could be used in some way with this affair. Just in case she greeted him warmly.

Rafnon returned the greeting, somewhat warily. He knew Careen well enough to know something was probably up. He had never gotten the kind of information from her that he had thought he could get (in fact, it had soon been apparent that Careen didn't notice much of anything other than herself). He had stopped seeing her when he realized she could do more harm to him than good. He knew he rode a fine line between Starpeace and the Power Movement but he enjoyed the conflict. His loyalty was all with Starpeace, but he knew his ways might sometimes be misunderstood.

He had heard that Careen and Shahvid had split (Careen had been making it known rather loudly wherever she could, and it wasn't to Shahvid's benefit). He had an idea her friendliness that afternoon might have something to do with that. After a few words he asked her where she had been headed so intently.

Careen answered without thinking. In fact, she had a vague idea that he and Valjar were somehow connected, though she didn't know how. She didn't realize Rafnon's feelings toward the man. "Oh, I'm off to see Valjar, he asked me for some information and it's important so I better get going."

Rafnon considered that. He disliked and distrusted Valjar, to put it mildly. And Sinat had told him about the man's following Neana. He'd asked him to find out what he could, and what else might be afoot from that group. They really didn't expect Caljn's death to be the complete downfall of the Power Movement, as nice as that would have been. Besides, Rafnon was still feeling a little guilty about his reaction to Neana at that Starpeace meeting. Now it looked like his time with Careen maybe hadn't been a waste after all. He had an idea he could find out what 'information' she had. They were soon in a quiet booth in a nearby cafe, having a drink and something to eat. And talking.

~~~ ~~ ~ ~~ ~~~

The sun was far over in the sky when I finally closed my sketch pad and promised those around me that I'd do it again another day. I was happily tired and couldn't decide what I wanted most, a cool swim or a cool drink, and a good meal. Instead I decided to go home first to see if Sushati or Jahon had called, and what the plans for the evening might be. Then I'd decide on the other options. I loaded my supplies into my pack and headed out.

It was too nice a day to hurry, so I took one of the lesser used, shady and more roundabout paths toward home. I did have a feeling that maybe I should stick to more public places right then, but I ignored that thought. As I told Shahvid, I wasn't going to hide out or give in to some unnamed possible danger. I'd spent most of my life walking anywhere I felt like in the town, and I wasn't going to change that habit.

~~~ ~~ ~ ~~ ~~~

Rafnon walked back into the Square, quite put out by the time spent with Careen, and the information' gleaned. Hardly what he had been hoping for. But he supposed he should at least warn Neana.

He walked over to where she had been sitting, sketching, earlier but she was gone. He quickly looked around the Square but there was no sign of her. He assumed she had headed home.

He tried to think of how long it would have taken Careen to get to Valjar, and for Valjar to get here. It was too bad he had stopped to visit with the friends he had run into. Damn. Now what? He didn't know of Valjar's intentions of course, but he had to agree with Sinat's uneasiness. They knew too much about the man to ignore it. There was nothing for it but to try to follow Neana as fast as possible. It would have helped to know which direction to go. He'd just have to take a best guess, at least he knew her well enough to guess, and hope she was home when he got there. With a somewhat frustrated sigh he hurried toward a wooded pathway.

This certainly wasn't what he'd had in mind for the evening, he grumbled to himself as he jogged along the quiet walking path. He wished he was in his vehicle, but he knew Neana would more likely be walking.

Rafnon passed a few people but hardly noticed, so intent was he on his purpose, and on trying to keep up the pace. Jogging wasn't his usual style and he wasn't enjoying it. He didn't even see the trees and life surrounding the path. He was too busy thinking about how long he could go before he would just drop over from exhaustion. Besides, he told himself irritably, the trip was probably useless, and nothing was wrong at all.

Then he rounded a corner around a large tree to almost run right into Valjar and Neana. They were both turned in his direction, having heard his panting, hurried approach. He wasn't in such bad shape that he didn't notice Valjar's look of anger, and Neana's look of relief.

"Why, hello," he stopped, breathing hard. "Figured it was time I started to get in shape, someone said this is supposed to be good for you." Not too creative a conversation but he couldn't think of what to say. Valjar's angry stare and his closeness to Neana had taken Rafnon aback. He was too well aware of the man's reputation. He also didn't care for the tight look on Neana's face, or the almost hidden smile as she watched him trying to catch his breath.

~~~ ~~ ~ ~~ ~~~

Valjar stood staring at Rafnon a moment then turned and stalked off without a word, back toward the Square. We watched him in silence while Rafnon recovered.

I turned to him then with a brief smile, "Nice timing. Thank you. How did you know?" I knew he wasn't out jogging for his health.

Rafnon hesitated, then explained, "Careen. Apparently she's been keeping Valjar informed as to your activities, whenever she knew them. She saw you in the Square today and was on her way to report to him when she ran into me. I found out what she was up to but couldn't find a way to dissuade her. By the time I got to the Square to tell you, you were gone. I guessed as to your direction and took off. Ever think of using a vehicle, or at least a bicycle?"

I laughed, half in relief, half at Rafnon. I sincerely appreciated that he had come after me, and Valjar. "I just might next time. I appreciate your good guess, and your timely arrival. I don't know if I was in any danger or anything, but let's just say I was uneasy. And was glad to see you. Care to walk on home with me for a glass of juice or something?"

"Thank you, but I should be heading back. I hadn't planned on this side trip this evening." Rafnon did want to know what had happened before he arrived, but didn't want to ask directly. Instead he carefully nonchalantly added, "Of course, if you're uneasy about continuing on alone I could walk you home. I assume Valjar headed back to the Square, but you never know."

I saw through his act but I was quite grateful for what he had done. I told him, "I feel quite safe now but why don't you accompany me home anyway. If you have time that is."

Rafnon agreed and we continued on our way at a more leisurely pace. I decided not to say anything more about Valjar and instead chatted about other things. I wanted to think about what had happened before discussing it with anyone, and when I did it would be with Jahon first.

~~~ ~~ ~ ~~ ~~~

Rafnon left Neana at the head of the lane to her house, none the wiser, and totally disgruntled with the whole affair. And now he had to walk all the way home. It didn't help that he met Jahon after a short way, riding his bike toward Neana's. They greeted each other politely but shortly, neither of them particularly happy with the sight of the other.

~~~ ~~ ~ ~~ ~~~

As Shahvid served dinner I finished telling Jahon and him about my day, and about the walk home. I ended with a brief description of my encounter with Valjar. I hadn't planned on saying anything about that yet at all, but when I came into the kitchen after my shower almost the first thing Jahon had said was to ask what Rafnon had been doing out this direction. Since he had preceded the question with a pretty friendly greeting, and I was still trying to recover my composure (a few brotherly comments from Shahvid hadn't helped), I hadn't responded as defensively as I might have at one time.

Jahon and Shahvid were silent when I finished my story. I hadn't expected them to take it as seriously as they apparently were, based on their frowns. Jahon rather forcefully scooped out some rice and banged it onto his plate. My mind irrelevantly went to the lady who had made the bowl the rice was in. I was brought back to the present by the chirp of the telephone.

Shahvid went to answer it and I asked Jahon about his day. He rather evaded the question, just touched on a few things he'd done, then brought the conversation back to Valjar. And Rafnon. He admitted gratitude for Rafnon's appearance but he didn't sound thrilled by it. And he didn't appear convinced that I had told him all there was to tell about the affair. Which of course I hadn't.

"What *exactly* did Valjar say?" He finally asked, "and what was his manner? Was he threatening?"

I took my time finishing my mouthful of food, trying to decide how to answer. I had glossed over Valjar's actions, not because I wanted to keep it from Jahon but because I hadn't had time to think it over for myself yet. And I was anxious to not make something out of nothing. Just because the man was obnoxious didn't mean he was dangerous. I conveniently ignored what he had been helping Caljn with just a short time ago, and what I knew about him and his friends. It was easier to admit danger to someone else than to yourself. It just wasn't a normal part of my life.

But I also knew that Jahon would not be put off. Just as I started to answer him I was given a short reprieve by Shahvid's return.

"That was Sushati asking if tonight would be OK. She knows it's short notice but she just got in touch with Chanthan, and it's tonight or not until Wednesday. I told her tonight was fine, I didn't think you'd mind, and that we'd head over as soon as we're done with dinner. I called Kasho and she'll meet us there." Shahvid sat down to finish eating.

"Tonight's a good idea." Jahon agreed. But he hadn't forgotten his question. He looked at me, prompting, "Well?"

"I don't know as it's all that important to get the meeting going tonight, but I guess it's OK," I grudgingly agreed. For some reason it seemed like I was jumping back into the affair without taking time to think about it first. I knew that was silly, I had never gotten out of it. And Valjar *was* getting on my nerves. Maybe that was why I didn't want to put into words what Valjar had said, and intimated doing. I didn't want to admit that there was more to this whole affair, that it wasn't over, and that I couldn't just step out of it. Jahon's and my relationship was too new. I didn't want to be distracted by anything else. Especially this thing with Valjar. I felt the old feelings of depression come down on me, like a virus caught from Caljn and his friends.

Shahvid looked from Jahon to me, then said calmly, "It's hard to get a good picture of the situation when we're so close to it. I think it will help to talk it over with the others." Then he unknowingly echoed Jahon's question, "What did Valjar actually say, Neana? How angry was he?"

With a small sigh, I straightforwardly and calmly told them what Valjar had said. "He said he was sure I had something to do with Caljn's death, that I had driven him to die. He talked about Caljn's work and how dangerous it was to have stopped it." I didn't look at Jahon, who had stopped eating and was staring at me. With my next words Shahvid joined him. "Then he said something about how Caljn needed to be repaid for what had been done to him." I addressed the bowl of rice as if discussing the weather. "That was when Rafnon arrived so I didn't have a chance to reply to him. But I guess you could say he was pretty serious about what he was saying. And yes, he was angry. But he often is."

"And your idea of that conversation was that 'He just wasn't happy about Caljn's death'!", which was what I had said earlier. Jahon's outburst brought a shrug and a defensive,

"Well, I just thought he was being over dramatic, he's like that. I don't think you should make too much of it." I was irritated by their reactions. I became more stubborn about it as my fears jumped up to meet theirs and I tried to pull them back down. I didn't like being afraid, and wasn't going to give in to it.

Shahvid said, "I can't believe you're taking this so matter-of-factly, as if it was hardly of import. Valjar isn't a man to be taken lightly."

Jahon was almost beyond words. "You know what he's been involved in, Neana. Do you want me to spell out more for you? It's not pretty but I'll do it if you aren't going to take this seriously."

I got up abruptly from the table and took my plate to the sink, emptying the rest of my dinner into the compost pail. The day had been so high, and now felt so low. I had thought I was over that kind of emotional seesawing. I washed my plate in silence. When I was once again in control I turned back to them.

Jahon stood and quite naturally folded me in his arms. He held me, saying, "Hey, I thought we agreed to share this thing. What did you think my and Shahvid's reactions would be? We happen to both think a lot of this woman and don't take threats to her lightly." I just shook my head.

Shahvid had also calmed down. He knew me well enough to just give me some time. "Maybe Jahon and I are overreacting a bit, Neana. You were there and we weren't. But Jahon is right you know. I think we all have to take Valjar quite seriously. Maybe he is just venting his feelings and isn't dangerous to you. But what if that isn't the case?"

"You may know the man better than we do in some ways, Neana," Jahon added, "but we also know what he and his friends are capable of."

I couldn't think of anything to say. Maybe they were right. Maybe I was. And they weren't enjoying this any more than I was. "I'm sorry." I said. "I honestly don't know what to think about Valjar."

"Why don't we go on over to Sinat and Sushati's, it'll give us all a chance to think about it on the way," Shahvid suggested. "Do you want to walk, bike or take a vehicle? It looks like it's clouding up and cooling off."

Jahon loosened his hold on me as I turned back to the sink. "I'd just as soon walk," he answered. "We can always borrow a vehicle if it rains later." He felt the need of physical movement. The coldness that had swept him when he had heard Valjar's words had abated but not left.

I said simply, "OK," and went to put on a warmer robe, socks and shoes. I was calm. The affair required at least one calm person at all times, and right then that person was me. I could handle it, in spite of Shahvid and Jahon's opinions to the contrary.

The walk was cool, fast, and mostly in silence, but a comfortable one. We all felt better by the time we knocked on the door and Sinat let us in. It had just started to rain and the comforting sound seemed to enclose the entire group as we made our greetings.

My eyebrows raised a bit in question as Chanthan greeted Jahon and Shahvid. The two didn't look at me as they returned his obviously familiar greeting. First Sinat, now Chanthan. Who else did these two know well that I wasn't aware of? I was relieved to see that neither Rafnon nor the others I had met at that first Starpeace meeting were there. I didn't want to have to deal with any uneasy relationships right then. I especially welcomed Kasho and Sushati's friendly faces and words. And it was nice to meet Myana, Chanthan's wife and partner.

There was easy conversation as we all made ourselves comfortable, and tea and juice was handed around. I settled myself cross legged on a large pillow beside Jahon's chair, leaning against it. Everyone seemed quite comfortable. Except me. I worked on my slight feeling of intimidation, for which I knew there was no reason.

~~~ ~~ ~ ~~ ~~~

Chanthan watched Neana and laughed at himself for not having recognized her that Sunday. She was obviously Shahvid's sister, which Sinat had informed him of after the meeting. He knew of her paintings but hadn't connected them with her. She was also apparently a close friend of Jahon's. It was probably just as well he hadn't known who she was that night or he may have been tempted not to let her get involved. Then he remembered she had gotten involved on her own, before she had come to them.

He was suddenly hit with sorrow that the affair had not ended with Caljn's death. But he had known it wouldn't. And they may as well get on with it, and do the best they could. It was past time for things to settle down for their community. He changed the direction of the conversation as he turned to Neana, he saw no reason not to be direct.

~~~ ~~ ~ ~~ ~~~

"Sushati told me of Valjar's attentions toward you," Chanthan addressed me, "and Rafnon told Sinat about today's affair, from his end anyway. I'd like to hear about it from your perspective now, and what actually happened before Rafnon arrived." Then he added with a smile as I tightened up at his words. I couldn't help it. "Or however much you feel comfortable sharing with us that is."

I didn't know why I felt so jittery. The people there were all friends whom I trusted and respected. I took a deep breath, then Jahon's hand came over to rest on my shoulder. He conveyed a lot with that light touch, and it helped. I proceeded to tell, again, about Valjar's numerous appearances in my life the past week, up to that day. I tried to be as factual and objective as possible.

There was some discussion but no one had much to add. All Kasho's informant had said was that Valjar had been acting a little funny since Caljn's death. But that was to be expected considering how close they'd been.

There wasn't anything special going on with the inner group that they could discover. It appeared that Caljn's death had quite disorganized them. There was no indication that the people of the town didn't think Caljn had killed himself. And no one knew what Caljn's friends thought.

I felt shy about continuing. My involvement with Caljn had been a conscious decision, and much easier to talk about compared to this thing with Valjar. I didn't like the feeling of not being in control of it, and for some reason I felt embarrassed about the whole affair.

Shahvid gave me a gentle push, "Well, Neana can add a little to that anyway. How much depends on how seriously you take Valjar's words." He smiled at me.

Jahon's hand hadn't moved and he gave my shoulder a gentle squeeze. I realized how unwarranted and silly my uneasiness was. So I told them of my day, my walk and my unexpected meeting with Valjar on the path. I looked off into the air as I repeated, again, Valjar's words. They sounded strange in the warm room, unreal. Certainly out of place. When I was done, ending with Rafnon's departure, there was silence in the room.

Chanthan had listened carefully, thoughtfully. Jahon and Shahvid were steady, their emotions controlled. Kasho stared at me in dismay, and had checked a movement to jump up. Instead she had reached out to Shahvid. Even Sinat and Sushati seemed shocked. You'd think they would hardly be surprised. But hearing it like that, the implied threats so calmly repeated, was a bit unnerving.

"Well," Chanthan broke the silence, "it appears that for Valjar this whole affair has not ended. So then of course, it has not ended for us. Now we have to decide what to do." Chanthan addressed Shahvid's earlier words, "As far as taking Valjar's words seriously, I know of no reason not to, and many reasons to."

His words broke the spell and the conversation once again flowed. "Good heavens Neana," Sushati exclaimed, "I hadn't really thought it would go that far when we talked about it Friday. I rather thought he was just being obnoxious. But this is something else." She certainly took Valjar's threats seriously, and looking at Jahon wondered about his control. She didn't think he would do anything rash, but she had an idea of his feelings and knew he was a direct acting person. She thought the plan he had put forth to Sinat that morning was a good one.

Sinat agreed, and his thoughts were along the same line as Sushati's. He didn't think that Jahon had mentioned his plan yet. He'd give it as much a push as he could. "Yes, this is certainly something else. As Chanthan said, there is no reason not to take Valjar at his word. We know what he is capable of. I don't care to describe some of his prior actions but I hope you will take my word for it that he can be a very dangerous character. We had hoped that with Caljn's death he would back off, that most of the influence had been Caljn."

"It probably still is Caljn," Chanthan said. "Valjar may be even more motivated by Caljn's death than when he was alive. We guessed that something like that might happen, we just didn't know which direction it would take."

Sushati added, "Of course, this may not be his only direction, though it appears he has zeroed in on Neana for now. And apparently is doing it on his own." She asked Kasho, "Have you heard of anyone else going along with Valjar?"

"No, in fact, I got the impression he was staying pretty much to himself. Even before he wasn't that close to any of the others. But no, I hadn't picked up anything like this." Kasho shook her head emphatically, as if to shake it all away. She was still a little shaken by my encounter. Before it had all seemed a bit unreal, like a play, but this was so direct.

I didn't say anything. I was rather taken aback by what they were all saying. It didn't seem to connect to me. I just looked from one to the other as they spoke.

Sinat glanced at Jahon for a moment, then he said, "I think the first thing to do is for Neana to get away for a while, out of Valjar's reach. Then we can get the rest of our people together and try to find out just what is going on, if anything, with that whole group. And to keep a close . . ."

I reacted emphatically and interrupted, "I'm not going to run away. I don't think that will solve anything. I can certainly find out more if I am here and involved than out hiding somewhere. And I'm not going to let any fear of Valjar chase me away." I could feel the color come up in my face as I spoke.

Jahon and Shahvid exchanged a look and both shrugged slightly. I caught the exchange and knew what they were thinking. It didn't help my disposition at that moment. I wasn't about to be bulldozed about this. And I wasn't going to let any of them push me into running away. That wasn't the way I lived.

"It's not running away, Neana," Kasho said, as if she had been reading my thoughts. "It's doing what makes the most sense. What good will it do to stay around here right now when Valjar has made his intentions pretty well known to you. And even discounting the danger, he has already harassed you so much you can't go out without wondering when he'll show up."

"Yes," Sushati added, "and if you think of it, that might just be the thing to do, to go right away. Having you suddenly disappear might just throw Valjar off. He's not very stable to begin with. We can set up our system to watch him closely, and hopefully be able to handle his reaction with the least danger to everyone."

She assessed the situation calmly and straight forwardly. "It's too bad we concentrated so much on the scientists, then Caljn, and ignored Valjar. We do not seem to have a very good picture of him. I sure wish we knew just what he had in mind."

I felt my bristles lay back down as she talked. Jahon and Shahvid tended to ride herd over me. But Sushati was speaking directly, person to person, and so had Kasho.

"True," Chanthan agreed, "but I think we have enough now to act on." He turned to me, and in his gentle manner said, "I can understand how you feel. And I want you to know we aren't trying to shut you out. But I believe there is a good chance that you are in very real danger now. I have to agree with Sinat that it might be good for you to be away for a time. It might be hard for us to do anything about Valjar while you are so close. We would all, understandably, be very concerned about your safety. If you could consider it, I think a trip away from here would be a good thing."

The rest of the bristles collapsed.

Jahon listened to Chanthan with renewed respect. It had been some time since he had worked with him and he had forgotten the man's ways. He leaned forward a bit to look at me and asked, "How about a vacation, Neana?"

I turned to him with a puzzled frown. It seemed a funny time to be thinking of vacations.

He grinned at me, "Now come on, does a vacation with me strike you so bad that you have to consider it that seriously?"

I could feel my face redden and I gave him an exasperated look.

Kasho laughed and said, "Well I can understand the problem, the lesser of two evils, you or Valjar. Tough decision Neana," she said with mock seriousness.

The tone of the whole room lightened as they joked. I gave up, gave in, and laughed with them, though my cheeks were still hot. My relationship with Jahon was still too new and tentative to be comfortably shared with others. I knew I wouldn't mind having a good long time alone with Jahon right then and that didn't help my embarrassment any. I certainly wasn't going to say that, and besides, his invite was rather roundabout.

"I guess if I could think about it, maybe I could plan a trip away." I thrust the thoughts of Jahon away and tried to consider the matter fairly. "I don't have any commitments right now so it would be a good time. If you honestly think I couldn't be of more use here. I'm not afraid of the danger."

Chanthan knew that the others were likely much more afraid for me than I was for myself. He certainly could relate to that. Besides, I had already shown what I could do, danger or no, with my involvement with Caljn and his death. But he only said, "I honestly do think it would be better if you could leave for a while since we don't know just what form that danger is in."

He didn't think it would be wise to add that he thought I shouldn't go alone, feeling there was some safety in numbers. It appeared that would take care of itself. It also appeared that it would be good to have Jahon away from Valjar. Something must have changed, he thought with a smile, since the affair with Caljn began.

Shahvid threw in some teasing encouragement, "You know you want to go, Neana, even without this situation with Valjar. And it shouldn't be hard to think of where. Your list of 'Someday I'm going to go exploring there' is endless."

Jahon added, "I don't have any deadlines right now either. Why don't we plan say a two week holiday, maybe a bike camping or backpacking trip?"

I finally agreed gracefully. I had a feeling it would

have been useless to fight it anyway. But for some reason that was OK. Later I was to wonder about the smoothness of the apparently 'sudden idea'.

They all joined in with suggestions and ideas until it almost became a group trip. Jahon finally voiced that thought, wondering wryly out loud if he and I were to have any say at all in the destination of our vacation.

I reminded him with mock shortness that this was supposed to be *my* holiday. Jahon just gave me a knowing grin with raised eyebrows and everyone laughed. I ended up with a red face again. This had to stop. Though with this crowd I hadn't much hope.

So the evening ended on an upper tone, as they all agreed that Jahon and I would decide where to go, and would be as inconspicuous as possible about going. Shahvid would let the rest of the group know our decision, and no one else would be informed. Except Tamoi and Binjer, Kasho reminded. Sinat said he'd meet with some of the other Starpeace members to organize a plan of action once a destination had been decided. It would be soon. Shahvid and Kasho would be included if they wished. They did.

It was still raining as we made ready to leave, so we accepted Sinat's offer of a vehicle. We made our farewells then Shahvid, Jahon and I road off with Kasho into the rainy night.

I woke up when we reached Jahon's house and sleepily agreed to stay the night there. Kasho and Shahvid left us with Skaduter and headed back to Shahvid's.

I was soon comfortably asleep in Jahon's bed, with the cat curled up safely between us.

~~~ ~~ ~ ~~ ~~~

Jahon laid awake for a time contemplating the woman in his bed. Apparently Skaduter didn't have any problem with the arrangement. And, he decided, neither did he.

~~~ ~~ ~ ~~ ~~~

I awoke late the next morning with the sun shining in and Jahon asleep beside me. Skaduter had long since deserted us. I laid there thinking of the last few days, and nights. Everything seemed unreal. Except for Jahon lying there next to me. He was definitely real. I watched him for a while, at once contented, awed, and excited. On one hand I felt it was all too fast. On the other, that it was so very natural and had been coming for a long time.

Inside I knew it was the right path, but still I argued with myself. I started thinking that maybe what I should do was to go off by myself, give everything time to settle out. But I didn't have an answer to the question that came back at me. If it was right, why should I wait? And for what?

Then Jahon opened his eyes and smiled at me.

It was some time later when we got up to greet the day, and get something to eat. Dinner last night had been too small and too long ago.

"I don't know, it just seems too fast." I tried to explain, between spoonfuls of berries and milk. "I know I agreed, and last night it made sense. It's just that this morning it seems farfetched." I shrugged and stopped to spread jam on my toast.

"What is, the threat from Valjar, or the threat of two weeks with me?" Jahon asked, half teasing. He finished eating and set his bowl aside. "They're probably equally dangerous, just in different ways. Valjar would probably just kill you. With me, well, you never know!"

"Oh, Jahon, be serious." I chided him. "You know what I mean. But to be honest, spending several weeks with you is a little farfetched too." I concentrated on my breakfast and tried to ignore his amused look. I knew I was blushing but couldn't do anything about it. Darn him anyway.

"I don't know why, we've camped out together before. There will just be fewer people this time." Jahon watched me until I looked up at him. "Seriously, Neana, I think we should trust Sinat, Chanthan and Sushati. I've worked with the three of them several times before and have great respect for them, and their judgment."

"Yes, I was going to ask you about that," I interrupted.

Jahon just smiled at me, "A man has to have some secrets in his life or there wouldn't be any reason for a woman to want to spend two weeks camping with him."

I hmphfd and made no comment, just finished my breakfast and got up to make some more tea. I had to admit this wasn't a bad way to spend Sunday mornings. I hmphfd again, told myself to be serious, and asked Jahon if he wanted more tea.

"That would be fine, same kind." Skaduter came through to see if there was any leftover milk. There was. "Neana," Jahon continued, "first of all, I would like to go away, right now, with you, where ever you'd like, as long as no one else is along. Maybe I didn't make that part very clear." Jahon didn't want to push, but he was anxious to get the thing settled and get on with the plans. And to get me out of town as soon, and as quietly, as he could. "Second, I take Valjar's threats very seriously, and I think you should too. Third, why not?"

I sat down with the tea, half smiling at his words,

half ignoring them. I decided to just take the third question. "I guess when you put it like that I don't know why not. But maybe it's because I don't want to just run away. And maybe it's because I'm not convinced it will solve anything."

Jahon looked at me a moment, then with a smile he leaned across the table and kissed me on the nose. "And maybe it's just because you are a very stubborn person."

I had to laugh. He might even be right. "Well, OK, say we go ahead with this crazy plan. Where would we go? Any feelings for one place or another?" I finally went along with my inner feelings and was soon caught up in the excitement of the trip. Even with the idea of getting out of town and on our way without being seen. We brought out ideas, tossed them out or put them aside until we were surrounded by them.

We finally agreed that our destination would be a wilderness area quite some miles away. It was a place we had both been to for short trips but never taken the time to explore fully, though we had both talked of it. It would be a backpacking trip since no vehicles or bicycles were allowed in the area, and because that was how we wanted to go. And we were sure to meet few if any people there. But how to get there, and when?

"There are lots of options. We could bicycle but that would take quite a while just to get there. And if we don't want to be seen leaving that rules out any public transportation." I listed off a few other ideas and threw them out also as too public. Air travel was out since there were no landing areas near where we wanted to go.

"How about a wagon ride?" Jahon suggested. "You know how the people who own teams are always looking for an excuse to go somewhere. I bet we could hitch a ride out that direction since that road is popular with the drivers."

I considered the idea. I had often gotten a ride out into the country that way. There were quite a number of people who had teams and who hauled people and goods around the countryside just because they preferred the animals to the electric vehicles. The wagons and carriages were so well designed, and the animals and their trainers such a nice group, that they had no lack of business.

The idea appealed to me. Our packs wouldn't take up much space so catching a ride wouldn't be that difficult. Between us we knew quite a number of drivers.

"I'd like that. It would be fun and it's a great way to travel. Let's go down to the stables and check around, or maybe leave a notice." The more I thought about it, the more excited I became. "We may be able to find someone going our direction this next week sometime."

"Well, actually," Jahon sort of cleared his throat and looked up at the ceiling. "There's a wagon leaving tomorrow morning that has room for us and it just happens to be going our way." He tried on an innocent smile as he looked rather tentatively at me.

I just looked at him a moment then started laughing. I knew I'd been had but right then I just couldn't get angry at him for it. I tried to get my smile under control as I asked him in mock indignation, "And just how long have you known about this chance coincidence?"

"Oh, only since yesterday. I was just trying to plan ahead. You know, be prepared and all that." Jahon thought he was in the clear but he wasn't real certain about it. "I'm sorry, Neana, I guess it was a little backhanded. But I've been worried about Valjar's intentions toward you even before yesterday's confrontation. I had this idea and spent yesterday sort of checking it out and lining up possibilities. I was hoping you'd want to go along with it, for several reasons which I think I've mentioned, and I wanted it all set just in case. Does it help that my intentions were good even if my methods were shaky?"

I just looked at him. Then I got up and went over to give him my answer, which I think he understood quite well. "Just don't do it again," I added. And, as I sat back down, "Do I know the driver?"

Jahon brought himself back to the kitchen, "Oh, yes, I think you do. He lives out by my folks and usually drives a team of black horses into town to deliver farm produce.

He knows you and was quite anxious to have us along. I didn't tell him everything, but he knows enough to understand the spirit of the thing, and I trust him."

I decided not to ask when the driver had planned this trip that we were going to 'hitch' a ride on. I knew the man, and the horses, quite well and had often ridden out to Jahon's parent's place with him, and back again. I agreed with Jahon's trust in him and also knew that Jahon had known him and his family quite some time.

"I know him," I agreed. "He and his horses have a good relationship. They'd be fun to ride with." Then I remembered that Jahon had said tomorrow morning. "But tomorrow Jahon? We can't be ready to go so soon. We have to get all our gear together, come up with food, and plan who's going to carry what, and all that. We can't possibly be ready by tomorrow morning, that's too soon."

"Do you have any other plans for this afternoon?" Jahon asked me. "We can run over to your place right now and pick up your things. Then bring it all back here and sort out and pack up." Then he added, almost as an afterthought, he hated to push his luck, "And I think we can come up with enough food, I have a pretty good supply."

I eyed him suspiciously, "You've got the whole thing all planned and ready haven't you?"

"Well, I guess you could say I have a good start on it," Jahon had to agree. "But I'm really not leaving you out of it or anything. I just wanted to make it easy. And I wanted to leave fairly soon. Do you mind too much?"

I had to admit I really didn't mind, not that I was going to let him know that. "Of course I do, but I'll let it go this time. Now that I've decided to go I guess I'd just as soon get going also." Then I added as I saw him relax a bit, "But don't think you're off the hook. I'm not going to forget this right away you know." But it was hard to put much into the threat with him sitting there grinning at me. I could tell this wasn't going to be an easy relationship.

When we got to my place Shahvid was out. Jahon sat down in the study to write him a long note, to let him know of our plans, in case we didn't see him before we left. I went to get my things. Thank goodness the clothes that I needed were all clean, Jahon had lucked out on that. All my camping gear was together. A quick check through and a few additions was all that was needed. That was the nice thing about backpacking, you didn't take much.

I felt funny about leaving on such short notice, with little planning and without saying good-bye to anyone. I wished Shahvid had been home. But it was time I stopped leaning on my brother so much. Instead I wrote him a note and took it in to leave in his study.

Jahon was just finishing and I asked him if Shahvid had mentioned to him his plans for the evening. He said no, but that he had told him to stop over that night if he, or he and Kasho, were free, if that was all right with me?

I smiled, agreed, and made a few changes to my note. Then we loaded my things into the vehicle and headed back to Jahon's. The rain the previous night had washed the world clean and shiny, and the sun was reflecting that shine all around. We couldn't have asked for a nicer Sunday afternoon. Or a better omen for our upcoming camping adventure.

~~~ ~~ ~ ~~ ~~~

When Shahvid arrived home early Wednesday evening there was a message waiting for him to call Sinat. After a short conversation he hung up then rang up Kasho.

"Hi, Shahvid here, have you had dinner yet?" At her reply to the negative he told her, "We're invited to an informal dinner party tonight at Sinat's, want to go? Good. I just have to wash up and change and I'll be on my way. I could meet you at the Split Tree crossing if you want? Fine, see you then." It didn't take him long to get cleaned up and ready.

As he wheeled his bike onto the lane he thought ahead to the coming meeting. He was anxious to hear what was going on with Valjar. He and Kasho had purposely kept themselves busy and out of touch the last few days. Half to avoid questions that might touch on where Neana or Jahon were (although they had come up with an answer for that) and half to keep from worrying about the whole thing.

His pace kept up with his anxiety and soon he came in sight of Kasho waiting at the crossroad. It wasn't much longer before they pulled into Sinat and Sushati's yard and parked their bikes.

Kasho gave him a quick hug as they walked up to the house, "Relax. It won't help to let yourself get worked up about this thing. Besides, while you're here worrying Jahon and Neana are out having a great time off in the woods. No doubt not even thinking of us here at all!"

Shahvid laughed and made himself calm down. "I am a little wired I guess. And you're no doubt right about those two. Now that I think of it, I'm jealous. Have any plans for the next few weeks?"

Kasho just laughed back at him as Sushati answered the door and let them in. Introductions were made as they met a few people they didn't know. Then they greeted Sinat, Chanthan, and Rafnon. Rafnon was a bit uneasy with Shahvid's presence but his greeting was friendly enough.

Dinner was buffet style and they were soon all settled with their food and drink. The conversation turned to the matter at hand - Valjar.

Sushati asked Shahvid, "I assume Neana and Jahon got off all right? We figured you would let us know if otherwise, but I had to ask." Rafnon and the others had already been told about the "vacation" trip.

Shahvid assured her and the rest that the two had arrived at their destination with no problems. The driver had gotten in touch with Shahvid as soon as he had returned to town, as had been agreed. He reported that he had picked Jahon and Neana up and delivered them to the wilderness area with no witnesses. He had waited to watch them disappear down a little used path into the woods before returning. He would pick them up at the same spot in two weeks. Shahvid trusted him and appreciated his involvement.

Chanthan asked what the others knew of Valjar's activities so far that week. There wasn't much. There was a lot of discussion, but the bottom line was that Valjar wasn't doing much of anything. He was still around a lot but seemed to be wandering without any direction. He wasn't harassing anyone, and hadn't asked any questions that they knew of about Neana's whereabouts. He appeared to be keeping to himself. All they had were bits and pieces of information with no connections.

"It's those seemingly small pieces of knowledge that often end up being important," Chanthan reminded them.

"Has no one heard anything about the inner group getting together? Or anything about any of them?" He was uneasy. Caljn may have been their leader but they knew a lot and had followed him pretty closely.

Kasho offered, "I don't *know* anything about their activities for sure, but I did get the feeling from what someone said that they have gotten together recently. Of course you'd think they would, that would be natural. And the person I talked to isn't that close to them so it was more of a hint than a fact. I just couldn't get any more."

"I don't think you should try to get very close. They may very well know that you're a close friend of Neana's." Shahvid had been worrying about that all week.

Kasho assured him, "I haven't felt any hint of danger or suspicion. My contact with them is pretty low-key. Besides, the only hint we have of any suspicion of Neana is from Valjar, and he appears to be on his own."

Sinat agreed, "I don't think any of them really know Neana much at all. I gather the only contacts she had with them, except on a very casual level, was with Caljn. And because of Caljn, Valjar. What do you think Rafnon?"

Rafnon started a bit. His relationships with Careen and with Neana had been going through his mind and he was still uncomfortable being in on this discussion with Shahvid there. "Um, well, I think you're right. No one else in that group seemed to have taken any notice of Neana. And I doubt that they would know of her life or her friends." Except for Careen that is, and he sure wasn't going to bring her name up.

Chanthan spoke to Kasho, "I would think that as long as you're in good touch with your feelings, as you seem to be, you'll recognize any danger. Can we assume you would back off and let one of us know if you felt at all threatened?"

"Of course," Kasho assured him. "I really think I'm in much less of a position to be noticed and perceived as a threat than the rest of you are."

"Well, we don't have any indication that they are

aware of us as a group," Sushati replied. "We are pretty
sure that their choice of Chanthan as their target was due
to his community leadership, not his Starpeace activity."
Then she added, "And I'd agree with you as to your lack of
notice were it not for Shahvid. And Careen."

Sushati was aware of the undercurrents coming from
Rafnon, but there were more important things to be
considered. Besides, she felt fairly certain that Careen was
now far behind in Shahvid's life. "I am thinking of Valjar's
visit to Neana. He knows you, Shahvid, are her brother
and where you live. Let's not underestimate him."

Sushati turned to Rafnon, "And you had said Careen
was reporting to Valjar Neana's actions and whereabouts
when she could."

"Well, yes, she did say she was doing that, and that
he wanted to know," Rafnon answered rather
uncomfortably. "But she wouldn't know now anything of
importance."

Shahvid agreed, "Careen isn't likely to know any
more than any of the people around town about Neana's
activities." He assumed they all knew that he and Careen
were no longer together. But he hadn't thought of Careen's
possible involvement. And why was she keeping tabs on
Neana for Valjar? He didn't like it. He said, "But she would
of course know who Neana's friends and my friends are. I
hadn't thought about that."

"Well, it's not a secret anyway," Kasho argued. She
wished Shahvid wouldn't be so worried about it. "We're
not that large of a community. I don't think there's any
reason to look for trouble where none is. Besides, what
would there be to do? Except to just keep aware, and I
think we're all doing that."

"You're right," Sinat agreed, "We don't want to miss
an important clue. But we also don't want to create by our
worries a situation that isn't there."

"I think as long as we stay aware that Valjar would
know of Neana's friends, and Shahvid as her brother, we
needn't concentrate on it," Chanthan calmly considered.

"And it doesn't sound like anyone else other than Valjar is questioning Caljn's death. Not that we should stop watching the others. I'm still anticipating some reaction from them. They've been too quiet. And," he added, "we don't know for certain that the handpiece of their weapon system which Caljn was holding was the only one in existence. We don't want to get so caught up with our worries about Valjar that we forget their original plan. Let's go over again, carefully, what each of us has heard."

They all agreed. As much as they'd have liked to forget that original, dark plan of Caljn's, they knew they couldn't, and wouldn't. Hopefully it had all gone down with Caljn, not to surface again. But they knew better than to stake their lives, and the community, on that hope. They each, once again, shared what they knew, what they had heard, leaving out no little bit of information that might help. Ideas and suggestions were exchanged. Possibilities discussed. But there didn't seem to be any hint that the Power Movement were planning any action, of any kind.

It was finally decided to just continue their surveillance. And for everyone to keep a low profile, especially Shahvid and Kasho. If anyone came up with anything they would let Sinat know and he or Sushati would arrange another meeting.

It was late and the group melted into the night. Shahvid rode with Kasho to her place then pedaled on home, feeling more and more uneasy with the whole situation. He didn't try to ignore his feelings but he did try to keep them in perspective. As he drifted off to sleep he decided he needed a longer talk with Kasho. About the Power Movement, and about them.

Thursday morning found Shahvid busy in his study working on drawings for his current clients. They were remodeling and he had spent quite a bit of time with them, discussing what was important in a home. He had worked up several different plans that he thought would fit their ideas and the house. But before he met with them that afternoon he wanted to make some more sketches. Not everyone could easily visualize the end product and he found his perspective drawings helped. Especially when, as in this case, the owners were going to be doing much of the work themselves. It seemed to help the project along when they had a clear picture in their minds as to where it was all headed.

When at last he was satisfied with what he had it was almost time to leave. He decided he had time to give Kasho a quick call to see about getting together that night, maybe for dinner.

But there was no answer at her end. His first reaction was disappointment, then worry came right on its heels. He tried again, then again. Then he got a hold of himself and realized how silly he was being. She certainly wasn't spending her time just sitting by the phone waiting for him to call. She had a full and busy life. He shook off his concern, laughed at himself, and decided he could call later from his client's place.

Shahvid loaded up his pack, threw some fruit and cookies in his bike bag and headed out, eating lunch on the way.

By the time Shahvid parked his bicycle once again in the shed it was dark. It had been a long session with his clients, continuing through dinner and into the evening. But he had their decision, and could now set to work on the final plans and drawings.

Normally he would be excited about getting started. He enjoyed this type of job and the challenge of coming up with plans that the owners could understand and build from, even though they weren't experienced builders. But he felt down. He hadn't gotten in touch with Kasho, though he had tried several times. He didn't know which was worse, his worry (unfounded he was sure but there nonetheless), or his disappointment. He hadn't realized how much he had counted on seeing her. He tried once more, then decided it was getting too late to call.

He was tired but knew he couldn't settle down to sleep yet. As he wandered through the house the feeling that it didn't fit ánymore rose up in him. Maybe it was time to move on. He felt pretty sure that Neana would be moving out soon, and he couldn't see Kasho there.

He laughed at himself as he saw his problem. Why not just accept it and work on some plans, right then? Come up with something that might fit the two of them. He had a pretty good idea of what she thought was important since he'd been helping her look for a place. With higher spirits he settled down at his desk and was soon lost in his drawings, sleep forgotten, his worries and loneliness receding to a far corner.

The telephone chirped Shahvid awake early the next morning. He was still half in his dream world when he answered. When Kasho's voice greeted him he responded more straightforwardly than if he had been fully awake. "Why hello, where have you been? I tried to reach you all yesterday but couldn't. I wanted to see you."

In the moment of silence that followed his words Shahvid woke up completely. He tried to think of how to rearrange what he had just said.

But Kasho simply answered his question without commenting. She realized she had wakened him with her call. "I was tied up all day at a client's home. We're trying to decide on colors and patterns for rugs, pillows and such for a new room. And we had lots of 'help' from friends and relatives. It was a long day let me tell you. The weaving will be a cinch comparatively, even considering some of the complicated designs we ended up with."

Kasho thought a minute before continuing, "Then last night I was trying to get some information from a friend and we had trouble connecting. Just one of those days I guess. But I'm sorry I missed your calls. I want to talk with you, too."

Shahvid had to apologize even if she had ignored his manner, "I'm sorry Kasho, you don't owe me a report of your day. You caught me half asleep and I'm afraid I said the first thing that came to mind. I didn't mean to."

Kasho laughed, "I'm not sure which is worse, your words or your being sorry you said them! Don't worry, I realize I woke you. What's your plan for today? Could we fit in lunch together?"

Shahvid collected himself and remembered what she had said about information from a friend. He certainly wasn't at his best that morning. Three hours of sleep just wasn't enough. "Sounds good to me. Where would you like to meet? Here, there or out would be fine, my schedule is loose today."

"Well, I thought I'd whip something up if you'd like to come here. I have to go out this morning but should be back by before noon."

"OK, I'll be there then. Can I bring anything?"

"Just yourself."

Shahvid rang off and decided he had time for a few more hours sleep. He certainly wanted to be more alert for lunch. It was nice to be with someone with a quick mind, but not when yours was fuzzy.

Two hours later the chirp of the phone once again brought Shahvid to the day. This time it was Binjer's young friend Mastal with a new problem with his bicycle. He politely asked if Shahvid might be able to show him how to fix it sometime. Shahvid agreed readily and said how about that afternoon?

He didn't know what Kasho's plans were but he knew that the boy depended on his bicycle to get him out to his uncle's orchard where he helped out a lot. And he had gathered that for whatever reason Mastal didn't have access to another bike through his family, only from friends. And he preferred not to borrow. He was quite determined to make his own way in this life. The last time Shahvid had helped him fix his bicycle he had insisted on paying, though Shahvid had assured him that he often helped friends with their repairs and didn't expect any payment. It was something he enjoyed. But a trade was worked out that suited them both. Mastal delivered some fresh fruit from the orchard the next day. And he agreed to make use of Shahvid's help, and tools, should he need them again.

Mastal said that afternoon would be fine with him. Shahvid told him he was going to be out for a while so if he wasn't there when Mastal arrived to just make himself at home. He didn't think Mastal would be comfortable going in the house without him there so he told him about a nest of baby birds hidden in the bushes that he might want to see. If he was quiet he might be able to watch the parents feeding them. Mastal's reaction to that assured Shahvid that he would be well entertained if Shahvid was late. In fact, he guessed the boy would be sure to get there before him.

Shahvid decided to eat before his shower and he was soon in the kitchen rummaging for something that would do for breakfast. The slim pickings made him consider going into the garden for some berries. But he just didn't care for picking the things, even under such a beautiful sky as there was that day. As he made his choices and sat down to eat, he tried to analyze the uneasiness he felt.

It *was* a beautiful day. He was going to be with Kasho in a few hours. And he was looking forward to helping Mastal with his bike, even if it did mean shortening his luncheon. It wasn't as if he wouldn't be seeing her again anyway. He didn't think his uneasiness had to do with Jahon and Neana. He knew they were safe, and he was happy that they were together. So what was it?

After he showered he sat down at his desk to do a bit of work before leaving. He wasn't any closer to figuring out what was bothering him. It wasn't that specific a feeling. He finally decided to just set it aside. He knew better than to ignore it, but he also knew that to dwell on it could be just as bad. He set to organizing his drawings from yesterday and it was soon time to leave. The uneasiness hadn't left but his spirits were high with the day, the ride, and the destination.

"Well, it's so nonspecific," Kasho explained. "I just can't get a handle on what it means, if anything. That's why I asked you to come over. I figured if I told it out loud to you maybe it would sort itself out. Or at least we could decide together if there's anything there worth bothering Sinat about." Shahvid and Kasho had finished lunch and were relaxing with cold drinks out on her porch. The sky was alive with fluffy clouds and sleek birds. It was hard to keep one's mind down to earth.

"Sounds like a good plan," Shahvid encouraged as Kasho stopped, "I'm listening."

"Well, I got a message yesterday afternoon from my informant friend that something was up. He didn't have much but was trying to get more. And that he would meet me as usual around dinner time. I won't go into it all now but it ended up being a frustrating evening of not meeting up with each other. When we finally did connect it was late. He had been jockeying all night trying to keep up with Valjar's activities and trying to contact me.

"Anyway, what he had to say was that the inner group had a meeting last night. But my friend had a hint that most of those members had met a few nights previously, and Valjar hadn't been included. He didn't know if Valjar knew. But Valjar had been acting really wired all day. My friend said that the meeting last night was stormy and that Valjar had angrily walked out of it."

Kasho stopped to watch the sky for a moment. Shahvid sipped his juice, waiting without comment. "That's it. I wish I knew what they'd argued about. But that's all I have. It makes me uneasy. I'm not sure if it's my feelings, or if I'm just picking up my friend's concern. And he *was* concerned, though he admitted he didn't know exactly why. Valjar never was close to the others and only got along well with Caljn I guess."

"It's not much I agree, but I wouldn't ignore your feelings about it." Shahvid thought of telling her about his own uneasiness that morning but decided not. No use

.confusing the issue at hand. "I don't think it would hurt to pass on the information to Sinat. Though I think they're watching Valjar pretty closely anyway, it might help."

"If they don't know already. But that's how I feel too, that it wouldn't hurt." Kasho grinned at him, "I guess I just needed someone to tell me they agree with what I think."

"Anytime!" Shahvid responded with a bow, "I'm at your service. If there is anything else I can agree with you on just let me know. Your wish is my command."

Kasho laughed, "I think I'll not take you up on that right now. But I may hold you to it later."

Their conversation drifted to other things. Shahvid mentioned some of the ideas he had come up with last night and they were soon deep in discussion about what each wanted in a home. When Kasho mentioned a covered bicycle rack Shahvid came to the present with an exclamation and a dismayed look at his watch. "I forgot all about Mastal!"

Shahvid quickly explained to Kasho. "I was supposed to be home an hour ago. I could call the house but I doubt that he's inside."

"Why not leave your bike here and take a vehicle. The garage isn't far, though I don't suppose Mastal is all that concerned about the time anyway."

"Probably not," Shahvid agreed, "but I still feel bad about having forgotten him. And I'm also sorry to cut short our discussion. There's a lot more I want to discuss with you."

Kasho smiled and gave him a hug. "Well, it can wait I'm sure. You better get going. And I have to get to work anyway." When Shahvid didn't let go she gave him a friendly shove and added, "Why not come back here when you're done, I'll be working in my shop all afternoon."

Shahvid reluctantly undid his hug and agreed. "How about we eat dinner out? You decide where. I'll see you later then." With the evening thus arranged he was soon on the road.

Mastal started out for Shahvid's as soon as he was through with lunch. His bicycle was working well enough to ride so he was soon near the lane that ran up to the house. He knew he was early so he debated whether to park his bike in the bushes along the road or leave it at the house and come back to walk quietly through the trees to find the birds. He wanted to come up to the babies' nest without disturbing the parents.

He finally opted for going to the house first just in case Shahvid was there. He rode up and parked near the shed, then walked to the front of the house. He thought he heard someone inside. But when, after a few minutes, there was no answer to his knock he decided he hadn't. He went back up the lane to enter the grounds near the road.

It wasn't a long way but he made it a long adventure, stopping to watch a snake, then a caterpillar. He was content that Shahvid wasn't home yet. He wanted to have time to watch the birds. He stepped slowly and carefully. His patience paid off and he came upon the nest, full of hungry open mouths wiggling around inside. He settled in to watch. It occurred to him that the parents were very likely used to humans watching, with Shahvid and Neana around, but that didn't dampen his enthusiasm any. This was his adventure.

He leaned back against a small tree. He could see

the house through the trees and bushes so was sure he'd notice Shahvid when he arrived. He relaxed, half asleep and half mesmerized by the warm day, the cool shade, and the cheeps, whirs and other sounds around him. There was no time and no thoughts.

Then something startled him fully awake. It took him a minute to figure out what was wrong. Then he realized that it was suddenly quiet all around him. Nature's critters were listening. Frowning he looked around, but instinctively stayed quiet himself. He didn't think Shahvid had returned. He didn't see any activity around the house or sheds. But he felt that something wasn't right.

Then two things happened almost at once. He saw someone run out of the back of the house into the bushes. And he smelled smoke.

Almost without thinking Mastal was on his feet and running up to the house. He yanked open the first door he came to, the one into the kitchen. The fire was burning pretty well in there. He yelled and called but the fire blocked his entrance into the rest of the house.

He quickly ran to the back and entered there, calling and searching as fast as he could. The fire was apparently just in the front part. He found a telephone in one of the rooms and quickly connected into the fire emergency system to report the blaze.

The smoke was getting thicker though the fire wasn't spreading very fast. He again searched and called as best he could, assuring himself that no one was in the house.

By the time the first neighbors arrived to help he had a garden hose propped up in a tree branch aimed through a window into the living room where there was a small fire. And he was getting another one to douse the fire in the kitchen. The neighbors wasted no time in pitching in. Someone with knowledge of fire fighting gave directions and the others put their efforts where they could.

The fire fighting vehicles weren't far behind. By the time Shahvid turned into his drive the fire was out, and preparations for cleanup under way.

Shahvid stood looking at the house, yard and people in shocked amazement. He gathered from the equipment that there was a fire, but not much else sunk in.

Mastal noticed Shahvid first, he'd been watching for him, and came running up. His excitement of the event and his relief at the sight of Shahvid made his words tumble out every which way.

But Shahvid got the gist of what he was saying. He assured Mastal that yes, he was here and OK, and no Neana was not around, she was out of town. Shahvid gathered that, though dirty and sooty, Mastal was fine.

A close neighbor and one of the fire squad saw him then and came up to talk with them. Between them all Shahvid soon had a picture of what had happened, or what they knew of what had happened. Not much was said about the man Mastal had seen leaving the house. No use speculating about it. That would be left for the inspectors, one of whom was already there looking around.

After much assurance that there really was nothing that he needed, but he would of course tell them if there was, and thank yous and appreciations on his part, the neighbors and unneeded fire fighters headed back to their homes. There was no problem with bystanders since people understood the need to stay out of the way of the workers, and the need of the owners for time to adjust and react to the event in their own way.

Shahvid asked one of the neighbors to give Kasho a call and tell her what had happened. He didn't feel he should leave to call her himself but he wanted to let her know. Maybe he even knew he wanted her there and had an idea that she would come when she heard. He didn't take time to analyze it.

With the inspector, Mastal, and one of the fire cleanup crew Shahvid took a tour of the inside of the house. The fire, and most of the damage, had been kept to the kitchen and living room areas. And due to the fast action by Mastal, the neighbors, and the first firefighters there was little smoke damage throughout the rest of the house. Most of the windows had been open because of the nice weather. And the doors to both Neana's area and his study had been closed.

Neana's rooms were untouched and fairly clear. But his study - what chaos! The fire wasn't the problem there. Someone had come in and emptied the contents of his drawers and shelves all over, overturned furniture, and in general made a mess.

No one said much about it except for a question by the inspector asking if he could tell if anything was missing. Shahvid looked around in some dismay, but quickly noted that as far as he could tell nothing big was missing. And, he added, he couldn't think of anything that someone would want to take. It appeared to be just an act of destruction in general.

The inspector nodded and looked carefully around before they left the room, closing the door on the mini-disaster. Shahvid wondered to himself what in the world Valjar had been up to. That it had been Valjar he had no doubt, Mastal's description fit him to a T.

The big fans were in place continuing the job of ventilating. There would be a lot of cleanup work of course, but overall the damage was minimal. Thankfully he had moved he and Neana's study and studio furniture back from the living room after the celebration party (was that only a week ago?) and hadn't done anything more to furnish the room. They were only material things but there were several pieces that he would have hated to lose, and was sure Neana would feel the same. It was too bad about the kitchen chairs though. Valjar had apparently built a bonfire out of paper, boxes and whatnot from the kitchen and added the chairs for good measure.

The inspector took Mastal through his story again, slowly. He listened closely, not saying much. He finally put out his hand to Mastal saying how very worse the damage would have been had it not been for his quick thinking and fast action.

The fire squad people and Shahvid agreed until

Mastal, very uncomfortable with the praise but glowing just
the same, said he'd better head on home. Shahvid excused
himself from the inspector and crew and walked out with
him to the shed.

"I know there's no way to thank someone for
something like this, but I guess I feel the need to try anyway."
Shahvid held out his hand to Mastal.

Mastal rather solemnly shook Shahvid's hand but
said, "I really don't know what the fuss is all about. What
did you expect me to do?"

Shahvid laughed, "You're right of course. This type
of event tends to make one lose sight of the obvious I guess.
Speaking of sights, I wonder if I should throw you in the
sauna before I let you go home. Your parents may not let
you come back again if this is the result of a visit to me."

Mastal just grinned but changed the subject as he
saw someone coming up the path, "Do you think all this
will upset the birds?" He had been worrying about it ever
since things had calmed down a bit. "I thought about going
to check but didn't know if I should."

"I doubt that you would disturb them," Shahvid
assured him, "and I don't think they will desert the babies
because of the commotion. But if you want, why don't you
come back tomorrow and check on them. I guess we won't
be able to get to your bike today after all, but I'll be glad to
help you tomorrow. You can borrow Neana's bike for now,
I'm sure she won't mind."

Mastal thought about it. He had wanted to go out
to the orchard in the morning, and if he had a good bike he
could then come back in the afternoon to check on the birds.
For some reason he felt quite attached to them. They were
so much easier to understand than everything else that day.
Especially the man he had seen, and Shahvid's study. No
one had said much about him or the destruction, and he
guessed he really didn't want to know anything. Not yet.
The fire had been exciting, but also depressing. He'd rather
think of the birds.

"OK," Mastal said, "that would be nice. I had planned

to go out to the orchard in the morning but I'll bring the bike back after noon."

Shahvid said, "There's no hurry on the bike but that would be fine with me. I'll plan on meeting you here, hopefully with less fanfare, and we'll work on your bike then. You can put it in the shed when you get Neana's bike out."

Mastal agreed and thanked Shahvid. He was soon on his way down the path.

Shahvid turned with relief to Kasho. He was sure glad to see her.

Kasho had waited while Shahvid was talking with Mastal, wandering around looking at and into the house, being careful to stay out of the way of the cleanup crew. Once she had assured herself that Shahvid was safe she turned her attention to the damage. Thank goodness the fire hadn't been bad enough to damage the trees and greenery around the house, and the people working on the fire had made little impact. It was almost as if they had hovered considering all the traffic.

She gave Shahvid a big hug and with few words they toured the house, stopping to help out here and there where they could. He told her briefly what he had learned of the fire. She gave him a quick look when he mentioned the man, and the job done on his study. But she didn't comment, until he opened the door and she saw what he was talking about.

"Shahvid, how awful!" Somehow the damage done by the fire didn't seem as bad to her as the utter chaos on the floor. "All your papers and drawings and plans." She started picking up one then another until Shahvid gently stopped her.

"It's OK, don't worry about it now. It'll take some time to straighten up but there doesn't appear to be any real damage. We don't need to bother with it now, it'll wait." He knew it was a bit of a shock at first sight, but he'd had a little time to adjust and think about it. "It doesn't seem so bad when you think about how much worse it could have been."

She had to agree. Since there were others around neither of them expanded on that thought out loud.

One of the women from the fire squad came up to them then and explained what they were doing. She said they were nearly finished with their work, but would be leaving the fans going to continue forcing fresh air through the house to help clear the smoke smell. And a few people would be staying around that night to make sure the fire didn't reignite.

Some neighbors and other volunteers had already set up a well-stocked refreshment center in the sauna for the workers, and Shahvid encouraged her to have them help themselves to anything else around that they might need or want. Neana's rooms were pretty much untouched and they were free to use them.

She thanked him, assured him they were all set, then went back to work. Shahvid felt he should help in some way, after all it was his house, but he also knew that they were well trained in their work and there was simply nothing for him to do. His mind started, almost automatically, assessing what repairs would be needed to get the house back in shape.

Kasho brought him back to the world with a low voiced, "Well, are you sure it was Valjar? Shouldn't we be doing something about it?"

Shahvid looked at her in surprise. It took him a minute to understand what she was talking about. Then it hit him. He couldn't believe he had forgotten. "Of course! I forgot all about him. Yes, from Mastal's description I'm sure it was Valjar. But what now? I guess we ought to talk to Sinat as soon as possible. But first I want to talk to the inspector. He was pretty quiet about it while Mastal was telling him, but I'm sure his mind was working it over. I didn't want to say much in front of the others."

"Good idea. Here he comes now." They waited as

the man finished talking to the fire fighters and headed their way.

He didn't waste any time, or words, "You know who the man might be that young Mastal saw?" Although he didn't know Shahvid well in person, he did by reputation and knew he could trust him. And he didn't play any games he didn't have to.

Shahvid understood, "Yes, I'm pretty sure I do. His name is Valjar." The inspector didn't comment but Shahvid sensed a quickening at the name. "You know of him?"

The man replied simply, "Yes." He was quiet for a moment as he thought. "Yes, I know of him." His voice was calm but with an undertone that told Shahvid much more.

Shahvid wasn't sure just what to say. The inspectors and Starpeace were going in the same direction, they just did so in different ways. They were independent of each other yet cooperated as they could. It was a balance that seemed to work. Shahvid didn't think he had anything to add that would help. The inspector wouldn't be interested in gossip or guesswork, that wouldn't be his way. He guessed the man knew quite a bit about the whole affair anyway. How much more he should be told would be up to Sinat or Chanthan.

Shahvid glanced at Kasho with a questioning look but she just gave a slight shrug. She couldn't think of anything to add. She also knew of the ways of the inspectors compared to the ways of Starpeace.

Shahvid said, "I guess there is nothing more to add that is concrete."

"But you're not surprised."

Shahvid answered honestly, "On one hand yes, I'm surprised at the event. On the other hand, no, I'm not surprised that Valjar would be involved."

"Your sister is not around now, is that right?" The inspector continued his pattern of thought.

"That's correct. She's out of town for a few weeks right now."

The inspector nodded with the comment, "That's good." He looked toward the front of the house, blackened with fire and smoke, then asked, "Are you planning to stay here? Several fire fighters and either myself or another person from our office will be here all night, and into tomorrow at least. So there's no need for you to be here."

Shahvid frowned, he hadn't thought of that, but he didn't think he cared to leave right then.

Kasho, however, agreed wholeheartedly with the inspector. "There's no reason for you to stay here. Pack up a few things and come stay at my place. You've got the vehicle here and your bicycle is already at my house."

Before he had time to reply the inspector said, "Good idea. If you'll give me your address and phone number I'll know where to reach him." As Shahvid looked at the two of them in surprise Kasho gave the man the information and he walked off with a "Be talking with you."

"Now just a minute," Shahvid found his voice.

But Kasho interrupted, "I don't know about you but I'm starving, and you promised dinner out tonight remember? Besides, your kitchen's a mess if you hadn't noticed."

Shahvid just shook his head and laughed, gave her a quick hug and said he wasn't real sure about her proposal but guessed he'd take what he could get. She responded with a hmph!, and suggested he get his things together while she made sure all was set, and that no one needed anything.

They took a last look around, told the people who were left how to get in touch with Shahvid, and set his overnight bags in the back of the vehicle. Neither of them had put into focused thought, but it was certainly there, a hint of anxiety - What was Valjar doing now? And what more, if anything, was he planning?

As they drove off Shahvid and Kasho debated what to do. They were both hungry and grimy, but they also knew that the first order of business was to let Starpeace know what had happened. So, somewhat reluctantly, Shahvid turned the vehicle in the direction of Sinat and

Sushati's. The sun was heading down with much fanfare. Nature's reminder that the day *was* still beautiful no matter what had happened in their lives. It was hard to remember that. Especially when the ramifications of Valjar's actions started to sink in.

Kasho finally tried to put it into words, "I guess it's just such a shock that I don't know quite what to do about it. It was such a direct attack, and if I let myself think about what could have happened if . . ."

Shahvid interrupted, "Don't dwell on the possibilities. Let those thoughts go. It didn't happen so no use thinking, or worrying, about it." Though, he thought to himself, if he was honest he had to admit he was having the same trouble. But to Kasho he said, "For some reason it's not bothering me too much. Probably just hasn't sunk in yet." He gave her a grin, "The result of living with your head in the clouds too much."

Kasho returned his grin but it faded fast. She just couldn't joke about it. It didn't help to say you shouldn't think about the possibilities. The thoughts were there, and they shook her.

Shahvid talked on calmly about the practical problems involved with the fire and what would need to be done. He knew he was avoiding mention of Valjar but he didn't know what to say. He didn't want to think about the other probable paths the event could have taken. And any mention or thought of Valjar brought those possibilities to mind too readily. So they drove on without talking about the real problem at all.

Kasho and Shahvid were barely out of the car when the front door opened and Sinat hurried down the steps toward them. With a strong hug to each he said, "There you two are, we're so glad to see you and that you are OK. I've been trying to contact both of you. I had just reached the inspector who is at your place," he nodded to Shahvid, "but he said you had left already. We were trying not to worry." With that greeting he ushered them quickly into the house where Sushati also greeted them with extra sincere hugs.

Shahvid tried to lift the mood a bit, "Sorry to arrive smelling, and probably looking, like smoked fish. Hope it's not too bad."

"That is the least of our worries right now, we are just so glad to see you. Come on in." Sushati motioned them into the living room where they were greeted warmly by Chanthan and Myana, and quietly but sincerely by Rafnon.

Sinat left to answer the telephone and Sushati offered them some tea or juice.

"A tall, cold juice and water would be great," Kasho responded as she glanced at the light colored cushions and pillows. She didn't know if she was all that sooty but she didn't feel comfortable sitting down on any of the furniture just in case.

Shahvid was feeling the same and said, "A cold drink would be great for me too. But would you mind if we washed up a bit first? We came right here from the house and didn't stop to clean up." Shahvid gathered that somehow they all already knew about the fire.

"Of course, I didn't think of that. We were just so glad to see you," Sushati repeated, but didn't elaborate. "Come along, I'll find something for both of you to change into. A few more minutes won't matter, and you will be more comfortable I am sure."

Neither Shahvid nor Kasho commented as they followed her up the stairs but they looked at each other with questioning frowns. What was going on? Neither the fire nor the ransacking warranted this type of behavior from these people.

When they were all settled back in the living room, with Kasho and Shahvid cleaner but more than a little curious, Sinat spoke. He explained that they had received the news of the fire but no details. He asked Shahvid what had happened.

Shahvid related quickly what he knew, and what he had guessed, about the event at his house. He had a feeling that there was much more going on and that this was just a small part so he didn't elaborate much.

They all listened intently and when he had finished Sushati put their thoughts into words, "Thank the gods that neither you nor Neana were home when he arrived. And that Mastal had not gone inside. Of course, there is no such thing as coincidence, but still, it is amazing how all the pieces fit together."

Shahvid looked at her in surprise, not only because of her words but because of her manner, and the others' too. He asked, "What's going on? There's more to this than the fire isn't there?"

Chanthan answered, "Yes, there is more, unfortunately. This afternoon one of the scientists who was a close associate of Caljn's, probably highest in rank next to him, was found dead in his lab office. The signs point to Valjar, though there is no hard evidence, at least not that we know of yet. There was a struggle, and it appears the man's desk was searched. There were papers all over, but of course no way of knowing if anything was taken. It is guessed that it happened before noon, and Valjar was seen in that area late morning. He hasn't been seen since. Except, it appears, by your friend Mastal."

The room was silent as Shahvid and Kasho took in what he had said. Their uneasiness turned to a sickening realization of what it meant. Kasho asked if he knew the name of the man who had been killed. Rafnon provided the name.

Kasho and Shahvid looked at each other. Then Kasho shared the information she had, her story of the previous evening and night. The man was the same one her informant friend had mentioned Valjar arguing with. The pieces were fitting all too well.

Sinat asked, "Can we pass that on to the inspectors? Would it put your friend in any danger do you think? We can of course wait till you check with him if you prefer, but I wouldn't mind getting that information in the hands of the people working on the case, even if it's just as an 'informed rumor'."

Kasho thought about it, then said, "Once he hears about the murder I think he will get the information to them himself. But for now, in case he hasn't, I would rather it be as an anonymous tip. And I'll contact him as soon as I can."

Sinat agreed and went off to telephone. Chanthan commented to Kasho, "I think it might be wise to keep a low profile. If you feel you must contact your friend then of course you must. But you might consider not doing so right now. Since he is so close to that group I would think he will know all about it soon."

Shahvid agreed, "I'm beginning to think we should have gone off into the woods with Jahon and Neana." And, he added to himself, it would be hard to express how glad he was that Jahon had gotten Neana away. He sincerely and fervently hoped it, whatever it was, would be all done and over before they returned.

Kasho gave Shahvid a quick smile, and thought about what Chanthan had said. "Yes, I have to agree. Not for my safety but for his. He knows how to contact me if he needs to so I'll leave it to him."

Shahvid asked, "And Valjar? What has become of him? You said no one has seen him since this morning?"

Chanthan slowly nodded his head. "Except for Mastal, no one that we know of has seen him since. I probably don't need to assure you that we are trying to locate him, as are the inspectors. To say nothing of the Power Movement people no doubt."

Shahvid now understood the silence of the others. There really wasn't much to say. They were all only too aware of what that meant. Or could mean.

Sinat returned and answered the unasked question, "No, no sign yet. They're necessarily keeping a low profile so as to not push him into something. But between their forces and ours I can't believe he could have disappeared. But because of who the murdered man was it is making it more difficult of course. Those close to him aren't exactly friends of the inspectors and aren't cooperating in any way. They are trying to keep it internal. Though they must realize that isn't possible now."

"Well, they are not known for their common sense," Sushati responded. "Anyway, there is nothing we can do right now except support our people in the field. And we will not be very good at that if we don't eat. If you will all move into the kitchen I will find some food."

They knew she was right. As much as they would all rather be out *doing* something, each of them was too well known to be effective right then. And, though no one put the thought to words, any of them could be a target for Valjar. There was no reason to take unnecessary chances. They were just too unsure of the man, what he knew, who he knew, and where he was going.

They all pitched in one way or another. It was a relief to have a project, even a small one. It wasn't long before they were settled around the table, eating and discussing. Trying to make sure there wasn't some point or hint or clue they may have missed. Anything that might help them second guess Valjar, and beat him at his game, whatever it was.

"Good heavens!" Kasho interrupted the talk with her exclamation, "We forgot all about Tamoi and Binjer. They are likely to hear about all this, well Shahvid's fire anyway, from Mastal and they're sure to be worried."

Shahvid tried to calm her concern, "If Mastal did tell them of the fire he would also have told them that I, and you, are fine. And if they heard about it elsewhere they would know that we'd be likely tied up at the house. And they aren't likely to hear about the murder."

"I know, but I think you should give them a call anyway. No matter what they hear, if anything, they'll be concerned and want to know what they can do. You know we'd feel that way if we were them."

Shahvid agreed, and went off to call, inform and assure his friends. He was glad he did. Kasho had been right.

No one felt like leaving. Even Rafnon had put aside his uneasiness around Shahvid. But as the evening grew late and there was no new word about Valjar it was apparent that there was no reason to stay.

They all agreed to contact Sinat if anyone came up with anything at all, and he in turn assured them he'd let them all know as soon as any news reached him. They were especially concerned about Shahvid, and Kasho. Chanthan inquired as to their plans for the next days.

"I hadn't given it a great deal of thought to tell you the truth," Shahvid answered. "I'm planning to be at Kasho's tonight, then spend tomorrow at my house. I promised Mastal to meet him there after noon to work on his bicycle. And the sooner I get to work on the chaos that was once my study the better I'll feel. I still can't imagine that Valjar was searching for anything specific. I can't think of what it could be if he was. Maybe I'll know once I get the mess sorted out. I think it was just a case of wanting to destroy. Further than that I don't know."

Chanthan nodded then looked at Kasho. She answered, "Like Shahvid I guess I hadn't thought that far yet. But my plan is probably to work in my studio and shop both day and evening. I have a new commission I need to get to work on."

Chanthan nodded again but his face was serious, almost to a frown. He was worried about Shahvid and Kasho's safety, but had to trust them to take care. They both knew what was going on and there really wasn't anything he could do, except urge them to be cautious. He was only too well aware of how easy it was to be concerned for others' danger but to minimize your own.

Shahvid understood Chanthan's frown, though for some reason he didn't feel any danger for himself. But his earlier uneasiness had not lessened and he realized he didn't want Kasho to be alone right then. Maybe he didn't want himself to be alone. But either way, he suggested, "Why don't you delay your work for a few days if you can and plan to spend the day with me. Maybe it would ease some minds if we were at least in the company of each other."

Sushati grinned, "Depends on what the minds are worried about! Seriously though, I think it a good plan for you two to stick together."

Kasho pondered seriously, "I'm not sure if being with Shahvid that much will have an irreparable adverse affect or not. But," with a sigh and a barely repressed smile, "I guess I could chance it." Then she added with a wry grin, "However, having seen his study I hope there's some fire cleanup work for me to work on instead."

Shahvid laughed. He rather agreed with her. It wasn't a project he was particularly looking forward to himself, except for it to be done.

The others discussed their plans and where they would be. It was agreed that all of them would keep in the company of others as much as possible, just in case. All except Rafnon. He said he wouldn't tie himself down. He needed to be out and around, and couldn't say where he'd be. He was sure he wasn't in any danger from Valjar. But he did agree to check in occasionally.

That settled, they went their ways, trying not to let fear rule their lives in any way. But they were all alert, very alert, to whatever was going on around them.

It was one of those few times that Shahvid was glad to be using a vehicle instead of a bicycle. He mentioned that to Kasho, saying he was almost ashamed of that but it was true. She shared his feeling, saying she didn't think it was a reason for shame at all, just using your common sense, and your inner feelings. They were both tired from two long days in a row. But they decided to take a roundabout route to Kasho's anyway. They were too keyed up to just go home. Their conversation fitted into the leisurely drive. By the time Shahvid pulled up to the house they were both calmly ready for sleep.

Shahvid and Kasho were deep into their work of sorting through the mess of papers in Shahvid's study when the inspector arrived. He greeted them briefly then went out to confer with the woman from his office who had spent the night at the house.

The last of the fire fighters were packing up their equipment to leave. They stopped in to talk with Shahvid. He joined them to inspect the damaged portion of the house and discuss what needed to be done. Shahvid hadn't had much experience working on fire damaged buildings so appreciated their ideas and experience. However, he would wait until Jahon returned before doing much to the house, other than that which needed to be done to make it weather-tight. He knew that Jahon had rebuilt several buildings that had been partially burned and would know what to do.

He again thanked the people for their expertise, talents and help, and bid them farewell, with the hope that they wouldn't meet again under these same circumstances. They laughed, agreed, and urged him to contact them if he had any further questions or problems with the cleanup. Then they picked up the last of their gear and left.

Shahvid stood looking at the blackened kitchen and living area for a few moments then turned back to his study. The inspector and Kasho were deep in discussion and both started a bit when he came in. Shahvid stifled a remark about what they had been up to (the inspector was a nice enough person but didn't seem to have a great sense of humor) and merely sat down, after removing one of the seemingly hundreds of piles of paper around the room.

"The fire squad people have finished up and left. They did quite a job, there really isn't any cleanup left to do. Just repair work now. Guess you're stuck in here," he grinned at Kasho, remembering her remark from last night. Then turning to the inspector, "Anything new I should know about? I take it last night was quiet enough around here."

"Yes, very quiet. Unfortunately. We would have preferred some action. But that doesn't seem to happen when you are most prepared." The inspector paused a moment and Kasho got up to look out the window.

It was cloudier than the day before, but not rain clouds, just nice shade clouds. The sun looked around one for a minute, momentarily highlighting Kasho as it danced into the room. Shahvid forgot the inspector as he watched the rays in her hair, the light brown curls escaping their bonds, as they usually did whenever she tried to wind them up onto her head and keep them in order. Sleek order was just not their way.

Shahvid was pulled reluctantly back to the room as the inspector continued. "Of course, we are still prepared as well as we can be. There was last night, and will continue to be for the time being, one or two of our people around your grounds. I hope that won't inconvenience you?"

Shahvid assured him it was not a problem. He would trust them to do what they needed to. "But," he asked, "do you really think he will return here? I don't know why he would. Then again, I don't know his purpose to begin with, with the ransacking and the fire. But my thought would be along the lines of just a threat."

"We don't know of course, but we want to keep the place covered just in case." As the inspector paused again, Kasho turned back to the room.

"I believe we have company, of a friendly sort thank goodness. Binjer is coming up the lane."

Shahvid rose to look and a smile came readily. He was happy to see his friend, as himself as ever, riding up to the house. For some reason it seemed to help bring things into perspective, helped to dissolve some of the worries and fears. If one wasn't careful one could think that the whole world was made up entirely of worries and fears, and lose the real picture.

Shahvid went out to greet Binjer and was greeted himself with a big hug. "That's from all of us, to use as you see fit. I had to come to make sure in person that you're fine, and Kasho too. Not that we don't trust you to take care of yourself, but we are beginning to wonder."

Shahvid just laughed as Binjer unstrapped a large basket from his bike. "And just to make double sure, Tamoi and I came up with a sure cure for anything, with lots of help from the youngsters as I think you'll see."

Shahvid led Binjer and his load through the back door. "Kasho and the inspector are in my study. Why don't we park that in here, then I'll take you on a tour. Half priced rates for friends you know."

He opened the door to Neana's studio and Binjer set his load down. They wandered through the rest of the house, discussing the event, the damage, and the cause. Shahvid had an easier time talking about it with Binjer. They understood each other well, as old friends do. Binjer was a great help in seeing the whole thing without the fog of emotions that seemed to be getting in Shahvid's way. By the time they arrived at the study Shahvid felt much buoyed by his visit.

Binjer and the inspector were introduced, then Binjer greeted Kasho with a hug as he had Shahvid. He and Tamoi had been sincerely worried about their friends, and he was very happy to see them both safe, sound and in good spirits. The study however was another story. Even with the hours of work that Kasho and Shahvid had spent on it, the place was still quite a mess.

Binjer pointedly looked around, "New filing system? Maybe I should send over some of our youngest friends to help, looks like they could figure it out pretty fast." Even the inspector smiled. "No offense, but it looks like you could use a break. Maybe you could come up with a better system after a good lunch."

So with appropriate replies, and assurances to the inspector that he may as well join them, there was enough for a small crowd and then some, they retired to Neana's studio for a welcome break and lunch. The meal was not only delicious but quite a spirit booster. The food had been prepared by Binjer and Tamoi but the wrappings were definitely creations of the children. Even the inspector's serious demeanor didn't have a chance between the two.

Shahvid and Kasho enjoyed it all to the fullest, with a great appreciation for their friends. They both needed and appreciated the boost.

As they finished the meal with some fruit the inspector cleared his throat and broached the subject he and Kasho had discussed. He directed his words to Shahvid, "I mentioned before that we would have people around here for the time being, and I have been thinking that it would be good if you were to move out for a while. It would be a natural thing to do while the house is repaired, though I realize not necessary since you have rooms that weren't damaged. But if you were to do so quietly, without advertising where you went, maybe that would be best right now."

Shahvid didn't reply right away, just looked at him, thinking. The inspector continued, "It is not that we think you would be in the way, just that it would be safer for you. And your friends. It may not make sense that Valjar would come back here for another, maybe different, attack, but I don't think we can plan on the man doing things in a sensible manner. And until we know where he is and what he is doing, we don't care to take any chances."

When Shahvid again didn't answer, Binjer said, "I tend to agree with him, Shahvid. There's no reason to sit here and be a clear target, assuming your friend decides he'd like a little more action. Besides, wouldn't it be easier to not live here while the repairs are being made? Although I know you have lived through your and Jahon's many fiddlings with this place I still don't think food heavily laced with sawdust is the best."

Shahvid laughed but was waiting for Kasho to offer her opinion. She remained silent however. She was waiting for him. He finally said, "On one hand I'd rather not move out, if just for the fact that I hate to think of the packing and moving. Not that I have all that much. But I don't think I'd want to leave many of my, or Neana's, things behind. But then, if I don't think Valjar will be back, why does that worry me? Maybe I just don't feel that it is necessary."

He tried to think the proposal through honestly and calmly. There was also much involved that he couldn't discuss out loud. And it just wasn't his way to act without thinking it through well first. "On the other hand I *can* see where it might be easier to work on the place without trying to live here too, at least in the kitchen. I'll have to think about it some more. I don't want to make a decision based on reaction to a fear that might not be justified."

The inspector nodded and got up to leave, "Well, think about it if you would, and let me know. I'll be around off and on, or you can contact me through the office. Thanks again for the well done luncheon," he nodded toward Binjer, "and you two take care of yourselves." With another nod for Shahvid and Kasho he left.

"I too shall be on my way. I wouldn't want to be the cause of any more delay in the great paper shuffle." Binjer started packing the cloths and bottles away. "I'd offer to stay and help but I'm *sure* you two have a great system going that I would only interfere with."

Shahvid laughed, "Oh, we could probably think of a suitable job for your talents, but considering the great meal you provided us I'll not offer. Seriously, this was a very nice idea and much appreciated. I hadn't realized how much I needed it."

Kasho dittoed Shahvid's words, "And the company wasn't bad either. Do thank Tamoi and the children too."

"I will and thank you also." Binjer picked up his basket and looked out to see Mastal riding toward the house. "And here comes your hero now. I guess I can leave you two in his care." Binjer turned back to Shahvid, "Seriously Shahvid, I hope you'll consider moving out. This whole thing with Valjar just doesn't feel right. It wouldn't take us long to get you all moved and settled. You know, we could move Neana's things out too. And I assume I don't need to tell you that you are more than welcome to move in with us, there's always room for more. But I also assume you would have other preferences." And with a grin, a wave, and a "Just let me know when - Binjer Moving is at your service," he went out to talk with Mastal before loading the basket on his bike and riding off.

There was a moment of silence as Shahvid thought about what Binjer had said. Then he looked at Kasho. "You've been awfully quiet about this. Especially considering that I think it was your idea?"

Kasho just smiled back and said, "Maybe we better wait until Mastal leaves before we discuss it further. I'll get back to work on the study while you help our friend." She gave him a quick kiss as she went by, leaving him to go answer Mastal's knock at the back door, while his mind followed her back down the hall.

A few hours later Shahvid joined Kasho in the study. He and Mastal had successfully fixed the bicycle, and the boy had gone off to check on the bird family before going home. Shahvid looked around at the orderly piles of papers around the room and commented, "Looks like I should have left earlier. Did you sneak in a helper when I wasn't looking?"

"No, just a lack of distractions and a goal. Does wonders. But I could use a break. Want to go admire Binjer's leftovers?" Kasho got up and dusted her hands off on her pants.

They settled themselves in Neana's studio with cold

juice and ample leftovers. Even with the fresh air whispering in through the windows, the smell of smoke was a constant reminder.

Kasho addressed the issue on her mind directly, "Shahvid, how about moving in with me, right now. I don't want to rush our relationship any, but this is beside that. Valjar is just too unpredictable and unstable to trust not to come back here to cause more trouble. You know he's not likely to confront you directly." She paused a moment, watching Shahvid's face. "I think my place would be safer. And I would like to be with you right now."

Shahvid smiled at her, "Put like that it'll be hard to come up with a reason why not." It was all a bit too fast for him but, he reminded himself, one had to allow one's self the freedom to move with the wind. And this was a pretty strong wind. With or without Valjar. "There's a lot more to talk over between us, but for now, I'd like also to be with you. I'd rather think of moving with a bit more planning is all. But I guess there is no reason I couldn't do it, I don't have that much to move. But do you really think you want to be that crowded, give up that much privacy?"

"If I didn't want to, I wouldn't have suggested it you know. It'll be tight for both of us but my place isn't all that small, we can fit. We could just think of it as an indoor camping trip!" Kasho smiled at him, "It's not permanent or anything. Neither of us is making a long term commitment here. It is just the right thing to do right now. Hopefully it will help keep Valjar off track. Or better, bring him in before he does anything else."

Shahvid nodded, "Yes, it could help in keeping Valjar guessing, though I doubt it will be much help in capturing him. As far as you and I, we can work our relationship out with or without the move. And take as much time as we want." He smiled at her, then added, "But I do feel like I'm running away. I don't like that. I'd rather stay and fight. Which is rather crazy. I don't think of myself as a fighting man."

"You and your sister!" Kasho teased him. "You two

grow up together or something? 'Running away' is sometimes the best solution. There is nothing wrong with it if it's the best course. It's the old ego thing. But if your ego needs some reinforcing I'll be glad to take care of that! Then it won't need to worry about how it'll look to move out. Besides," she added, "there are lots of ways to fight, you know that. It's not the first time you've fought the Power Movement."

Shahvid had to agree. And quite frankly he could look forward with pleasure to moving in with her, cramped quarters or no. Wasn't that what he had been thinking so much about lately? One shouldn't ignore the god's answers to your wishes. But out loud he just said, "OK, I agree. So, what do we do now? I take it you've been thinking of this and probably have some ideas. But first, I think a more formal agreement would be in order."

After a bit they set about planning the move. Shahvid called Binjer who said he just happened to have the perfect vehicle right at hand and would be right there, then rang off before Shahvid could comment. Shahvid just shook his head, laughed and relayed the message to Kasho. They decided to stop by the inspector's office later, on the way to Kasho's, to let him know of Shahvid's plan. No use advertising his destination on the telephone, just in case. The same for Sinat.

They set to work organizing and packing Shahvid's possessions. They decided they'd figure out where to put it all when they got to Kasho's. They packed and labeled the boxes keeping in mind that Shahvid would be living out of them for a while, and some would not be unpacked again before another move.

When Binjer arrived with the moving vehicle, Tamoi, and more boxes, Shahvid and Kasho had things pretty well organized. They sat down in Neana's studio for a cool drink and a snack, and to discuss what needed to be done. They had worked together enough on numerous projects, and were all let's-get-to-it-and-get-it-done type people, so a plan of action was quickly organized. But there was one detail that was still unresolved. Neana.

Shahvid voiced his concern out loud, "I don't think it's a good idea to leave Neana's things here, but there wouldn't be room at Kasho's for it all. Plus I don't know how I feel about moving her out of the house without her even knowing about it."

"Her clothes wouldn't take up much space, but her studio would be hard to fit into my place," Kasho agreed. "But I also don't think we should leave it here. Especially not her paintings." She looked around the room and said, "I'm just glad Valjar didn't come in here when on his destruction outing. Can you imagine what a mess he could have made?"

"I don't even want to think about it!" Tamoi waved the thought away emphatically.

Binjer agreed, "What he did to Shahvid's study was quite enough. Not to mention the fire. So, I think we can all agree we should not leave Neana's things here. We would fit them in at our place if need be of course, but I think a better, and easier, solution is at Jahon's."

"I don't know how you manage to fit in what you do at your homestead, we don't need to add to the problem," Shahvid told Binjer and Tamoi. He and Jahon had designed and retrofitted enough storage nooks into their house to know how well utilized every spot was. The only way to put more in was to kick something, or someone, else out first. "And yes, there would be room at Jahon's. But you know Neana. If we just move her in with Jahon without her input we will have more problems than just storage."

Kasho laughed, "Now, Shahvid, she may be independent but she's not unreasonable. Besides, it's going to happen anyway."

Tamoi said doubtfully, "We all may agree that is what is to happen, but that doesn't mean Neana is going to accept it that easily."

"I don't know why not," Binjer argued, "I've been waiting for those two to get together for ten years. I'm too old to wait any longer." When the laughter died down he added, with finality, "I say we move all of Neana's things to Jahon's. Then we do the democratic thing and leave Jahon to work it out with Neana when they return."

Kasho added, "If this whole affair with Valjar isn't settled by their return we aren't going to want Neana moving back in here anyway, fire damage or not."

That settled it. They went to work with high spirits and much laughter as they carried on a four way disjointed conversation that continued as they passed each other in and out. It was decided to get Shahvid moved in with Kasho, then come back and move Neana to Jahon's. They would deal with Neana's reaction when the time came. What Jahon's response to the move would be didn't appear to concern any of them.

There was still light in the sky when a happy but tired crew closed the door of the moving vehicle on the last item. It wasn't a large van but they had managed to pack in all that was to go.

Binjer and Tamoi had to get home to the children so it was decided that they would all meet in the morning at Kasho's to unload, but not too early. With thanks and hugs Tamoi and Binjer left in the small vehicle that Shahvid and Kasho had used, and they in turn left in the moving van, going first to the inspector's office and then to Sinat's.

It seemed a long time later that the weary couple finally sank into bed, any discussions put off as they instantly fell asleep.

Sunday morning arrived with an overcast sky and Binjer and Tamoi at Kasho's door, almost too early. They had settled the children with friends and were ready for a busy day. And a busy day it was. The weather cooperated by withholding its rain and the cloud cover made for cooler conditions, for which they were all thankful.

They started by unloading Shahvid's world into Kasho's home without doing any unpacking or organizing, except for those choices which were obvious. Then they headed back to Shahvid's to pack up and move Neana's.

At Jahon's they made a more organized job of unloading since they wouldn't be the ones to have to find, sort and unpack everything. They moved things around and organized the two homes into one, while trying not to have it look quite as obvious as that. Skaduter was kept busy supervising the new additions and arrangements, carefully and critically checking out each one. Thankfully neither Jahon nor Neana were into accumulating things any more than Shahvid. All in all both moves went fairly fast. Once they got into it Shahvid felt comfortable with the thought, and the actuality, of moving.

By the end of the day there was not much left at Shahvid and Neana's old home. Just those things in the storage shed which needed to be decided on between them later. And the tools needed yet in the garden, which Shahvid was sure Neana would not want to just desert. The man who was keeping the berries picked while she was gone said he would be happy to keep a general eye on the rest of the garden too, picking anything that needed to be harvested.

During a short break in the moving day Shahvid had made a quick trip to the neighbors to let them know what was going on. He was vague about their plans, just that they had moved out for the time being. It was an understandable move and no one commented about it except to offer help in whatever way they could.

It was late when Binjer closed the door on the now empty moving van for the last time. "I vote for a long overdue dinner at the Grape & Stew. Assuming we can drag our weary bodies through the door."

The vote was unanimous. They all trooped back into Jahon's to wash up. A final check with Skaduter and they were on their way. The Grape & Stew was very kind about serving the weary and grubby, and without undue comment. Though Dainon did say, after a thoughtful look at the group, that he had just the right wine for them that evening - they looked like they needed it.

Kasho and Shahvid woke late Monday morning to a soft, gentle, comforting rain. They lay in bed listening and talking for some time, letting nature massage their tired bodies and spirits. Nature was an excellent masseuse.

When they finally made their way, literally, to the kitchen for breakfast, both aspects of themselves felt refreshed and ready for whatever the day was to bring.

Although there were parts of the community who weren't fully at ease that day, life went on as usual with no great interruption. Shahvid and Kasho spent the day organizing and rearranging, all to the gentle sounds of the warm rain. It was hard to imagine people like Valjar, and Caljn, and their scientists being a part of the same world. Not just once did they wonder to each other what Valjar, what someone like Valjar, thought of a day like that day. What they would be, what *he was*, doing.

By Tuesday evening both Kasho and Shahvid had their own places in the house to work and think. And the rest of the house had been blended to accommodate them both, together. And no word came of Valjar, or any of the Power Movement people.

The next two days found the two of them back to work on their respective projects. Life was continuing in a business-as-usual fashion, but with a certain sense of unreality. The sun shone, the plants grew, and Shahvid and Kasho wondered what was going to happen, and when. That question echoed over and over in many minds. They were glad they were together, and they comfortably and happily kept to themselves. No one else noticed, it was only a few days, but to them it was a much longer time.

The weekend came. It was Sunday morning. Starpeace sat looking at one another with a bit of dismay. They were ready, they had continued to be ready, all set for action. All week. But nothing had happened. Nothing to report on. No sign of Valjar. No activity from any of the Power Movement. Jahon and Neana were due back Tuesday. But it didn't matter. It was as if their feelings about the whole series of events with the Power Movement had blocked further action, had prevented anything more from happening, had canceled the whole thing. It wasn't an easy feeling.

It was time for Kasho and Shahvid to go. They were going to ride out with the driver to pick up Jahon and Neana. Their overnight camping gear was in the vehicle waiting outside Sushati and Sinat's home. They rose to leave.

"I assure you we'll be careful," Shahvid repeated again. "We can't, and won't, hide out. And we want to let Jahon and Neana know what's going on, or isn't maybe I should say, before they get back to the community."

"Not that it will be any fun, right?" Sushati teased.

Kasho smiled, "Of course! Why else? We better get on the road, though, or we'll be left behind." Hugs and assurances were repeated as they made their farewells.

"I envy them," Chanthan admitted as Kasho and Shahvid drove away. "No reason, just honest envy."

Sushati laughed, hearing his remark as she returned from answering the telephone. "If it would help, you can come with me. I'm on my way to welcome a new person. Maybe, if he or she decides it is time. The last time I went over the baby had changed its mind. The parents are certainly ready though." Sushati continued as she gathered her things together, "I am not sure if the babies are trying to teach patience or just seeing how much their parents can stand." A kiss for Sinat and a questioning look for Chanthan, with a smiling, "Well?"

He just laughed and waved her out. He, and they, knew where his talents lie and it wasn't with slippery newborns.

"If I didn't doubt strongly that he had it in him, I'd think Valjar was deliberately trying *our* patience," Sinat spoke wryly to Chanthan and Rafnon after the others had also gone. "In any event, I feel like going out. Care to join me for lunch somewhere?"

Chanthan readily agreed but Rafnon declined. "I think it's best not to be seen in public with you two. Plus I have some contacts I want to check with. Someone *has* to have an idea where Valjar is and I think I might have some luck if I get out and around. I have some ideas in mind." With a quick nod to each he was out and off in his vehicle.

Rafnon seemed the most frustrated of them all with the lack of progress, and action. He just couldn't believe he couldn't find out where the man was. He didn't stop to think about how strong the incentives were for Valjar to stay well hidden - and not only from them.

Sinat left a message for Sushati, then he and Chanthan walked down the path toward the Grape & Stew. They were used to Rafnon's ways and hadn't expected him to join them. They didn't let their worries keep them from enjoying the day, the meal, or the company.

Meantime, it wasn't long before Shahvid and Kasho were settled in the wagon behind the two beautiful black horses. The animals were as content to make the trip that day as they had been two weeks earlier. And their two new passengers were more than a little content themselves.

The driver made a final check of the entire outfit, confirmed that Shahvid and Kasho were ready, then swung up onto his seat. A quiet word to the horses by voice and through the reins and they pulled out. Temporarily leaving behind the community, the problems, and the frustrations.

~~~ ~~ ~ ~~ ~~~

"Well, I won't say you haven't smelled better," Shahvid teased as he held me at arms' length after a long hug. "But if one looks deep enough one could say you look just fine." He gave me up to Kasho as he turned to Jahon with an equally sincere hug.

"I don't know what you're talking about," Jahon protested, "she looks great! I mean, compared to yesterday."

Kasho laughingly looked Jahon over, "And you? What should we compare you to?"

"What ingrates! After all the work we went to getting spruced up for the homecoming! That stream this morning was *cold* too." I suppressed a laugh as I dug in my pocket for the treat I'd saved for the black horses, and in mock indignation stalked over to my less vocal friends. "At least these two aren't such snobs." The horses confirmed that compliment as they nuzzled me and accepted their tip.

"Ah, well," the driver calmly added as he surveyed the party, "at least I shouldn't have to worry about complaints concerning my companions' manners." This as one of the horses drooled rather generously over my shirt as I turned my attention to his partner.

I just laughed and gave them each a final scritch, then turned back to my human friends. It had been a beautiful and rewarding two weeks, and much too short. But it was also great to see Shahvid and Kasho, and the driver and his team.

As the bantering continued we loaded our packs into the wagon. The four of us settled ourselves behind the driver, and the horses carried us all down the road. The wagon was a lightweight, well-designed carrier with a removable cover to shield from the sun or rain, and side curtains if it got stormy. There were plenty of cushions for seating and an excellent suspension system. It was easy to relax into the ride.

The sun shined intermittently on our happy group as we traveled along. Jahon and I told stories of our adventures of the past two weeks. Well, not the personal ones. But I could tell by the smiles and comments that Shahvid and Kasho were both reading between the lines way too well. I was too happy to care. And really, why shouldn't they know?

There was no mention of Valjar. He and his life didn't fit into the party. I didn't want to be the one to bring his name up, though I admit I was curious. But no one else mentioned him either.

As the sun was setting, the horses pulled us off the main road along a trail. It ended near a small, quiet lake. It was a rest area that had a simple log shelter for travelers with attached lean-to for the animals and wagon, snuggled in naturally among the trees.

We all stood a moment by the wagon in silent appreciation of the view. The last rays of the sun found their way around the clouds and ran out to play over the surface of the lake, then slowly bid all farewell as twilight, and the clouds, settled in. I didn't even think of wanting to paint the scene. A human being couldn't.

After the horses were taken care of and all set for the night, we humans did the same. The rain was just starting as the last trip out was made, and we five gratefully settled in around the table for dinner.

By now the driver knew, more or less, the reason

behind our vacation. He had accepted the confidence and trust with little comment and much understanding.

We finished our meal, cleared the table and washed the dishes. No one seemed to want to approach the subject, though it had to be done.

Jahon did it. "Although I do dislike having to come 'down to earth', we may as well get to it. In spite of the other distractions of the last two weeks, I have to admit the subject *has* crossed our minds occasionally." He shared a look with me and I returned a smile mixed with a shrug. "So, what has our friend Valjar been up to while we've been away? Can I assume he's the reason for the early welcoming committee?" Jahon replenished everyone's mugs then settled back down at the well worn wooden table.

Kasho and Shahvid looked at each other, then at Jahon. The driver just sipped his drink.

I added, "Not that we don't appreciate seeing you before we arrived home. It was a relief to see that you're both OK." When neither Shahvid nor Kasho spoke, I asked, "Well? Is something wrong? What's happened?"

Kasho and Shahvid shared a look, then Shahvid smiled and said, "For some reason I had rather forgotten that you two would know anything about Valjar. In a way it seems like you've been gone for months. I'm not quite sure where to begin." He stopped, looking again at Kasho. She just shrugged and made a gesture leaving it with him.

"Nothing is 'wrong', and nothing has happened," Shahvid answered my last question. Then quickly added as Kasho looked at him in amazement. "I mean, nothing devastating or anything. All of us and our friends are fine."

Jahon looked from one to the other then suggested, "How about if you just start at the beginning. We don't have any other plans for the evening."

I watched Shahvid look again at Kasho, and a small feeling of dread settled in my stomach. He had said all of our friends were fine, and he and Kasho appeared to be OK. What then?

With a small sigh Shahvid pulled his chair closer to

the table and, leaning on his arms, he began. As he continued with the events of the past two weeks, with occasional help from Kasho, my astonishment widened, and Jahon's frown grew deeper. Valjar, Mastal, the fire, the ransacking of his study, the scientist's death.

Shahvid ended with his moving in with Kasho for the time being. "And that's about it. No one has seen hide nor hair of Valjar since. And believe me there are plenty who are looking. So you could say that things are quiet at home right now. Though I admit it's a pretty uneasy quiet."

I just looked at him in amazement. In spite of all that had gone on with Caljn and the Power Movement, and Valjar, I couldn't assimilate these latest events. It didn't seem real to me.

We talked and asked questions, discussed and commented. Through it all the driver said little. He just calmly watched and listened, not unlike he would watch his horses. Not detached, just not involved. But in a very friendly manner. It was comforting somehow, helped to keep everything in perspective.

"Well, I have to admit I'm having a hard time taking it all in, in spite of all your words," I finally told them, accompanied by a sudden yawn. "Which is probably just as well considering the ramifications. I think I need to get some sleep before I can think clearly about any of it." The day had started early and I was tired.

They all agreed and we set to cleaning up as the driver went out for a final check on the animals. We each claimed a bunk to spread our sleeping bags on. And it wasn't long before the only sound in the room was the rain drumming lightly on the roof.

~~~ ~~ ~ ~~ ~~~

Careen wandered across the Square toward her Aunt's house, thinking. It wasn't something she had done much of, at least not very deeply, but these last days had been different. And this cloudy Monday seemed to demand her mind's attention.

She had heard of Shahvid's fire and been surprised at how upset she'd felt. She realized now that for all her differences with Shahvid, and Neana, she hadn't wanted anything bad to happen to either of them. It had been her home too, for nine years, even though she'd never thought of it that way when living there. She had never been satisfied with it, even after all the changes Shahvid had made. Maybe she even understood a little that the dissatisfaction had been with her life, not with the house. Maybe not.

But what was bothering her the most now was Valjar. She'd also heard of the scientist's death. And she knew, though she'd tried to deny it, that Valjar was involved in both incidents. And maybe, just maybe, she had been involved some herself. She wasn't sure if what she'd done had contributed, but it worried her.

At one time she would have gone to Shahvid to talk it over. He had always been a comforting listener. But she knew that those days were gone. She wasn't sure when she'd lost them, but it had been awhile. Now, she decided, she would talk it over with her Aunt. Even though the woman had a sharp tongue where Careen was concerned, she knew that she would listen fairly enough. She had let Careen move back in with her after she'd left Shahvid's, and with surprisingly few comments.

~~~ ~~ ~ ~~ ~~~

In another part of town Valjar was having his own struggles with his thoughts and feelings. It had been easy before, right after Caljn had died. He'd set himself a goal, a direction. But now he wasn't sure. Caljn had always been the thinker, he'd always told Valjar what to do, what *they* were going to do. And Valjar had been a loyal follower. But now? He knew that Caljn was gone completely. That's what the Church had drilled into him. When you die, you're dead, no more, no less.

Then why did he keep feeling Caljn around? It had to be those demons Caljn had so often talked about. And it was because he'd not yet completed his mission, his goal. The one he had set for himself. It was a rigid, no way out path he'd defined. He would avenge Caljn's death.

Well, he had taken care of that pompous scientist. He wasn't sure he had anything to do with Caljn's death but he must have had some connection. After all, he was the one who had designed and given Caljn the small hand destroyer. The one people said Caljn had killed himself with. The one that was supposed to have hit Chanthan.

There was a nagging thought that kept coming around, and each time Valjar angrily threw it out. That it was true. That Caljn *had* somehow killed himself. It was a possibility Caljn had mentioned more than once. But all that didn't matter. The scientist had thought himself as important as Caljn, so he of course had to be killed. He was sure Caljn would have directed it had he been here. But he would not believe that Caljn would have directed his own death. They were wrong.

But the woman. The picture of her standing at her door, saying to him with more sincerity and kindness than he could ever remember hearing, '*I understand. And I'm sorry Valjar*. He got up angrily, grabbed the first thing he laid hand to and hurled it across the room. The heavy dish crashed into the wall but fell to the floor unbroken, its contents scattered about.

Valjar paced around the small room, then threw himself into a chair, his head in his hands. She was responsible. He knew she was responsible. She had to have been the one. But every time he tried to think of how he should kill her that damned picture came to mind. Again and again. He wished he'd go crazy enough to not be able to think of it, or anything else. That or die.

Of course, that was the other thing. That was one of the rules of this game. Either he killed her, or he killed himself. He was sure it was what Caljn's ghost demanded. That was the way it had to be. He had made the rules and he couldn't, or wouldn't, change them.

There was a hint occasionally, a glimmer now and then, that there was another way. But he'd spent too many years of his life believing otherwise, and those beliefs were not about to easily give up and stand aside for any ray of light, no matter how bright.

~~~ ~~ ~ ~~ ~~~

"Good morning to you too and I am sorry if I woke you."

Sushati's voice brought a smile from Chanthan as he shook the dreams from his head and answered into the receiver, "You're welcome to wake me any time, as I hope you know. What can I do for you today? I'm quite awake now."

Sushati responded directly, "I had a dream last night. It was a mixed reality type and I was not directly involved, more of an observer. But I remember recognizing Neana and Valjar. Other people too and horses. There was a great competition, one of those old 'only one can win' type of events. I feel like the horses won. It is all somewhat hazy now, not the kind of dream you can easily translate. But the competition made me very uneasy. And that feeling was still with me when I awoke this morning.

"Sinat and I have been discussing it, but we are not sure of the message, if any. He did not recall any dreams of anxiety or danger last night. We decided to check with you. I thought you would be awake now or I would not have called yet." Sushati added rather wryly, "Having the telephone bring you awake is not very conducive to dream recall,"

Chanthan chuckled at her tone. "That's true, but actually I was awake once already this morning and had just dozed off again. So I do remember a lot of my night's activities but nothing that would be along those lines I believe." He was silent a few minutes thinking. "No, I can't fit any of my dreams to yours, sorry to say."

"Of course it would be easy to just put it down to natural concern," Sushati said. "I guess we are all thinking of Neana and Jahon's return today. But it feels like more than that. I *know* there is more to that dream if I could just unravel it."

Chanthan spoke to the frustration in Sushati's voice, not a common thing from her. "Even if you could 'unravel' more of your dream Sushati, what would you do with it? Shahvid and Kasho and the driver are sure to be with Neana and Jahon by now. And they are all aware of the danger, in the form of Valjar. If it was a dream of warning then it's very likely you were not the only one to be tuned into, or involved in it. Our friends are very aware people, they won't ignore such a warning."

Chanthan's calm words did much to help Sushati back to her usual steady level. She smiled at herself and agreed, "I know. The feelings were so strong and so much still with me when I woke that it was hard to step back at all. And Sinat and I share our feelings with each other maybe too easily."

Chanthan smiled at her words. She and Sinat did have a special relationship, one that their friends recognized, appreciated and enjoyed. But neither of them were apt to ignore reality no matter their emotions. "So, what do you have in mind?" Chanthan asked.

"Well, it is a beautiful day for a carriage ride out into the country with some friends," Sushati answered. "We could pack a lunch, make a day of it."

"And don't forget the rain gear," Chanthan added as he looked out at the cloud filled sky.

"Oh, we will try to go prepared for anything," she assured him.

Chanthan laughed, "I'll check with Myana and get back with you. When do you plan to take off on this unplanned adventure?"

Sushati half-jokingly reminded him, "Be careful what you label this trip! I am considering it just a friendly picnic."

"I best not analyze that any deeper then," Chanthan commented.

Sushati just laughed, they both knew the game, and the rules. "Sinat is on his way now to the stables. He is going to call from there to let us know if anyone is heading that direction soon, or is willing to."

Chanthan rang off with the promise to get right back with her. Though he was sure that Myana would be agreeable to the trip he wouldn't take her thought or feelings for granted. He went out to the kitchen to share the conversation and plans. In spite of the lightheartedness in which the talk with Sushati had ended, he could feel the seriousness of the journey.

~~~ ~~ ~ ~~ ~~~

The rain had stopped sometime in the night but the day arrived still covered with clouds. Jahon slipped quietly out of the cabin and down to the lake. He stopped for a moment, feeling the early morning, before diving through the surface to the world below, barely startling a long-legged bird standing in the shallows on the other side of the water.

The day was noticeably brighter, though no sun showed yet, by the time he had swum himself out and stood once again, dripping, on the shore. He turned and headed back to the cabin with a wave to the driver, who had stopped to watch the water-person then with a smile continue on to tend to the horses. Jahon stopped a moment to listen to the animals' greetings, then let the chill hurry him in. The anxiety that had accompanied his waking that morning was still with him.

Shahvid and Kasho were coming out just as he reached the door. After morning greetings they continued on to their own lake baths, by way of the outhouse. They were soon followed by the driver.

I was the last to arise. I met Shahvid and Kasho coming back in on my way to the lake. My dip was short but refreshing. It felt good to wash the road dust off, and it certainly woke me up.

By the time we were all gathered once again in the small cabin Jahon was setting breakfast on the table. To the delight of the crew of hungry, and very awake, people.

The talk at the table was energetic. The events of the past two weeks were hashed out again, with just an occasional comment from the driver. It was all still like a story in a book to me, events happening to mythical characters, not people I knew. Or a house that I knew. I was glad that my studio hadn't been harmed. Of course Shahvid's safety was far and above that, but there were a couple of paintings in progress that I would have been sorry to lose. And some special furnishings. As far as the rest of the house, I was sure that Shahvid and Jahon would put it to rights soon enough. And I could live in my rooms until then. After the last two weeks out in the wilderness it would seem like quite the luxury.

We didn't rush but didn't waste time either as we finished eating, cleaned up, and readied the shelter for the next guests. After an appreciative farewell to the place, we once more climbed in behind the black horses and headed down the road toward home.

The sky was still filled with clouds but the rain held off, and we were all comfortably dressed for the coolness. The animals in front also seemed to be enjoying the weather and the day. We lapsed into a natural silence. Each involved in their own thoughts and feelings.

But each thought and feeling also wove in and out of every other thought and feeling of the group. In spite of the beauty and joy of the moment there was an overriding feeling of anxiety shared by all. No one could come up with a way to express it, so the words weren't spoken.

The sounds of the horses' hooves regularly meeting the dirt, the creak of the leather and wood that they pulled, and the wheels turning round and round fit in with the wind to surround us and carry us on down the road. The whole affect was quite mesmerizing. I thought of Valjar and wondered what he was doing right then.

~~~ ~~ ~ ~~ ~~~

Valjar had made his decision. It wasn't that he knew exactly what he was going to do. But he knew his intent and was filled with it to the exclusion of all else. Almost without thinking he silently made his way to the dead scientist's lab. In fact, the only way he made it there without being detected was by instinct, not by thought.

He knew what he wanted, and he searched with that one thought in mind. He hadn't found it before. But he had to find it now. He panicked when he was once again unsuccessful. His search grew more desperate. Then he found it. It was there. It was in his, Valjar's, hands now. A thought/feeling intruded momentarily, that same little ray of light, that there was indeed another way. But he knew now what to do with such things, and it wasn't a problem for him again.

The air outside was heavy for him and he had to work just to get through it. But he pressed on, as fast as he could. Nothing distracted him. His mind and body were fully focused on his intent.

~~~ ~~ ~ ~~ ~~~

"We could stop here for a bit if you want." The horses slowed down as the driver spoke into the non-conversation behind him. We all startled back to the day, a little ashamed that we had wandered so far and been ignoring the beauty of the world through which we were traveling. It didn't seem that long since our last rest stop.

Jahon spoke, "I guess I don't feel the need to stop, unless you or the horses or the others wish to of course. I do admit I'm feeling anxious, but nothing seems to say that we should delay our trip. How do you feel?" He put the question out to all of us.

Shahvid agreed, "I share your anxiety. I've been trying to pin my feelings down, but no luck. But I guess I also feel like continuing on. Almost as if just to get it over with. Whatever 'it' might be."

Both Kasho and I agreed. The driver nodded his head in assent, shook the reigns lightly, and the horses picked up speed once again.

I also felt anxious. But not in any way I could put into words, or wanted to try. I didn't feel like discussing the facts or the possibilities any more, and I doubted that anyone else did either. I looked out past the driver to the horses, watching their sleek black coats moving over those great muscles. I felt connected to them. Maybe I wanted some physical activity myself. It would have felt good to jump out and run along beside them for a while. Beside me Jahon shifted his weight and brought me back into the wagon. I smiled and fell into the comfortable, though somewhat uneasy, silence around me. We all sat watching the life around us as we trotted by. I could feel the clouds moving in a little closer.

The driver felt the horses slow down before they did. He consciously sharpened his already highly aware senses. In a moment those behind him also felt the horses' hesitation, their senses suddenly alert.

I saw him first. And quietly asked the driver to stop, almost before I could fully take in what I saw.

Jahon, then Shahvid and Kasho were not far behind me. Jahon reached for me but I gently stopped him. I think I was the only one who saw, or was aware, of what Valjar held in his hand.

I didn't have to guess about it. The picture of Caljn, that last day of his life here, holding that same item, pointing it out at Chanthan, was so strong in my mind that I could almost feel the warm breezes in the Square.

~~~ ~~ ~ ~~ ~~~

The look on Neana's face brought such feelings crashing into Jahon that he almost couldn't handle it. Almost. But he knew what she was seeing, what Valjar held in his hand. And he knew that his life here depended on playing this event with Valjar with the very best of what he had in him. For the moment also brought, without thought, the fact that Neana *was* his life to him. He very consciously didn't look around at the others, and held out his mental hands for all the help that was available.

~~~ ~~ ~ ~~ ~~~

Valjar was almost surprised to see Neana coming toward him in the wagon. His resolve faltered a moment, but just a moment, before the well armored self he had created took over.

He lowered the weapon to the horses as the driver pulled them to stop at Neana's soft requested. Valjar assumed he was responsible, he and the weapon. The horses and the wagon stopped. His anger grew as he tried to control his shaking hand, and couldn't. And the sudden quiet almost unnerved him completely. Even the wind was silent, for a moment.

~~~ ~~ ~ ~~ ~~~

The driver carefully and deliberately sent calm assurance to the horses, and support to the people. And he kept an extremely sharp focus on Valjar. Both physically and mentally. The reins held firmly, not too tightly, not too loosely, in his well-callused hands.

As Neana moved to climb down, the others instinctively reacted against that. Jahon so strongly that he almost reached out to grab her but she silently held them off. They all kept their places as Valjar's hand raised shakily to her once more.

They knew they had to support Neana as strongly as they could, from within. They knew this was her game. But they had to struggle harder than they had ever had to before in this life to keep that in mind, and stay physically still. Jahon's feelings at that time could not have been put into words, nor Shahvid's or Kasho's.

~~~ ~~ ~ ~~ ~~~

I could feel the horses' fear, or feel them catch the humans' fears, as I started to climb down. I wasn't afraid for my friends, or rather I knew I had to maintain my focus entirely on Valjar. I was well aware that if I allowed myself even a moment of fear for those in the wagon I would lose my stability. I had to keep this between myself and Valjar.

I concentrated on him as I climbed down to the ground and walked up by the horses. I worked on seeing the event as it was - *Valjar's* game, not mine. I struggled to center myself, and not get caught up in his view of the world.

I put my hand up to the black, satiny, coat beside me for support. The support was given. I found the strength to put aside my picture of Caljn, and the knowledge of the weapon Valjar held in his hand.

"Hello Valjar." I was startled by my voice. It was surprisingly calm. I almost wondered where it came from. It threw me off my concentration for a moment. But the feel of the tension around me, the almost overwhelming love and fear, brought me back. I kept my hand on the horse's warm side. I couldn't see where to go. I couldn't find a level in Valjar to connect with.

~~~ ~~ ~ ~~ ~~~

It was a decidedly one way search. Valjar had carefully built up a sturdy, and ugly, brick wall to avoid any such contact. He had to. He knew he couldn't allow himself to break down into the kind of thoughts that had invaded his mind recently.

And here she was, just as he had planned. So why couldn't he just do it?

His desperation increased, made all the more intense by the lack of verbal response from anyone. He knew they must hate him, why didn't they show it? He wanted some action so bad he could taste it, or was that his fear? He wasn't in a position to analyze it. He just knew he was unable to move.

He struggled to remember his goal, his responsibility, Caljn. But she just stood there looking at him, and he couldn't take his eyes from her. Why didn't something happen?!

The clouds responded. And the rain spattered down around him. He felt every drop, but no one else seemed to even notice. His mind swirled to make sense of what was happening, to put the scene into the narrow confines of his world. The one he had so carefully created.

Then his mind latched onto something. Something it could identify. He whirled around to see another team of horses coming around the bend, pulling a carriage full of people.

~~~ ~~ ~ ~~ ~~~

Jahon's muscles jerked to propel him over the side of the wagon, and in the next instant jerked him back to non-motion as Valjar spun back to Neana, the weapon in his hand waving wildly. Jahon felt his emotions scream inside him as he clamped down hard on himself. Shahvid and Kasho held each other in a bruising tension. And the driver deliberately and firmly kept touch with the horses.

~~~ ~~ ~ ~~ ~~~

I heard another wagon coming, but I drew on everything available, and stayed still. My eyes never leaving Valjar, the horse holding me up. As if from a distance I saw him lunge for me. In the same instance I felt my world move as my horse and his partner both reared up, and I lost my support.

As I went down I heard a mixture of screams but couldn't distinguish the sources.

~~~ ~~ ~ ~~ ~~~

The people in the other carriage were on the ground before their driver had pulled her horses to a complete halt a few paces from their black friends. It took her a moment to calm the team as they reacted to the other horses' feelings. Both drivers sat firmly in their seats, the rain and wind unnoticed as they worked to settle their horses, and themselves. As the chaotic scene on the ground wrenched itself apart, then carefully came back together.

~~~ ~~ ~ ~~ ~~~

Jahon pulled me from beneath my black friend's belly, the horse forgiving him his lack of control as it stood quietly, shivering.

My muffled words worked their way out from around Jahon, "I'm OK, really, I'm OK." I worked my way somewhat free of his arms, to be engulfed by Shahvid and Kasho.

The feelings broke and soared around us as we struggled to set our world right again. Chanthan, Sinat, Sushati and Myana not too calmly gave us the needed time before assuring themselves, personally, that we were all, indeed, OK.

As the rain washed the tears, and fears, into the ground, Chanthan and Sinat stepped away from the group to the body that had landed by the side of the road. The horse's contact had been complete, and final.

Myana handed Chanthan a blanket from the

carriage and he laid it over Valjar. There was nothing to say.

Sushati pointed to something in the grass lying a few yards from us and we all watched as Chanthan walked over to Valjar's weapon. He pulled something from his pocket and aimed with a steady hand. A quiet crack, a flash. The weapon lying on the ground was gone.

He walked quietly back to the tight group by the wagon, and looking from us to the instrument in his hand said, "Rafnon came by just as we were leaving. Said he didn't know why but that I should bring this along, he felt we would need it." He rubbed the black horse's neck, "Guess he hadn't foreseen this fellow."

Putting it back in his pocket he gave me a gentle kiss, "We're happy to have you back."

I looked over at the blanket, then buried my head in Jahon's chest, adding my tears to the already wet shirt. The rain spattered down around us unnoticed.

~~~ ~~ ~ ~~ ~~~ ~ ~~~ ~~ ~ ~~ ~~~